ABOUT 1 HE AUTHOR

Thorne Moore lives in a north Pembrokeshire farm cottage on the site of a medieval manor, with an excellent view of the stars, but she grew up in Luton and studied history at Aberystwyth. Nine years later, after a spell working in a library, she returned to Wales, to run a restaurant with her sister, and a craft business making miniature furniture.

She took a law degree through the Open University, and occasionally taught genealogy, but these days, she writes, as she had always intended, after retiring from 40 years of craft work.

Besides her psychological crime and historical mysteries, including *A Time for Silence* (finalist for the People's Book Prize and Bookseller Top Ten best seller), she also writes science fiction.

For some years she ran the Narberth Book Fair with fellow author Judith Barrow, and she is a member of Crime Cymru.

Published in Great Britain in 2024
By Diamond Crime

ISBN 978-1-915649-43-0

Diamond Crime is an imprint of Diamond Books Ltd.

DIAMOND
BOOKS

Acknowledgements

Many thanks to my good friends Judith Barrow, Trish Powers and Catherine Marshall for their suggestions and encouragement, and especially Trish for her eagle-eyed proof-reading.

Thanks, too, to the boys (both my cats, Tod and Eddie, as well as Steve, Phil and Jeff at Diamond Crime). Events in this book, like the characters and places (mostly) are fictional, but it is easy to find all too many examples of the missing and never found.

Cover design: Thorne Moore

For information about Diamond Crime authors
and their books, visit:
www.diamondbooks.co.uk

For Becky, as always.

COLD
IN THE EARTH

THORNE MOORE

"Faithful, indeed, is the spirit that remembers
After such years of change and suffering!"
Emily Brontë

Contents

PART 1: ESSEX

August 1992
Hayford Green, near Harlow

Lolly Dawson is perfectly happy; she has a friend to play with, which is something that doesn't often happen. It can't last, of course.

"I'll have to go home," says Emma, pulling a face.

"My aunt's come and we've got to have lunch together. Boring."

Lolly's stomach stirs at the thought of food. "What are you having?"

"The usual, I expect. Quiche or something."

Lolly doesn't know what keesh is, but it has to be good if It's the sort of thing they eat in the posh house with the wide gates where Emma lives. In fact, any food would be good. "That's nice."

Emma is fingering the string of acorns that Lolly has given her. Two of the nuts are cracked, but it's still impressive. "Can I keep this, then?"

"Yes, It's a present."

"All right. You can have this, if you like." Emma fiddles with the charm bracelet on her wrist and unclips a charm. It's a metal ring with a bit of glass in it.

"Thanks!" Lolly would have preferred the four-leaved clover but the ring is nice.

"It doesn't really match the others," says Emma. "I don't want it."

She's seen a woman walking up from the road.

"Oh, I've got to go now. Mum's coming."

She holds her string of acorns up to show her mother.

"Yes, very nice. And who's this?" asks her mother, in the sort of voice that pretends to be friendly and isn't really. Lolly knows that sort of voice very well.

"Her name's Lolly," says Emma.

"That's a very odd name. Where do you live, Lolly?"

Lolly half-turns, pointing vaguely across the common, past the woods, hoping she won't have to say anything, but Emma jumps in with "She lives in a van."

"I see. I thought as much."

"Can she come over to our house after lunch?"

"I think you know the answer to that, Emma. Lolly had better go back to her people, and you come along home, Miss."

She's already shepherding Emma away. Half a dozen paces and Lolly can hear her saying firmly, "I don't want you messing with that sort, please."

Left alone, Lolly tries the ring on. It's a bit big, but okay on her thumb. She heads back across the common for home because there's no one else around, not even a dog, and nothing to do.

Home is an old horse van. It's full of junk and filthy. It probably smelled better when a horse was in it, but Lolly lives in it now with her mum Cara and with Dan. Neil's with them too, but he has his own transit van. Neil is really Lolly's father, not Dan, according to Cara, although Lolly doesn't much care, either way. None of them pay much attention to her, unless they want her do something. Cara doesn't pay much attention to anything anyway, because she's usually out of her head cramming pills or jabbing stuff in her arms. They all do that, and they all slap Lolly around.

She can hear them now, Dan and Neil, arguing in the muddy layby by the woods where they've been squatting for the last three days. Dan sees Lolly coming.

"She's back then, your girl. Like a bad penny. Don't know why I'm raising your brat for you."

"Didn't think you were raising her." Neil grins, looks at Lolly. "Fancy coming with your real dad for a change? Dump this loser and come to London with me, eh?"

Lolly says nothing. There's no need because whatever she answers, they won't be listening. What she wants to do is go to Emma's house and maybe have some keesh, if there's any left. The two men are throwing joke punches and they've already forgotten about her.

Dan turns his back on her. "Right, I'll fix the deal, make my own way back. You do the business and head off. Meet up to settle in Sheffield, yeah?"

"Sure." Neil bangs on the side of the horse van.

"Cara! You going to sleep all day, dozy cow?"

The door of the horse van opens and Cara's standing there, swaying, her eyes swimming as she tries to focus. She waves Neil away as he reaches out to catch her, then she sees Lolly. "Oh. You're back." She grips the door for support.

"She's back and you didn't notice she'd gone," said Neil. "Take her off your hands, shall I? Save you the bother of noticing if she's alive or dead?"

Cara stares at him, trying to make sense of whatever he's saying. "What you want to take her for?"

"Oh, you're listening, are you? Right, I'm off. Got that? Cara! London." He spits with disgust as she swivels on her heel.

"Go back to bed, for fuck's sake," says Dan.

Cara understands that much. She staggers back into the van.

The men head for Neil's transit. The mud churns up under the wheels as they head off up the road, black fumes billowing from the exhaust.

Left alone, as usual, Lolly wonders if it's past lunchtime yet. She climbs onto a stile. There's a footpath leading right through the woods. It comes out on the other road, with the big houses where her friend lives. Emma did ask if Lolly could visit, didn't she? And her mum didn't actually say No. Lolly jumps down and sets off along the path. No one sees her vanish into the shadow of the trees.

* * *

When does the present tense become the past, irretrievable, lost forever?

* * *

Dan flung open the door of the horse van and heaved a heavy bag in.

"Right, get up, woman. We're moving out. Now! Where's the brat?"

Cara struggled up, blinking in the darkness. "What?"

"The brat. Your daughter. Lolly. Are you deaf? Where is she?"

"Lolly?" Cara's eyes widened as a confused memory drifted past her. "Neil took her. That's right, innit? Taken her to Lunnon? That's what he said, wo'nnit?"

Dan swore as he shoved her back in and climbed into the driving seat. "He can have her, as far as I'm concerned. Come on, we're out of here."

He drove off, gears clanking. In the abandoned layby the litter stirred, then settled in the shadows of the overhanging trees.

* * *

The constable prepared to take notes, perched gingerly on the edge of the sofa, deeply conscious that Mrs Ogilvie was eying his boots with distaste. "And you say it was gypsies?"

Mrs Ogilvie sniffed. "Yobos, anyway. Parked up in that disgusting van. I've complained to the council, but they're gone now. Well, of course, now they've got what they came for."

"A diamond ring. Just that, was it?"

"That's enough, surely! It was extremely valuable. My mother's engagement ring."

"But no sign of a break-in."

"No, no, they got their hands on it by using one of their brats to trick my gullible daughter into handing it over. I thought she'd have more sense, but what can you do? She's only nine."

"Just to get this clear, did they snatch it, or are you saying she gave it to them?"

"Only because she didn't understand how valuable it was. But *they* will. They knew what they were doing, all right."

"You didn't make a note of the van's number, I suppose."

"No, I did not."

The constable stifled a sigh. "Can you give a full description of the ring? Any chance you have a photo?"

"Of course! For the insurance."

"Good. We'll circulate the details, but I wouldn't hold out much hope of recovering it."

"Useless!" muttered Mrs Ogilvie.

PART 2: ONLY CONNECT

The Inspector

Welsey Police Station, Lincolnshire

Detective Inspector Malcolm Cannell glanced at the clock. Nearly six and there was still a pile of paperwork awaiting his attention. Two weeks back on his old stamping ground and it was going to take him longer than this to go through Welsey's case load. No point trying to tackle more today. Better to start afresh in the morning. He reached for his coat and rummaged in the pocket for the list of things Barbara had asked him to pick up after work. Were any of them really urgent? He would much rather just go home and pour himself a beer.

DS Hugh Brody poked his head round the door.

"Good, you haven't gone yet, Guv. Busy?"

"Just getting things in order. Nothing urgent. Something up?"

"We've got a report of a schoolgirl gone missing."

Malcolm let his coat drop. "Missing? How long?"

"An hour or so?"

"Ah, a neurotic mother, is it? Likes her daughter home on the dot and not hanging around on street corners with the wrong sort?"

"I don't know about neurotic, Guv. You can judge that for yourself, if you like. She's here now, at the desk. Helen Wakefield. Her daughter walked home from school with friends. They stopped off for sweets on the way. She went on alone and never arrived. She's eight."

"Eight!" Malcolm frowned. "That's young. Too young to be off with a boyfriend, anyway. Even so, an hour. That doesn't really warrant bringing in the dogs. Sgt Nicholson knows the form, doesn't he?"

"Yes. Yes, of course, he does, but…" Hugh was shifting from foot to foot.

"Come on," said Malcolm, resuming his seat. "What is it that's upping the ante on this for you?"

"Thing is, Guv, It's not the first missing girl around here. There've been two others in the last couple of years while you were at Stamford. DCI Claypole was sent down to take charge."

Malcolm shut his eyes, rummaging through half-remembered reports. "Fleetham village. Was that one?"

"Yes, Guv."

"Architect's daughter. We heard about it. Didn't Claypole nab some local paedophile for it?"

Hugh sighed meaningfully. "Derek Cryer. The guy was caught snapping shots of lads in the public toilets. He had form and it was always teenage boys. Jodie Fitzpatrick was a little girl, seven, nearly eight, and there wasn't a shred of forensic evidence connecting Cryer to her disappearance, but Claypole… I mean DCI Claypole wouldn't…" Hugh paused to choose his words.

"Had a bee in his bonnet and wouldn't let it go?"

suggested Malcolm. "Yes, that's Keith. Tunnel vision is one way of putting it."

"We all knew it wasn't Cryer, but..." Hugh shrugged. "By the time we expanded the investigation it was too late. Jodie Fitzpatrick had been waiting in the park for her parents, after school. Mother was expecting and the dad had driven her to hospital for a check-up. There were plenty of other kids and their parents around but no one saw the girl vanish, and there's not been a trace of her since." Hugh's quivering nostrils indicated how resentful he felt about it.

"Still an open case then. And you say there was another?"

"Yes, Guv. Here in Welsey, about six months later. Rachel Redbourn. Same age, more or less. Lived in Abbey Close. She was supposed to be going to some Saturday club at school with her little sister, but there was a bit of a family argy-bargy and she finished up going alone to join a friend. Only half a mile, down Millfield Road, but she never arrived. Broad daylight."

Hugh pressed his lips together.

Malcolm winced. "Claypole again?"

"Yes, Guv. Some of us suggested there might be similarities with the Fitzpatrick case, but the DCI wouldn't hear of it. Cryer was locked up on remand on other charges, and Claypole was still determined to pin the Fleetham girl on him. He flatly refused to believe it could be a second abduction. He decided Rachel Redbourn must have fallen from the Millfield Road bridge. Had us dragging the river for two days. Nothing. We investigated the father, something of a bully with a temper, but there was no evidence against

9

him. No nothing. It's still officially an unexplained misper."

"I see. And now this." Malcolm nodded. "Three means it can't be coincidence. This one we take seriously and we pull out all the stops. Might be a long night, Hugh."

"I don't mind that, Guv, if it means we do it properly for once."

"Okay. Pat will already be organising door to door, I expect." Malcolm rose again. "I'll speak to the mother now." He screwed up the paper in his coat pocket. The shopping would have to wait.

* * *

Helen Wakefield had square shoulders and strong cheekbones. That was what Malcolm noticed first as he entered the interview room. She looked like a fighter, not a panicking wreck, which was good news because it meant she'd be able to give him the details clearly and calmly, instead of dissolving in a pool of hysteria. He was sympathetic – he could understand hysteria if it broke out, in the circumstances, but it would make his job a lot easier, if it stayed in its box.

Helen stood up as Malcolm came in, her eyes drilling into him.

"Mrs Wakefield. I'm DI Malcolm Cannell. Shall we-"

She held up one hand to silence him and laid the other firmly on his arm.

"Find my daughter. I know what you're going to say. It's only been a short while, I shouldn't worry, she's probably out playing and she'll turn up any moment. I've heard all that. Don't go through it all again. Please. Laura wouldn't do that. She knew she had to be home promptly. She promised. You see it's Kevin's birthday – my husband – and she was dying to help me ice the cake. She was excited about it. That's why she didn't go into the shop with her friends. I asked them. She told them, she was going straight home for Daddy's birthday."

Malcolm looked into her eyes and realised it wasn't strength oozing out of her. It was despair.

"Please," she whispered. "Help us."

Donna's Special Moment

The rain had eased off, no longer sheeting down the windscreen or beating a deafening drum roll on the roof, but it was enough to send the temperature plummeting as soon as the engine was off. Donna Gay hadn't envisaged this special moment happening in Lee Bristow's borrowed car, but there wasn't anywhere else. She shivered and wriggled to get her leg free from the gear stick as Lee struggled with his zip. He was trying to turn to her but he was half pinned by the steering wheel, no more experienced in the logistics of this situation than she was. Maybe they should have got into the back, despite the dog hairs and the dogshit stench. She groped for the lever under her seat that would let the back down and—

"What the…"

A blaze of light flooded the car, and she pushed Lee off, frantically wriggling her t-shirt back down. "Shit, shit, shit!"

"No!"

The two teenagers stared into the Chevette's mirror in disbelief as an HGV pulled into the lay-by behind them, stopping, with a hiss of brakes, just a couple of inches from their bumper. Lorries almost always used the bypass. It had no business on the old road, but there it was, the driver leering down at them. Donna couldn't see him, not with one headlight spearing right through the car and almost blinding her, but she just knew he was leering.

"Fuck! He can't park up here." Lee was zipping himself up, hurriedly, squealing as a hair caught. "Shit!"

"I'm not staying here," said Donna, on the brink of tears. "Get me out of here. Take me home."

"Yeah, look, okay…" Lee groped for the keys which had fallen into the footwell. "It's all right. I know a place. It will be quiet. No-one goes there, not this late." Twilight was already giving way to full darkness.

"They'd better not, that's all." Donna shrank back in her seat as the Chevette, long past its best, coughed into life with a belch of poisonous exhaust.

Lee pulled out, back onto the Fleetham road. "Not far," he promised, squinting into the gloom as the headlights flashed on sodden hedges, banks and the occasional tree. "It's here somewhere. There!" A turning appeared and his sigh of relief gave way to a grin as he swung the car round onto the narrow lane. It ran straight and unflinching across the wide, featureless landscape of harvested stubble. "Okay!"

Donna peered back over her shoulder, to gauge how far they were from the main road. A car's headlights flashed past. Still too close for her comfort.

"A bit further," she said, as Lee slowed. "Just a bit. Look, there's a bend. Once we're round that, okay?"

The lane ahead swung sharply to the right and Lee took the ninety-degree corner at speed. Donna bounced in her seat, grabbing at the console for support and he laughed, his adolescent voice breaking. "Yeah!"

"Shut up! Slow down, will you? There's no need…" Donna stared ahead. The lane ran straight again and a couple of hundred yard on, through the blur of the rain, they could make out the shape of a stationary vehicle. Their headlights just illuminated its side window, revealing it as a small van, its panels glinting blue black.

"Why does it have to be there?" she wailed.

Lee had slowed to a crawl, biting his lip with frustration, but the vehicle suddenly burst into life, juddering backwards and then swerving round, off along the lane and away from them. Through the chilling evening air they could hear its tyres screeching, its engine roar.

Lee laughed. "Another, you know, like us, I reckon. Still, we've frightened them off."

"All right," said Donna, cautiously. "Maybe." Her special moment was losing its magic fast. Lee was driving on and that was fine by her. She didn't want them stopping too near the blind corner in case others had the same idea of making use of that lane and interrupting them in their turn.

They passed a field gate, set into the bank. It must have been where the van had turned. Lee was slowing, looking for somewhere to park up.

"Stop," said Donna, a creeping chill working its way up from her stomach.

"Yeah, just up there."

"No, stop here." Her voice was small. Frightened.

Lee slammed on the brakes. "What?"

"There was something there."

"Where?"

"In the gateway back there."

"What do you mean, something?"

"I don't know. I think…"

She didn't know what she had seen. It wouldn't compute yet, but something had hold of her. It wasn't cold making her shiver now.

"I think we should go back. There was something there."

Lee was looking unnerved now. "I didn't see anything."

"Go back and look."

"Right!" He flung open the door and cold air shot in.

"I'll bloody look then!"

"Don't leave me here!" Donna was virtually screaming. "Can't we reverse?"

"Fuck," he muttered under his breath. He boasted, at school, that he was such a natural at the wheel that a driving test would be a waste of time, but reversing in the dark didn't count as natural. He swivelled in his seat, mouthing a string of obscenities as he peered into the gloom barely illuminated by their rear lights. Gingerly he edged back.

Back. Back. They were level with the gate. Donna sat frozen in her seat. Lee leaned across and pushed her door open. The car's interior light came on, not much but enough to cast a glow across the shadowed gateway, showing…

Donna began to whimper and shake. "I want to go home."

* * *

The house was fusty and it smelled of cabbage or Brussel sprouts. It made Donna feel even more nauseous. She wanted fresh air, but that would mean going outside and she never wanted to go outside again. Out there, past the sagging curtains, headlights flashed past, and blue lights strobed, constantly now, competing with each other. Light sabres at war. They hurt her head, made her want to shut her eyes, but when she shut her eyes…

She heaved.

The old woman slipped a washing-up bowl on Donna's knees and pulled a blanket round her shoulders. Donna stared at the bottom of the bowl, waiting for her shaking to subside. The shivering slowed.

A hand gently touched her arm through the blanket.

"Any better now?"

Donna looked up at the earnest face of the young policewoman who had been assigned to take charge of her. She wanted to smile, because smiling would make it all right, make the image go away, but when she tried to smile, she burst into tears again.

"How about that cup of tea?" suggested the policewoman.

"Oh yes." The old lady tottered off. She seemed to have recovered from the shock of having a Chevette screech to a halt, scratching along her garden wall and two hysterical teenagers screaming for her to phone the police. Now she no longer seemed paralysed with fright, just eager to be part of the drama and catch every word.

"Yes, I'll make tea."

"All right, Donna. Take your time." The policewoman was hunkered down in front of her, peering up to see if she was regaining control. Donna sniffed, accepted a handkerchief and blew her nose violently, then wiped her eyes.

"Do you think you can answer a few more questions?"

Donna nodded. She looked up to see Lee hunched in an armchair, white-faced and nervous, a policeman standing over him, patting him on the shoulder. Or maybe holding him down.

"All right then, Donna, you came round the corner and you saw a van."

"Yes."

"No chance you got the number, anything like that?"

"No. It was too far away."

"But it was definitely a van. Big? Small?"

"I don't know!" Donna had had enough. They were getting at her.

"Well, was it like a removals van? Or a postman's van."

"More like a postman's. But it wasn't red."

"What colour was it?"

"I don't know!"

"Light? Dark?"

"I told you," said Lee. "It was black, like. Or blue. Or maybe grey. A Ford Transit, I reckon."

"You know much about vans, do you, son?" The policeman standing over him was smiling.

"A bit, yeah."

"How old are you?"

"Six… Seventeen. So?"

"Passed your test, have you? Got a driving license?"

"Yeah!"

Donna could see the sweat beading on Lee's face. The policewoman turned to her companion, shaking her head.

"Not now. Okay, you reckon it was a Ford?"

"No it wasn't," said Donna. "My Dad's got one. It wasn't a Ford. It was just, you know, like a car, only no back windows." She concentrated on conjuring up the image of the van, turning in the lane ahead of them, so that other images wouldn't creep in. "It was dark. Might have been blue or black."

"Good! And did you see the driver?"

"No!" She drew her shoulders in, to keep the thought out. She didn't want to see a face in the van. If she had seen it, she wanted it blotted out. Like everything else she'd seen.

The policewoman gave her a last pat then stood up.

"Okay, get onto the guv. Tell him no number plate or description of the driver, but it's a small van, dark, possibly blue or black, could be an Astra or a Fiesta, something like that." She leaned back over Donna. "Did you see anything else, love?"

Donna raised her face, trying to see the policewoman, the neat dark hair, the silly hat, but all she could see – all she could see…

"Yes!" She screamed. And screamed and screamed. "Blood!" It was there before her, blood, blood, blood, and it would never, ever go away.

Shock Welsey Murder: Body Found.

"I was waiting for the potatoes," said Barbara. "Never mind, I'll do pasta instead."

"Sorry." Malcolm considered the can of beer waiting for him on the kitchen worktop, then decided it was unwise. "We've got a flap on. I was wondering what my first serious case would be, back here in Welsey. It's a missing girl. Eight years old."

Barbara paused before opening the freezer. "Oh hell! The poor parents. Do you think she's just lost, or something worse?"

"I don't think there's any chance she got lost." Malcolm leaned on the draining board, shaking his head, then poured himself a glass of water.

"She goes to Lacey Road Primary, walked back with friends to the sweet shop on the corner with the High Street. Crossed the road safely with Lollipop Linda. It's, what, two or three hundred yards from there to Kingston Avenue where she lives? Plenty of people out and about there and none of them saw Laura Wakefield in the avenue. She's well known and liked by all the neighbours."

He thought of the photo Helen Wakefield had shown him – dancing eyes, dancing fair hair, dimples, mouth wide in a smile that revealed gaps of missing baby teeth. A child brimming over with life and joy.

"Happy girl who bounces a lot, that's what they all

say, and somehow she's vanished into thin air."

Barbara was wiping the table absently. "How awful!"

"Yes. When it's a child, you know… Hard not to suspect the worst, in this case. We've spoken to neighbours, friends, teachers, shopkeepers. Not a clue. We're expanding the search, bringing in a dog team."

"And you'll be going back, of course." Barbara opened the bread bin. "Time to snatch something to eat first, or shall I make you—" The warble of the phone interrupted her.

Malcolm picked up the receiver. "Cannell."

"Sorry, sir. A body's been found."

He straightened, switching into professional mode.

"Is it…?"

"It's a child, sir. A girl."

"Right."

No, it wasn't right. Not right at all. But if Laura Wakefield really was the third victim of a serial abductor, then at least they had a tangible lead to work on, this time. A dead body was as emphatic a lead as you could get.

"Is it the missing girl? Laura Wakefield?"

"Looks like it, yes, sir. DS Brody is on his way to pick you up."

"Right. Okay. I'll be ready." He returned to the sink and swilled cold water over his face. "Sorry, Babs."

She was already holding his coat for him. "Go."

Malcolm opened the front door as Hugh Brody loomed into view through the glass.

"Sorry to have to call you out again, Guv."

"Don't worry, I wasn't planning an early night."

Malcolm followed him down the garden path to the waiting car.

"Okay. Fill me in."

"Piper's Lane. Do you know it?"

"Cuts across to Bartlet Lane and the abattoir?"

"That's right. Not the most romantic spot but a couple of teenagers were looking for a bit of privacy, which is what you'd expect to find round there. It seems the murderer was expecting the place to be deserted, too. They interrupted him before he could remove the body."

"Him? You mean they got a description?"

"Not exactly. Didn't see the driver, but they caught him having to do a hasty turn in the road in order to get away."

"Number plate?"

"No such luck, sorry, too far away. But they did describe the vehicle. Said it was a small black van. Black or dark blue, they thought. Noisy engine. Brakes screeched."

The words pricked a memory immersed in a kaleidoscope of random images. Brakes screeched... Drugs? No, not drugs. Malcolm had a horrible feeling it was important but he shelved it for now. This was immediate and urgent.

"Right. Let's get out there and see what we can do before HQ descend on us."

* * *

Piper's Lane was not one of the drunken rolling roads of Saxon England. Running with mathematical precision across the flat acres, a straight line staggered by sharp turns at field corners, there was nothing to distinguish it from other tracks through other flat acres. Apart, that is, from the incident tape blocking access, the police cars already in attendance and the flash of cameras. A cold wind slapped Malcolm in the face as he climbed out.

Sergeant Pat Nicholson was in charge. "No really much doubt it's the Wakefield girl, Malcolm. Face is slashed but hair and clothing matches the description her mother gave."

He led the way to a field gateway, set back in the sparse hedgerow.

Concrete slabs crossed the drainage ditch that edged the lane. The girl's body was splayed across them, ghoulish in the artificial light. Blood was congealing on the fair hair. A single slash disfigured one cheek. Dead. No life. No joy. Malcolm swallowed bile.

"Killer was disturbed," said Hugh. "Didn't have time to finish the job."

"Whatever the job was." Malcolm stared down at the child. Fully clothed. That was something. At least, he supposed it was something. Would Mr and Mrs Wakefield find it remotely gratifying to learn that their daughter was merely mutilated and murdered?

"Any more on the van?"

"Just tyre prints. It churned up the verge, making its get-away. The kids who found her, the boy, reckons it might have been a Ford, but I think he was just after a bit of extra credit. And the girl, well she's done nothing but puke. Mind where you step."

"Right. You've got everything in hand, Pat?"

"Yes, doc's been. And a team's on its way over from HQ."

"DCI Claypole?"

Nicholson smiled grimly. "No. Superintendent Lake, this time. From what I've heard, he's on the ball." He added, under his breathe, "For once, thank God."

Malcolm decided not to hear. "Right. Have the parents been notified?"

"Not yet. I was just going to send a couple—"

"No. I'll speak to them."

* * *

The house in Kingston Avenue was a respectable family home, detached but not large, garage with a pink girl's bike propped against it. Lights were on in most of the windows. Neighbours were out, hovering in the street, looking both serious and curious, as the car pulled up and Malcolm got out. PC Sandra Thorpe accompanied him up the drive. He rang the bell.

A figure was already silhouetted through the dimpled glass of the front door – someone who had seen the car arrive and had stepped into the hall in readiness, but who couldn't now bring himself to respond.

Sandra reached up to press the bell again. Malcolm stopped her.

Finally, the figure within moved. The door opened and Kevin Wakefield was standing there, holding his breath, his face grey.

"DI Cannell, sir, and PC Thorpe. Can we come in?"

Kevin nodded, stepped back. He shut the door

behind them, his hand shaking.

"Perhaps your wife could join us?"

"Helen." His voice croaked. "Can you come?"

The kitchen door at the end of the hall was open, and Helen Wakefield was standing there, mixing bowl in one hand, wooden spoon in the other, beating the contents to death and refusing to look up.

"Helen."

"I've got to do the icing. Got to do it. Laura will—"

"Leave it." Her husband had joined her and was wrestling the bowl from her grip. He steered her through to the sitting room and sat her down on the sofa.

A teenage boy came sliding down the stairs. "Is it Laura?"

His father tugged him over to the sofa and sank down with him, legs giving way. The boy stared up but both parents looked down at the carpet, every muscle clenched, waiting.

I'm very sorry to have to tell you..." began Malcolm.

"No. No. No!" Helen Wakefield was shaking uncontrollably. She raised her face and screamed. "No!"

☐

Single Mum: No One Listened.

It was the mention of screeching brakes. Some memory had unlocked, and Malcolm needed to prise it open. He caught Sgt Nicholson as he was about to grab a cup of tea. "Pat, can we have a word? I need to pick your brains."

"Sure." Nicholson followed Malcolm to his office. "What's the problem?"

"Do you remember a case two or three years back? Two and a half, it must have been. I was still DS here. It was just before I was made inspector and moved south. It was the same time as the Ellington drugs bust."

"Our big moment in the limelight, eh?"

"Yes, the whole station was fixated on Ellington. But a mother reported her daughter missing at the same time. Mile End estate?"

Nicholson wrinkled his nose, thinking. "Let me see. Knowles. Was that the name? Nothing like this case, though, was it? Wasn't it resolved? Custody battle or something. The father had taken her."

"Yes. Or no. I was sent to make enquiries at St Thomas's Junior. The head told me the parents were separated but she'd seen the father at the school gates the day before, talking with the girl. Ashley. Yes, I'm sure her name was Ashley. It was followed up and... I can't remember. I have a feeling we did get confirmation she was with her father, but I moved on before I heard the end of it. I just want to check that it really was settled."

"I'll have a look. Jack Harris was in charge of records, and you know he was ill, dropped dead a month later. His methods had got a bit haphazard. I'll find the file."

"Thanks. Preferably before we're invaded by the big boys."

"At least they'll have something definite to work on this time. How did it go with the parents?"

"How do you think?"

"Yeah, right. I'll get that Knowles file sent to you."

* * *

Detective Superintendent Lake, taking charge of the incident room in an immaculate pin-striped suit, was a thin stork of a man. He walked without bending his legs, and spoke in clipped phrases.

"Mutilated body of child. Girl reported missing last evening. Second in Welsey. A previous one seven miles away in Fleetham. DCI Claypole dealt with those disappearances. Suspected a known sex-offender for the first and concluded the second was a case of accidental drowning."

Lake studied his notes, expressionless, while grunts and mutters went the rounds.

"DCI Claypole is on extended leave, at present. You've got me instead. I've looked at the notes on the two previous—"

Malcolm interrupted him. "I think It's possible there were three previous, sir."

"Three? Explain."

"Rachel Redbourn went missing a year ago, from Welsey. Jodie Fitzpatrick disappeared six months before that, in Fleetham. A third girl was reported missing nine months before that, in '94. Ashley Knowles. Eight years old. Vanished from the Mile End estate here in Welsey and I'm thinking now that she might have been the first."

Lake flicked through papers without looking at them.

"There's no mention of Knowles in Claypole's files."

"We hadn't made the connection back then. It was an oversight."

"An oversight."

"Yes, sir. I'm afraid... 1994, there was a big drugs case on, plus a fire on the industrial, suspected arson."

"And a missing girl."

"Yes, sir. Enquiries were made. The girl lived with her mother, a single parent. The father was a lorry driver. He'd walked out on them a couple of years before, but he was seen with the girl at school the day before she disappeared. We intended to interview him, of course, but another driver with the same haulage firm reported seeing him, the day after, at the port, boarding for Rotterdam, accompanied by a young girl. That seemed to confirm that Ashley was with him, except that..."

Lake was expressionless. "Go on."

"The driver who reported seeing them was just responding initially to queries about the father's whereabouts. It was only some time later that he heard that Ashley was missing and he gave an amended statement to police in Harwich. It appears that when he'd said the father was travelling with a young girl, what he meant was someone in her late teens. Not an eight-year-old."

There was a general groan in the room. Malcolm was ready to join in with it. He could remember the case well enough now – remember being impatient at having to deal with a domestic squabble when there was bigger game afoot. Everyone was anxious to assume it was the dad. He hadn't pressed for more, just made his report to the DI and left it at that. The social services would sort it out. And he'd no longer been around when that amended statement had come in. Sgt Harris, on his last legs though no one had realised it at the time, had merely filed the statement away.

"The revised statement was passed on to us, but it wasn't followed up, sir."

"But now you suspect she's our murderer's first victim."

"Yes, sir. Same age. Similar appearance – fair, shoulder-length hair. In Ashley Knowle's case, neighbours reported hearing brakes screeching and seeing a van with a roaring engine speeding out of the estate. I'm afraid that wasn't regarded as particularly significant at the time. The Mile End estate is a bit of a rough area. Kids go joy-riding all the time."

"Details of the van?"

"Only that it was small, black or dark blue."

"Like the one reported in this latest case."

"Yes, sir."

"Perhaps you'd like to follow it up now."

"Yes, sir."

* * *

Malcolm got out of his car and made certain it was locked. It didn't do to leave anything of any value within reach of slippery fingers round here. Half the residents claiming benefits, drugs exchanging hands on every corner, women on the game... He stopped himself before he could finish the full list of prejudices against the Mile End estate, and looked around. A bit of litter, but no more than anywhere else. A couple of cars had passed him on his way in, men on their way to work. Muffled sounds of a few radios. He recalled his visits here as a lowly DS, and it had seemed properly sinister at night, but this was early morning and everything was sleepily quiet. He braced himself as he strode to the entrance of Newton House, a low-rise block, and headed up to Flat 14.

There was a long silence when he rang the bell. He waited a minute, then knocked. The door finally opened and he found himself facing a dishevelled woman, wrapped in a dressing gown, shadows under her blank eyes.

"Mrs Sharon Knowles?"

"Not Mrs, thank God. What do you want?"

"I'm DI Cannell."

"I thought the pigs might come calling. Everyone's saying a girl's been murdered." She trailed back into the flat and he followed, into a living room that reeked of tobacco and whisky. She was already lighting up a cigarette. "So?"

"I'm hoping to be able to clear up some details

29

regarding your daughter, Ashley."

"My dead daughter, you mean."

"Is she dead?"

"What do you think? She went missing more than two years ago and you lot never lifted a finger. Of course she's dead."

"We can't be sure of that." Malcolm had a grinding sensation in the pit of his stomach. He was bullshitting this woman and he had no right to do so. She'd been given nothing last time. Didn't she deserve a bit better, now?

"We suspected at the time that your partner—"

"Ex-partner. Yeah, you decided that Callum had taken her off to Holland, except that he was really with his latest tart, not Ashley. I thought Mikey had put you right on that, or couldn't you be bothered to read his statement?"

He decided to tell the truth and bear the pain.

"Unfortunately, it was overlooked."

"Yeah, well, you can find Cal and confirm it. He's still shacked up with Loulou or whatever she's called. In Amsterdam, if you're interested."

"The headmistress of her school did see him talking to Ashley just before she went missing."

"Yeah. That's right. Like I said at the time, if anyone had bothered to listen. He did the decent thing, for once. He came to say goodbye to her because he was leaving the country. Made a change from just disappearing without a word."

"Yes. I really am very sorry about that. We should have asked the Dutch police to find him and confirm that initial report."

"Yeah. You should. Like you should have searched the area. Like you should have gone looking for that van. We reported it. We looked. Everyone round here, we were out looking for her, and all you lot did was knock on a few doors and decide she must be with Callum. Kept going on about what sort of a crap mother I was and latchkey kids. I worked, okay. I was on late shift at Tesco's and Ashley was supposed to be going to tea with a friend. I didn't just leave her to fend for herself. Got that?"

"Yes, of course. I understand."

"And then going on about Ashley having been in care."

"Yes, I did notice that in the notes."

"You know why she was in care for a bit? I was in bloody hospital for a month. It was either that or let Callum take care of her and I wasn't having that. Go on, ask social services, if you give a shit. But you don't. You never did."

She picked up a framed photo from her cluttered sideboard and stared at it. So did Malcolm. A photo of mother and daughter, smiling, happy, cocky, the girl with a broad cheeky grin, the mother confident, almost glamorous – and young. She must have been very young when she'd had Ashley. She'd aged badly since that photograph had been taken. Malcolm struggled to believe it was the same woman standing next to him, but the change was not surprising, considering that she had been doubly betrayed, by whoever had taken her daughter and by the police. Why hadn't he asked more?

"She was my darling daughter," said Sharon,

replacing the photo. "My Ashley. I wasn't a bad mum.

We were all right, Ashley and me. I loved her, right, and you lot didn't give a shit." She stubbed out her cigarette, aggressively. The despair smothering her bitterness doubled Malcolm's sense of guilt. Tripled it. She wasn't spitting with rage, just numb with the pointlessness of saying anything.

"I am sorry. Truly. Very sorry. The case was never closed. We are still looking. We've had further reports of a van similar to the one seen when Ashley disappeared and we'll be—"

"It's true, then. You've found this last girl. Dead."

"Yes."

"How did she die?"

"We can't be sure yet."

"I want to know what he did to Ashley."

"We can't be certain—"

"Oh fuck off." She turned from him to the window, nursing her cigarette. "I know she's dead, and you lot did nothing.

"I'm sorry. I'll keep you informed if we find..."

"Just fuck off." She waved him away without looking at him.

Malcolm crept away. Muddled memories had clarified in a horribly clear light by now. There'd been much back-slapping and congratulations over their success with the drugs bust, one of those countywide cases that was destined to make national news. But all the time there had been the noises off, the images in the background – the vociferous women of the Mile End estate, invading the station and clamouring about a dark van and why weren't the police looking for it?

Was he going to admit, even to himself, that they hadn't pulled out all the stops because too many lazy assumptions had been made, about the area, the mother, the girl... They had better things to do. Malcolm wondered if they would have been as casual about it if Sharon Knowles and her daughter had lived in the same street as the Wakefields? If the police had focused properly, asked the right questions, paid the proper attention back in 1994, would three other girls be safe at home with their families now? It might not all be down to him, but he felt as if it was.

Latest: Irnby Man In Custody

Margaret Gittings stood at the sink, methodically wiping down every surface, scrubbing the bowl, wringing out the cloth. Everything in the kitchen was neatly, precisely in its place. She looked out at the garden. Just the same, or as much as she could manage in a year: cut grass, trimmed bushes, neat rows. Order and cleanliness, childhood habits drilled into her from the cradle, embraced still as if order out there could counteract the turmoil within.

Take control. That's what she had to do. Act normally. She forced herself to be calm, put the kettle on, reach for the pot and the tea caddy. She switched on the radio, because that was normal. Not because she had to hear the news. Not because she was afraid to hear the news. Stupid music playing, that was all. Wasn't that kettle boiling yet?

"*And now we go over to the newsroom for the latest on the murder...*"

She listened, shaking, fists clenched. "*...looking for a dark van, believed to have been...*"

Margaret lunged for the off switch. Be still, be still, be still. She put a frying pan on the hob, switched it on, opened the fridge to take out eggs, bacon, sausages. Tim would need his breakfast, wouldn't he? He couldn't stay in bed all day, whimpering under the covers.

No, she couldn't do it. She switched the ring off again. Tea. Just tea. She filled the teapot, her hand shaking so much that the boiling water splashed on her hand. She didn't care. It was just pain. Everything was just pain. Everything had always been just pain.

She went through to the front room, stood there willing herself to step up to the window. Furtively, she twitched open the lace curtain. Twitched it back as soon as she saw that nosey Grayling cow opposite, watching from her window. Cow. Margaret moved to the other side of the window, twitched the lace again, peered out down the road. All quiet. A lorry passed. Nothing to worry about, no one around. Then…

She saw it. No blue lights flashing, but she knew a police car when she saw one. Acid welled up inside her. No. No, no, no! They couldn't. Not again.

"Timmy!" She shouted, then she screamed it. "Timmy! Get up! You've got to get up now! Please, Timmy, do as Mam says. Please!"

* * *

Small, dark blue or black. The police might have failed to follow it up when Ashley Knowles was reported missing, but that van was their priority lead this time. Patient questioning of the traumatised teenagers who had found the body suggested it might be a Bedford Astra Van. Or might not. It was somewhere to start. Vans registered in the area were to be checked. There were a lot of them. A lot of irritated and resentful owners to be questioned.

"Looks like they've got something a bit suspicious

out at Irnby, Guv," Hugh Brody informed Malcolm. "Woman very reluctant to cooperate, apparently. You want me to check it out?"

"No, I'll go." Malcolm needed to be doing something positive.

He took the old road out east from Welsey, passing the turning to the Wakefield's house on Kingston Avenue, remembering the outburst of eviscerating grief. God, he hated making those calls. If he could just come up with some answers for them. He drove on to Irnby, a dreary non-place, three miles out of town and halfway to the large, prosperous village of Fleetham. It was no more than a random siting of houses, without church or school, pub or shop or garage, out in the wide fields, among a web of drains. A drab post-war terrace of five houses on the right, three older cottages on the left and that was it. If it had ever had a purpose, no one could remember what it was.

A police car was parked at the far end of the terrace, and Malcolm pulled up behind it. A constable hurried along to speak to him.

"Woman at No.5, sir, Margaret Gittings. She's the registered owner of a van but neighbours say it's only her son who drives it. She claims he's away on business. Went on Saturday and won't be back till the weekend. She's quite adamant about it. Too adamant, if you know what I mean. Won't let us in. There's a locked garage."

"I see. Right." Malcolm got out, shrugging his coat on. As he did so, he caught an elderly woman, propped painfully on two sticks, hobbling out to the gate of the cottage opposite. She waved a stick urgently at him.

"I'll just see what this lady wants, first."

He crossed the road. "Good afternoon, madam. Can I help you?"

She was breathless from the effort to get to the gate.

"Waiting for you lot to come."

"Yes?"

"Are you a policeman, then? Like them over there?" She nodded towards the constables who were trying to negotiate with a barely opened door.

"I am. Detective Inspector Malcolm Cannell." He was groping in his pocket for identification, but she waved him impatiently to stop. She wasn't interested in bits of paper.

"You're here about him, aren't you? Timothy Gittings. Him and his van. Noisy smelly thing." Her voice croaked, as if she didn't get to use it much. She coughed to clear it.

"We're checking on all owners of dark vans in the vicinity, Mrs…?"

"Grayling. Eileen Grayling. It was him, you know. Him as did for all those girls."

"You think so?"

"Yes, I do, my ducks, and don't you go thinking I'm just a daft old woman imagining things. I watch, you see. Ask round here. They'll tell you I'm a nosy old cow, and maybe I am, but I don't sleep, see. Not with the arthritis. Pain gets too bad, so I sit in my chair and look out. Watch my neighbours, watch the birds, watch the foxes."

"Yes, yes, love, and what did you see?"

"I saw him come home like Old Nick and all his imps were on his tail. Last night. After dark. Left that van of his half across the road and off he goes, running into the house. Whimpering like a child, that's what he was doing. I had the window open. I could hear him."

"I see." DI Cannell nodded, eyes narrowing as he looked from one side of the road to the other. Her window seemed mostly blocked by a lilac bush that had got out of hand. Was she fantasising about what she might have seen? The murder had been occupying the local radio all morning. They'd had more than a few calls from people trying too hard to be helpful.

Eileen Grayling was watching him intently, to see if he'd dismiss her as a senile old biddy or listen properly. She had more to say and she was going to say it if it killed her. Every attempt at speech was interspersed with a racking cough.

"He's a weird one, that boy. Timothy Gittings. Face all mashed up. Never looks you in the eye. And not right in the head, either. Won't say a word one moment and swearing at you the next for no damn reason. Can't do anything wrong in his mum's eyes though. She'll go for you like a wild cat if you as much as tick him off. She was there, last night, bundling him into the house. Then she came out and moved his van round the back. It's a dark one, all right. Dark blue if you can see through the filth. They've got a shed back there. She was coming and going with buckets and there were lights on in the house, on and off, all through the night. I saw them. Like bloody Morse code. On, off, on, off. Then, after midnight it was, she was out the back, at the incinerator, burning things."

"Burning things? What things?"

"Looked like clothes to me." Eileen was getting

caught up in her own excitement. She needed to calm herself.

"And you can see round to the back of No.5 from here?" Malcolm glanced across the road again. There was no line of sight round the side of the end terrace from where he was standing.

She wanted to tell him, but her coughing increased. All she could do was point with one of her sticks to the bedroom window.

"Can I go up? Take a look?" He took her cough for permission and bounded through the open door, up the stairs to the front room. Old sagging brass bed and a chamber-pot under it. An armchair by the window and a small table with a plate of crackers and cheese. This was where the old girl must spend her days. God knows how she managed the stairs.

He moved the table away from the window and looked out. From that vantage point, he could see straight up the side of No.5 to a corrugated iron shed, its double doors padlocked. And there was the incinerator next to it, just as she'd said.

He rushed back down the stairs, nearly tripping in his haste. This had to be it. He was on the verge of clearing up four probable murders. Please God, there would be no more lost girls.

"Right, thank you, Mrs Grayling. Someone will take a statement from you very soon. For now, just go in and make yourself a nice cuppa. Okay?"

She wanted to resist, but he guided her firmly back to her door, before heading back across the road to No.5.

The two PCs were still trying to talk to the occupant,

who was pushing against the door. Would have slammed it on them if a police boot were not in the way.

"I told you, he's not here. Go away."

"Margaret Gittings?" said Malcolm, smiling politely.

"He's not here. I told them, he's away. In Nottingham. All week. So leave us alone."

"I'm sorry, Mrs Gittings, but we have a witness who claims to have seen your son come home last night. I think both he and your van are on the premises right now, and I have reason to believe that you have already been destroying evidence, so…"

Margaret Gittings finally flung her door wide open. Not to admit them, but to shoot a look of snarling venom at Eileen, still propped in her own doorway. She spat.

Eileen spat back.

Angry Parents Slam Police

Piggot's Drive, Fleetham

It was the looks from his neighbours than alerted Peter Fitzpatrick, as he opened the bedroom curtains. No obvious gloating, but a thoughtful frown from John Taylor across the road as he prepared to drive off to work; then the Layton women, mother and daughter, from the house beyond, hurrying past and risking a furtive glance, one with her hand over her mouth as the other whispered in her ear.

Nothing of major significance, but Fitzpatrick was alert to every nuance. Something was up. He sat back on the crumpled bed and switched the radio on. Local news.

"…child thought now to have been the fourth victim of a serial offender. The police have not yet issued an official statement, but we understand that two people have been taken into custody and are now helping police with their enquiries."

He jumped up, rage rippling through him. Not yet issued an official statement? To hell with that. Did they seriously expect him to wait for that? He grabbed yesterday's clothes and headed for the bathroom, drenching his face with ice-cold water, and braced himself on the basin, waiting for the nausea of burning tension to fade.

He raised his eyes to the window, staring out into

the unkempt garden. Somewhere in that long grass there had been a rabbit hutch. Eyes shut, he could still see it, that day, the last day he had seen his daughter Jodie. His solemn and serious little girl, standing there, feeding her pet rabbit. She was going to be a vet, she'd told him, so she could look after lots of rabbits. She'd have done it, too. Except that she never did anything again. She was gone. The rabbit was gone. The no-expense-spared showcase garden was gone. Let the place go to wrack and ruin. Who cared? Not him. Not his wife, Lorraine, who was a nervous wreck, living with her mother now. She'd lost her daughter and then she'd lost the baby she was carrying, and Fitzpatrick had lost everything. Everything except rage.

* * *

Abbey Close, Welsey

Jennifer Redbourn slammed breakfast dishes into the washing-up bowl. "You heard. You heard it, didn't you?"

She turned to face her husband Alan, who was sitting slumped at the kitchen table, his head down, fingers twisting the corner of a place mat.

"I said, you heard it, didn't you? Or do you just have the news on as white noise, to blank me out?"

He looked up, not at her. "I heard. What difference does it make?"

"They've caught someone, that's the difference. So are you just going to sit there?"

"What am I supposed to do?"

"Go there! Ask them!"

He was looking down again. "Easy for you. They never suspected you. How do you think I felt?"

"Oh for God's sake! You pathetic man." She bit back tears, of frustration, of rage, of grief. "Well, I am going to ask. No, not ask. I'm going to demand. Just like you should be doing. Like you should have done a year ago, instead of deflating like a punctured balloon." She marched to the kitchen door and shouted up the stairs.

"Luke! Amy! Down now. We're going to the police station."

Her son peered down over the banister. "What about school?"

"School can wait." Jennifer was already pulling her coat on. She opened the front door and stared out down the road. Every time she opened that door and looked out, she saw it all again – sturdy, responsible Rachel in her blue anorak, heading off to gym club, because little Amy, screaming in a tantrum on the sofa behind, was refusing to go, and Alan, huffing and puffing like a sergeant major, was blaming Jenny for mollycoddling the kids. *"Go on, Rachel, left, right, left, right. You'll be all right on your own. You don't need your mother to hold your hand at your age."* And that laugh floating back from Rachel, because of course she was all right on her own. Except that she wasn't and Alan should have known that, and Jenny would never ever forgive him.

"I'm going," she snapped. "Do what you like, but I have to know."

* * *

Malcolm Cannell felt relief mingled with tension. Things were moving to a conclusion, at last. They didn't just have a lead, but a suspect in custody – one who did more than merely fit the bill. The parents hadn't been told officially yet, apart from Kevin Wakefield, because the police were still trying to pin down precise details, but the station was abuzz. Even the Ellington drugs case couldn't match this. They had their man, everyone knew it. Not just a killer but, it seemed almost certain, a serial killer.

He caught a babble of raised voices in the lobby. It sounded as if the press conference, scheduled for four o'clock, was already underway. But Malcolm knew what it was more likely to be. Word of the murder had spread round the town in a couple of hours, so news of a suspect in custody would also be in circulation by now.

He went out to the desk. It was exactly as he had supposed. Peter Fitzpatrick was there, father of the girl Jodie who had gone missing from the park in Fleetham. One moment the parents had been nagged with pregnancy anxieties and the next they were engulfed by a horror beyond comprehension. Malcolm had read up on all the cases now. He'd seen Fitzpatrick described as a mild-mannered, professional guy at first, hopelessly unaware that as the father of the missing child he would be one of the first suspects. His alibi had been watertight, but that couldn't have been much relief, thanks to DCI Claypole's obsession fixation on

Derek Cryer.

Malcolm recognised Fitzpatrick from photographs in the file, but there was nothing mild-mannered about him now. He was burning with a resentful fury. Of course he'd have headed straight for Welsey police station at the first rumour of an arrest.

Jennifer Redbourn. He recognised her from the files too. And, he realised now, from her previous visits to the station. She'd been in twice since he'd returned at DI, although he hadn't enquired why. The desk sergeant had dealt with her. Apparently, she'd been haunting the place for the last year, demanding updates on an investigation that was still official open but no longer being pursued. The files had described her as a meek little housewife, under the thumb of a blustering husband, but any meekness had evaporated under the weight of grief and not knowing. She had turned to steel. Word was out and Jennifer Redbourn had come for answers.

She had her two remaining children with her. Maybe she didn't dare let them out of her sight. Luke, the boy, eleven or twelve, was sullenly braced against the wall, his back to them, silently ripping the edges of a poster. Six-year-old Amy, tear-flushed face buried in her mother's coat, was sucking her thumb like a three-year-old.

There was another parent present, with them and yet apart. Sharon Knowles had turned up, too. She was sitting alone, smoking compulsively. Fully dressed now and made up, but the make-up only emphasised the impact of the last two and a half years. She was still in her twenties, but she looked over forty. Hollowed out by grief.

What were they waiting for? A sudden lightning bolt of justice? Permission to move on with their lives? That was something none of them had been able to do, and God knows if anything would be different now.

Fitzpatrick was shouting. "Yes, and you know why? Because I heard it on the radio."

"Well, it's—" The desk sergeant was trying to calm him, without success.

"No one came to tell me. No phone call. Don't you think I was at least due a phone call?" He turned to Jennifer. "You'd think they would, wouldn't you? They've got a body this time. And now they've got the bastard!" He ignored the sergeant's coughing attempt to qualify the claim.

"It was on the radio." Jennifer Redbourn was standing stiffly, almost to attention, fists clenched, ready to punch anyone who got in her way. "They said the girl was…" Jennifer's jaw clamped, as she tried to control her voice.

Malcolm stepped forward, their eyes instantly fixing on him. "Mrs Redbourn, Mr Fitzpatrick, Sharon. I am DI Malcolm Cannell. You'll have heard there's been a murder and naturally you want to know more. I do understand that, but I'm afraid there's very little we can tell you for now."

"You've got the killer, though!" insisted Fitzpatrick.

Malcolm held his hands up. "No one has been charged yet. Two people are helping us with our enquiries. That's all I can say, at this stage."

"Yes, yes, but they said there's been an arrest. Is that true or not? Tell us you've got him. The bastard who took our girls."

"We are pursuing enquiries, and we're about to interview the suspect, but, please, understand, as I said, no one has been charged yet, and until then, we can't say that we definitely have the right man. If he's charged... As soon as that happens, you will be informed, I promise. A police officer will be on your doorsteps—"

"Ha!" said Fitzpatrick. "More liaison officers pretending to be sympathetic while they spy on us to see what we're hiding? No thank you!"

"I'll tell you what," said Malcolm. "*I* shall be on your doorstep to let you know exactly how the case is progressing."

"And where he's put our girls," demanded Jennifer.

"That is one of the things we hope these interviews will determine. Believe me, I am absolutely resolved to find them all. Laura Wakefield's parents will have a chance to say goodbye and lay her to rest. I swear I will do everything in my power to make sure you will have the same, for Rachel, Jodie and Ashley."

The list prompted Fitzpatrick and Jennifer to turn and take proper note of Sharon Knowles's presence for the first time. They stared at her as she sat, saying nothing.

Fitzpatrick turned back. "It's true, is it? What they were claiming on the radio? The bastard took three girls before this one? Not just our two, but three?"

"Yes, we now think it's possible."

"Jesus! And how much time have you wasted getting nowhere?"

Jennifer stepped up to Malcolm. "You've got

somewhere now. Don't let this monster slip your fingers again, or I'll hunt him down and rip him apart myself."

"I understand," said Malcolm.

Behind them, Sharon Knowles rose and walked out.

Exasperated, they followed her.

The desk sergeant gave a sigh of relief. "I thought they'd be in. Wasn't looking forward to it. For my sake, as much as theirs, you get the answers."

"I'm on my way now," said Malcolm.

* * *

Timothy Gittings' lank hair was long, hanging over his face, probably to disguise reminders of past injuries. His left cheek was dented and scarred, the eye distorted and his nose was out of joint. He still wore the same expression of sullen resentment that he had displayed when they'd dragged him down from the loft in Irnby. Not fury, not fear, just sullen resentment. He looked down, up, away, anywhere but directly at people, blocking them out. Even the duty solicitor who accompanied him to the interview room received no acknowledgement. Superintendent Lake's team would have the pleasure of interviewing him. Malcolm got to interview the mother.

Suspect's Mother Questioned

Margaret Gittings was a small woman, transparent somehow, the sort people would pass on the street without registering. If he hadn't heard her snarling and screaming on her doorstep, Malcolm would have thought her the sort who wouldn't dream of raising her voice. No screaming now. She was folded in on herself, shoulders in, hands clasped, knees locked together, quite motionless except for her thin lips working constantly. Her pale blue eyes were fixed on Malcolm, waiting for the butcher's knife, but with a gleam of defiance rather than fear. Some interviews were easy. He recoiled from this one.

"Now, then." He shuffled papers. "Mrs Margaret Anne Gittings. You know why you're here, Margaret?"

"I know you've arrested my son and he hasn't done anything."

A slight Welsh accent. It had been more obvious when she'd been in full throttle. He glanced at the file again. From South Wales apparently, although she'd lived in the Welsey area for three years. She and her son.

"He hasn't done anything," she repeated, through her teeth.

"You know that isn't true."

"It is true! He's done nothing!"

"If you really thought that, why did you persuade

him to hide in your loft when we knocked on your door? Why did you tell our officers that he'd been away all week in Nottingham? Driven there on Saturday, wasn't it? Wouldn't be home till the weekend? Why did you say that, when his van was in your shed and he was in your attic?"

"Because I knew you'd come accusing him. You'd be bound to pick on him, just because he's got a van."

"No, Margaret. We merely came calling on you, very politely, because we've been calling on everyone in the area with a dark van. We're picking on him, as you call it, because his van has blood in it."

"No, it doesn't!"

"Yes, it does. We've found traces, despite the scrubbing."

"Well then, so what. Of course it has blood. He works at the abattoir."

"Not animal blood, Margaret. Human."

"His, then. He's always cutting himself."

"Not his blood group. But it does match Laura Wakefield's blood. Laura Wakefield. Eight years old. Here's a picture of her, Margaret. School photo. Pretty little thing, isn't she? No?" Malcolm pulled the photograph back, since Margaret Gittings refused to look at it. She kept her eyes fixed on him, unblinking.

"No. She wasn't pretty when we found her. Was it you, tried to clean the blood in the van? Not your son. You put a lot of effort into it, didn't you? Always dirty, we've been told, but it was positively sparkling when we found it. Not quite sparkling enough though. You were working in the dark, of course, and you missed a few bits. A smudge of blood, a couple of fair hairs. Not

50

surprising that you missed some, working all alone because your son couldn't have helped you. He was in too much of a state when he came home. Wailing and wittering, according to a neighbour."

"That's not true! It's Eileen Grayling, isn't it? She's a liar. A lying bitch!"

"She's an old lady in a lot of pain. Keeps her awake at night, so she looks out and she sees things. Like you going out to the shed in the night with a bucket. Like flames flickering in your back garden in the early hours. If you didn't think your son had done anything, why did you burn his clothes, Margaret? Is that how you normally deal with dirty laundry? Saves on the washing powder, I suppose."

"It's none of your business what I do in my own home." She was still not blinking, tense as a cat, ready to parry every blow.

"It *is* my business if what you're doing is destroying evidence of a crime. A murder. And not the first, was it? Have a look at these pictures, Margaret. Rachel Redbourn. Jodie Fitzpatrick. Ashley Knowles. Little girls. What did he do with them, Margaret? Because he killed them too, didn't he? Did you scrub the van and burn his clothes each time? Look at them, Margaret."

She leaned across the table, refusing to look down, fists clenched. "The only child I want to look at is my son. I want my son. You're not taking him from me, you hear me? You're not sending him down for murder, because of the lies of some stinking old witch!"

Malcolm leaned back, folding his arms. "You know what, Margaret? I'm not even sure he'll go to trial." He saw the flash of desperate hope in her eyes. "Because, let's face it, your son isn't right in the head, is he? Insane, even. Is that what you think?"

"No!"

"Then why does he go around killing little girls?"

"He doesn't. There's nothing wrong with my son."

"What, then? You think he's putting it on - angling to plead insanity? You realise, Margaret, that if he is sane, he's nothing but an evil child-killer."

She stared at him, lips pressed together, the desperation stoking up inside her. A mother's desperation. Malcolm had seen enough of that, before.

"You don't believe that, Margaret, and to be honest, neither do I. He's a sad case, that's my thought. Got enough of a grasp to know what he's done is wrong and he needs to hide the evidence, but beyond that, not really aware. Hasn't really come to terms with the world. He's, what, twenty-three? Old enough to drive, old enough to hold down a job, but inside he's still a little boy. Your little boy. He'll always be that, won't he, Margaret?"

He kept his voice steady, low, sympathetic. Watched her eyes suddenly swimming with tears, the tic in her cheek as his words wormed under her skin. He fought down the urge to lean over and throttle the woman.

"Someone made a bit of a mess of his face, didn't they?"

She drew in her breath. "That bastard!"

"It can't have been easy for him with those scars. And people can be cruel. Do they laugh at him, call him names? Call him stupid? Call him Scarface, maybe. Who's responsible for those scars, Margaret? Did he get beaten up? Bullied? But whatever other people have done, you've always stood by him, haven't you? You've always been there to protect him, and he'll always need you to take care of him. Make his tea and wash his shirts. Clean up after him. He needs help, really, not punishment. He needs you. His home. They're interviewing him now. Do you think he'll even be able to understand what they're asking, without you there to help him? When we arrested him, he was like a child. Had to be dragged like a child. Babbling. Didn't seem to understand what was happening, just wanted to find his toys, his book…"

The briefest intake of breath. The momentary flicker of her eyes and he'd caught it. Timothy Gittings had mumbled about his toys and book and Malcolm had suspected he was just playing dumb, but had there been a world of meaning in those words? They hadn't found a knife. A sick mind might regard a murder weapon as a toy. Was the book a diary of sorts? There was something deeply significant in the words and Margaret had been unable to hide her alarm when he'd mentioned them.

"Does he have a favourite book, Margaret? Favourite toys. Tell me where they are and I'll have them brought in for him, how about that?" Play it cool and she might not grasp that she'd given anything away.

But it didn't work like that. She grasped it, perfectly. Of course she did. The shutters came down. Her lips tightened.

"Or what about favourite clothes?" Keep trying. "Or something to eat. Tell us what he likes, Margaret, and we'll see if we can make him feel more at home."

"He wants to be at home. With me. Not in your filthy cells. He's not a child, he's a man. He doesn't have time for books. He doesn't play with toys. Give him back to me."

"Can't do that, Margaret. You know we can't. And if you won't tell us where to find his things, we'll have to find them for ourselves." There was no point pretending innocence any longer. He could see that from the set of her jaw, her clenched teeth.

"What's in his book, Margaret? Does he like to write about the girls he's taken? And the toys? What are they? Weapons, perhaps? Or trophies, is that it? Mementoes of his kills? You know, don't you?"

She stared back at him, blindly, blocking him out.

"Come on, Margaret. You're his mother and I understand what that means. It means you love your son, no matter what. You'd die for him. You'd do anything to protect him. But he doesn't need protecting now. He's safe, he'll see doctors, he'll have treatment. You can visit him. When he's better, maybe he can come home to you. You want him back, of course you do. God, how you must want him back. So you'll understand how those other parents feel. Their agony. They just want their children back too, and you can give them that. Think of them and what they've been going through, Margaret."

She said, very slowly and clearly, "I want my son. I don't care about them. I don't care."

He looked at her sadly. Then lunged forward and thumped the table under her nose.

"But I do care! I've got Jennifer Redbourn out there,

can't keep away from this place; comes in every day to ask if we've found her daughter. Her heart has broken. Her children don't stop crying for their sister. There's Lorraine Fitzpatrick, lost a baby and barely conscious even after a year, she's so stuffed full of tranquilisers. Hardly ever sees her husband anymore, because he's out every night, driving round Fleetham and Welsey, looking for their daughter, Jodie. I've got Sharon Knowles given up on life, smoking herself to death. I've got Kevin Wakefield crying like a baby at the morgue and his wife's in hospital because she had a complete collapse last night. Those are the parents I care about. At least the Wakefields have their daughter to bury. What about the other parents, Margaret? Where are their children? Tell me where your son hid them, so that they can at least say goodbye."

She said nothing. She'd flinched when he'd banged the table, but she'd recovered the power of resistance, stubborn to the death.

"We'll find them, Margaret. Because we'll find Timothy's toys and his little book. No good thinking he's got them safely stashed under some floorboard. We'll take the whole house apart, looking for them."

Another flash, brief and bitterly sharp. The slightest twitch of a smile that she couldn't hold back. Whatever had happened to those incriminating items, they weren't going to find them in the house. She'd put them out of their reach. They could burn her at the stake but she wouldn't talk. He'd hooked her and he'd lost her.

"You know what, Margaret Gittings? Your lunatic son isn't the criminal. You are. If we still had capital punishment, you're the one they should hang."

Welsh Connection: Miner's Daughter Missing

They were stripping out No.5 Welsey Road, Irnby, just as Malcolm had promised. Carpets, lino, floorboards, plaster, cooker shifted, every inch searched for any evidence, including Timothy Gittings' record of his crimes. The corrugated barn was taken apart, the contents of the incinerator raked, the immaculate garden dug up, in a vague hope that some of the missing bodies might be buried there. Improbable, since Gittings and his mother had only moved to that address after Rachel Redbourn's disappearance, but forensic tests were being run.

They already had enough to charge Timothy Gittings with the murder of Laura Wakefield. It was just a question of tying that in with the other disappearances. Malcolm was praying they would do better than that and find the missing girls. He had almost been persuaded by Margaret Gittings" confidence in the interview that her son's damning evidence must have gone up in flames, along with his clothes. But then she'd had one more thing to say. As she'd been escorted back to her cell in the custody suite, she'd guessed that Timothy was being interviewed nearby. It was probably as close as she'd ever be to him from now on. She'd stopped suddenly, resisting the PC herding her down the corridor, and shouted – screamed – at the top of her lungs as she was firmly dragged away. "Timmy! It's Mam! Don't you worry. You hear me, Timmy? I'll look out for you. I'll keep you safe! Trust me! I'll never betray you, Timmy!"

That, at least, was how Hugh Brody heard it, as he emerged from the interview room with Malcolm. But what Malcolm heard, unless he was deluding himself, was "I'll look *after it all* for you. I'll keep *it* safe." He was sure there was a book out there still, with all of Timothy Gittings' ghastly secrets recorded in it. If they searched thoroughly, surely it would come to light.

"I don't know about you," said Hugh. "But I'm still feeling unclean, dealing with those two. What do you reckon? The son's obviously mad as a hatter, but if you ask me, the mother is, too."

"Timothy mad? Certainly. Don't you have to be mad to go round murdering little girls? But do you have to be mad to protect your own child, whatever he's done?"

Hugh pulled a face at the thought. "I'll be making damned sure mine never do anything bad in the first place."

Malcolm smiled. Brody's two girls were ten and thirteen. Plenty of time yet for homicidal tendencies to show themselves. He checked for updates on the searches, which were not confined to Irnby. Margaret's previous home, a terraced house at the top of Millfield Road, had been ransacked too, and the concrete yard behind, without yielding anything. But neighbours reported that Timothy Gittings had used a garage accessed by a narrow lane adjoining the terrace and that was now receiving full forensic attention.

News of Timothy Gittings' arrest no longer needed word of mouth to get around. Lake had held a news conference announcing it to the world. The likelihood of Gittings being a serial killer was enough to make it headline news in the nationals and on TV. The Welsey Herald had only carried news of a murder in the last weekly edition, but it was busy now garnering every detail, quote, insinuation and gossip that could be wrung from the locals for a special edition being planned. Malcolm didn't dare imagine how the parents were coping with it. If they had reporters knocking on their doors, waiting to ask "How do you feel?" Malcolm might be tempted to call in an armed response team.

"Malcolm." Sgt Nicholson hailed him. "I think you'll want to deal with this. Guy's come in, says Gittings took his daughter too."

"What? I thought we'd been through the list of missing kids with a fine-tooth comb. All the others are teenagers. They don't fit the pattern at all. What makes him—"

"We've only checked up on the locals, though, haven't we? This one's from Wales."

* * *

Bryn Davies was a man in his forties, strongly built physically, but psychologically in pieces – pieces that he was desperately trying to hold together so that he could charge forward. He didn't wait for introductions. "He took my girl. My Bethany. It all makes sense now. We always thought they had it wrong. People talked at the time, but the police wouldn't listen, said she'd drowned."

"Mr Davies, please, sit down and let me get your story straight." Malcolm glanced at PC Sandra Thorpe, brows raised. She nodded and went off to fetch them tea.

"Right, now, you believe Timothy Gittings is responsible for your daughter's disappearance. Bethany, yes? When did she disappear?"

"November 10th, 1990."

"And this was where?"

"Brongarn." The man's fists were set solidly on the table, as if he were pinning down the facts before they could escape. "Hafod Terrace. That's where we lived, and he lived on Long Street, just below."

Malcolm checked his notes on Timothy Gittings. Neither Gittings nor his mother had been willing to provide the police with any information, but their past locations had been traced through tax record and other means. They had come together to Welsey in the late summer of 1992, from Essex, where Margaret Gittings had worked since January 1991, and before that they had lived in Brongarn, in Blaenau Gwent. It fitted.

"I'm sorry if I have to go over what must be painful memories for you, Mr Davies…"

"Go on! Pain. I know all about pain. I'll tell you how it was. They packed their bags and left, two days after Bethany went missing. She – that woman, Margaret Gittings – she told people the depot was closing, along with the mine, and she needed to look for a new job, but it wasn't true. The yard's still running now. She worked there, in the office, but she upped sticks, overnight, and took that boy of hers with her."

"I see. Tell me about Bethany. How old was she?"

"Eight years, five months and three days."

Malcolm winced at the precision of the answer. "Can you give me a description?"

Davies opened his jacket and fumbled in the inner pocket. He laid a school photograph on the table.

Malcolm only had to glance at it to know Davies had got it right. Smiling, cheerful, shoulder-length fair hair... She might not be the identical twin of any of the other girls, but they were all close enough of a match to be sisters, all of a similar age. 1990: Timothy Gittings would have been seventeen. Assuming this Bethany Davies was the first, he'd been killing girls for six years. How many more might there be, if that were the case? What had he been up to in Essex?

"All right, Mr Davies. Can you tell me everything? What happened?"

"It was a Saturday, no school, see. She was at home, playing with a friend, getting... you know what kids are. Getting rowdy, letting off steam, running around. Debbie, my wife, she'd had enough and she packed them off to play on the swings. Made Bethany promise to be home for tea, and that's the last Debbie saw of her. Can't forgive herself, can Deb, for making her go out. Blames herself. I said, Beth could break every stick of furniture in the house and bring all the ceilings down, if we could just get her back. But we knew, she was never coming home."

"And no one saw her again?"

"Not after she left her friend, Kerry. Except him. He took her."

61

"I presume there was a police investigation? There must have been."

"Oh yes," said Davies, his jaw jutting pugnaciously. "Police." He put a world of scorn in that word.

Malcolm guessed it was not just because his daughter hadn't been found. Brongarn, mining village, mines closing, the memory of the strike still a bloody communal sore. Malcolm had been a humble PC in "84, thanking his lucky stars he wasn't involved in policing the dispute. He'd had a couple of colleagues from training who'd resigned over it.

"We searched," said Davies. "Everyone searched, the whole area, knocking on doors, out on the hills, to the mine… all the miners turned out, everyone. Then they found her bonnet. On the riverbank. Pink, it was. Police decided she must have fallen in and got swept away. Said she must have gone playing… There's a patch of ground where Hafod Terrace comes down to Long Street." He was drawing out a map with his finger on the table now. "Slopes down to the river. But she never used to play there. Always went to the playground with her friends. That's what Kerry Williams said they'd done. Why would Bethany go playing down there on her own, instead of coming back for tea, eh? But that's where he lived." Davies was stabbing a spot on the table that signified, as far as Malcolm could make out, a house on Long Street not far from the suspected waste ground.

"Then Margaret Gittings left and people started talking – the ones who knew her from the depot, her and her son. She got him work there, a couple of days a week, driving a forklift truck. They knew about him not being right in the head. About his temper, how it would flare up for no reason. How he never said much, always kept his head down and then suddenly he'd be shouting and swearing. We told the police, said they should check him out, and they did search his house. Didn't find anything. All cleaned out. They were convinced my Bethany had drowned and they wanted to leave it at that."

Malcolm nodded. Had the police been reluctant to descend on a mining community and start searching for suspects? An accident would have saved a lot of ill-feeling. "And they never found any further evidence?"

"No. Nothing." Davies shrugged wearily. "What could we do? We had nothing. Just… Nothing."

Malcolm nodded his understanding. He knew exactly what Bethany's parents had gone through because others had gone through the same thing since. Rivers were very convenient scapegoats, as DCI Claypole had concluded, too. "I am very sorry."

"Yes, everyone's sorry," said Davies, sagging in his chair. Then he sat up again. "But then I heard, on the news. Timothy Gittings, arrested for the murder of a little girl and he's probably killed more. That's when I knew for sure. Of course my Bethany didn't drown. They'd have found her eventually if she had. It's not the bloody Amazon. No, she was just taken, by that beast. Killed by him, same as this one. I'm right, aren't I. You don't know what it's done to my Debbie. She knew the woman, used to give her lifts home sometimes, on her way back from one of her cleaning jobs. Used to talk to her all about Bethany, our golden girl. How do you think she feels now? She just wants her daughter back.

So do I. They know where she is, don't they? Can't they tell us? Make them tell us, that's all. It's all we want. Don't tell us we're clutching at straws, because I can tell you It's a poisonous fucking straw if that's what it is."

* * *

Superintendent Lake waited for the team to settle before turning to face them, pivoting on his stork legs. "You've done a thorough job. All leads followed. All evidence secured and analysed. The pattern is there for all to see."

His back was to a map on the wall, a map they all knew in minute detail, red flags indicating such a clear and obvious pattern, now they knew. The Gittings' previous home on Millfield Road that Rachel Redbourn would have passed on her way to Saturday gym club.

The route to Gittings' first job out at Fairley Chicken Farm, which would have taken him past Ashley Knowles on the Mile End Estate, in his dark blue Astra van. His next job at the canning factory on the far side of Fleetham, passing the park where Jodie Fitzpatrick was waiting.

Next job at the abattoir on Bartlet Lane, with one possible route to his new address in Irnby taking him past Laura Wakefield, walking home from school. Irnby, where he and his mother had rented a house two days after Rachel Redbourn's disappearance. With all the connections pinpointed on the map, it seemed painfully obvious. Too obvious for anyone to doubt his guilt in every case, and yet…

Lake paused, staring down at papers, then he looked back up at his audience. "Conclusion seems clear that he was responsible for the abduction and murder of four girls in this area. Four girls of similar age, similar appearance. Another girl, Bethany Davies, was a likely fifth victim, in South Wales, 1990. South Wales police now concur. We have missing years. Gittings worked as delivery driver in Essex '91 to '92. That's an eighteen-month gap before he arrived in Welsey. We know the targets he selects: girls, seven to nine, fair, shoulder-length hair and we've liaised with Essex police. DI Cannell?"

"They've been through their records," said Malcolm. "They haven't got any missing children matching the description of our victims on their books, in that time frame. I find it hard to believe that he didn't kill there, too. There has to be at least one more victim we haven't identified yet."

Lake nodded. "But no concrete evidence to go on, so we concentrate on our own cases here. DNA and other forensic tests are now complete. The blood in Gittings' van has been confirmed as that of Laura Wakefield. The two hairs caught in his seatbelt are a match to Jodie Fitzpatrick, and the gym shoe found in an oil drum at Gittings' old garage off Millfield Road has now been positively identified as that of Rachel Redbourn. Her initials are legible inside. RR.

"The Crown Prosecution Service is satisfied that, despite the absence of bodies, the murders of Jodie Fitzpatrick and Rachel Redbourn can be added to the charges. Regrettably, no other remains have been found and..." He waited for the mutters of irritation and anger to subside. "There is no forensic evidence to support our supposition that Gittings was also responsible for the disappearance of Ashley Knowles and Bethany Davies, which means they will not be included on the charge sheet." The mutterings rose again.

"I appreciate you are disappointed, but the CPS considers the evidence against Gittings for three murders is sufficient to ensure he's locked up for the foreseeable future."

"If he even comes to trial," growled Hugh Brody.

Lake nodded. "His psychiatric state is being evaluated. He has, however, demonstrated, if only in denial, that he knew his actions were unlawful and he went to great lengths, with assistance, to cover them up. I suspect that he will be judged unfit to plead, as his state of mind seems to have deteriorated, if anything, while in custody, but there will at least be a trial of the facts."

He raised his hands to quieten everyone again. "I want to thank you all for your energetic and determined dedication in this case. Had we been able to find Gittings" written account of his crimes, which we have strong reason to believe he kept, we might have been able to add two and maybe more murders to the charges, but we must be content with three."

Content? Malcolm returned to his desk with a sigh. He was never going to be content with this conclusion. Neither were the parents. And what was he to say to Sharon Knowles and Bryn Davies, when he informed them that their girls would not even be named as victims? And their bodies never found. He looked at the five photos he'd taken down from his board. He'd left a space between Bethany Davies and Ashley Knowles because, evidence or no evidence, he was convinced there must have been a sixth victim in Essex. Six little girls with their own characters, thoughts, hopes, potential. Six girls who should have gone on to live normal, happy lives and five of them couldn't even be buried decently. It shouldn't end like this.

And yet it probably would.

Part 3: PILGRIMAGES

Twenty-six years later

Tea and Parkin

October 2022 Holmesby, Yorkshire

It was raining. Of course it was. It splattered on the pavement, on roofs, in gutters, turning everything grey and black. Huddled under the inadequate canopy of the police station, Rosanna Quillan pulled up her collar, thinking that she couldn't conjure up a single memory of her hometown in anything other than rain. Or maybe it was just the memory of a dark cloud that had overshadowed her early life. It still followed her around. Always would, probably.

She peered up at the clouds now, debating whether to wait for the rain to stop or raise her hood and make a run for the carpark.

"Ros!" The woman hurrying up the street under a large umbrella sped up as she hailed her.

"Shelley! Hi!" Shelley Nelson, or Shelley Barlow she had been at school, was Rosanna's oldest friend, and still her closest. "What are you doing in Holmesby? You haven't moved without telling me, have you?"

Shelley laughed. "No, Dave and I are still living in Leeds. Just taking a day off. Mum phoned, said you'd called in, last night, so I came over." She held the umbrella over Rosanna as they headed together for the car park. "I was going to phone you, but I really need to have a proper chat, and as you're in the area... Do you have to rush off, or can you stay for a coffee?"

"Yorkshire tea, please! Is Peggy Sue's teashop still there? Did it survive the lockdown?"

"Just about. Still does the parkin. Okay, what's brought you back to Holmesby? Mum said something about your father's case, but I thought it was all settled."

"I suppose it is." Rosanna walked faster, clasping her hood tight. It helped dampen the surge of anger that still rose occasionally to the surface at the mention of her father. Craig Quillan had been a popular guy in Holmesby, always ready with a joke or a bright idea. Life and soul and all that. As a child, Rosanna had sometimes felt she was the only one who'd been able to see him for what he was – a mean, brutal bully.

The only one, that is, apart from her mother, the victim of all his physical and psychological abuse. Her mother, who had escaped into drink and then into the grave by accepting her husband's invitation to throw herself under a bus. Rosanna had witnessed it. No one witnesses a thing like that without it becoming a defining issue in life. It would always haunt her and so would the injustice that followed. Rosanna's complaints against her father had been treated as the over-imaginative fabrications of an angry child.

Craig Quillan had escaped any censure for her mother's death, but his latest woman had been less easily crushed. She'd reported him to the police and, finally, they'd acted. "He got a supervision order as well as a fine," she said. "That's better than nothing, I suppose."

"They should have sent him to prison," said Shelley, sympathetically.

Rosanna shrugged. "ABH, first offence – in the eyes of the law, at least. Nothing for my mother."

"That is so unfair. They should have thrown the book at him."

"I don't really care about him," said Rosanna. "He's been revealed for what he is, and that's what matters. But what I really want is my mother's inquest reopened. I hate it being put down to suicide while under the influence, without any explanation of what drove her to drink."

"Any luck?"

"No. I'm not naïve enough to think it's likely to happen, after all this time. But you know me. Who cares how long it takes. I have to keep chipping away at it."

Rosanna the Resolute, Shelley's parents had called her.

They'd reached the teashop in the lane leading from the carpark and turned in, shaking rain from coats and umbrella. A waitress guided them to a free table by the steamed-up window.

"Tea for two and parkin, please."

The waitress trotted off and the two women settled themselves comfortably.

"Now tell me, are you going to stick with library work?" asked Shelley. "Not thinking of going back to your old job?"

Rosanna's old job. What career do you choose if you're obsessed by the notion of injustice? The police, of course. Except that, in that one field she had discovered she wasn't quite resolute enough to stick it out. "No. That's over."

"But you always wanted to be a detective, get at the truth and all that?"

"And all that."

"And you're still doing it in a way, aren't you?

"Working in a library?"

"Reference library. Finding stuff. Digging out the truth."

"That's stretching it a bit. I spent most of the time charging for computer printouts."

"Oh, maybe, but it's more than that, isn't it. There must be some investigation involved."

"Maybe, sometimes."

"Well then! Detection like before, the same sort of thing, only different."

Rosanna smiled. "Very different. Anyway, I've finished at the library. It was only maternity cover for six months, and the proud mummy is now back at work. Which gives me time to please myself while I'm between jobs. And that's why I'm here, pestering them about the inquest."

"Yes, all right, but…" Shelley frowned at her, earnestly. "You'd still be willing to take on a bit of detective work, wouldn't you? Mum told me how you tracked down Hilary Taylor's daughter for her."

"Oh, that." Rosanna shrugged. "Yes, okay. It was hardly a case for Sherlock Holmes. She'd run off in a strop to Manchester."

"But finding her there couldn't have been that easy. Big place, Manchester."

Rosanna balanced a sugar cube on the back of a spoon, aware that Shelley was desperately struggling to push her into something. "I was lucky, that's all."

"Well, I think it must have needed brains and…" Shelley sat back as tea, cups, milk and parkin were offloaded onto their table. "Lovely. Thanks."

Rosanna automatically lifted the teapot lid and stirred the contents. "Give it five minutes."

"Okay." Shelley broke off a piece of parkin and sampled it. "Still good. Yummy. But what I was wondering was, would you be up for taking on another search?"

Rosanna shook her head. "Shell, I'm really not cut out to be a private eye."

"But you found Becky Taylor. You knew how to go about it. This would be something like that. Well, a bit like that. Okay, not like that at all, really, but you'd be looking for someone. Or have you got another job lined up in the wings? Mum said…"

"Nothing yet. I expect something will turn up, when I go hunting for it. Go on. Who do you want me to look for? Another runaway?"

"No, not exactly." Shelley dribbled milk into their cups in readiness, frowning. "You said it didn't matter how long some things took, didn't you? Well, this is old. Have you heard of the Timothy Gittings case? I don't remember it, myself, but we'd only have been kids at the time. 1997? Lincolnshire, I think."

"I don't remember it either but I have heard of the case. Child-killer. Deemed unfit to plead?"

"Yes. Sent to Broadmoor or something. He was convicted of three murders and they suspected him of another two, but only one body was ever found."

"That must be shitty for the families."

"Yes, very! That's the point. It's where it gets rather personal, you see. Dave's dad, his cousin's husband, Andrew, is a brother of one of the parents."

"Hang on, let me get that straight." Rosanna opened her bag and produced a notepad and pen. "David's dad's cousin's husband... Should I draw a family tree?"

Shelley laughed and began to pour the tea. "No, it really doesn't matter, except that we know Andrew and Kate, that's the point. I don't suppose you remember them. They came to our wedding and we keep in touch. It's just that Andrew is really worried about his sister, Jen. She's dying, you see. Brain tumour. Inoperable."

"And she's the mother of one of the victims? Poor woman. Life can be bloody cruel, can't it?"

"It has been for her. Rachel Redbourn – that was her daughter – went missing one day on her way to some club or something. I didn't know much about it. Andrew never talked about it until his sister got so ill, but now he's got it fixed in his head that he doesn't want her to die without knowing where her daughter is. He's got boxes and boxes of newspaper cuttings about the case, but where does he go from there? He's an accountant. He doesn't have the first idea how to go about it, what to do next."

"And you want me to find the body of a child, buried somewhere quarter of a century ago?"

"That really would be the answer to his prayers! But

no, It's much simpler than that. According to the newspapers, the police had this idea that Timothy Gittings kept a book with details of his killings. It was never found, but they suspect his mother might have it. She wouldn't say a word and she was sent to prison for obstruction or whatever it's called. When she was released, she just vanished. No one has any idea where she is. Andrew's afraid she might be dead, because if she is, that's that."

"But if she isn't, you want me to find her?"

"Well, yes, because that seems to be the only chance of finding the book, if it really does exist."

"I see." Rosanna sipped her tea. Good and strong.

"Andrew has been to the police, begging them to start the search again, but they say they can't without new evidence to go on. He's so desperate, he was talking of hiring a private detective, and I thought of you. He can pay."

"Oh well, as to that…"

"You'd want expenses, at least. And while you're looking for another job…?

Rosanna thought about it, as she dunked a bit of parkin in her tea.

Shelley pulled a disapproving face, then grabbed her hand. "Will you take it on? Say yes."

"Yes, of course. Any chance of having a look at all those press clippings he's collected, to save a bit of time?"

Shelley was already groping in her handbag. She produced a memory stick. "He's scanned everything. It's all here. If you want a down payment…"

Rosanna shook her head. "I'm not expecting any

new job to come along for a couple of weeks at least. Give me that much time to look over this lot and see if there's any serious chance of me getting anywhere with it. If I think there is, we can discuss expenses then."

Shelley sat back, with a sigh of relief. "Thank you, thank you, thank you. I'll tell Andrew you're onto it. I knew you'd come up trumps, Ros."

Flowers

Welsey, Lincolnshire

Rosanna stopped at a service station, ostensibly to grab a decent coffee and fill the tank. In reality, to choose, right or left. A junction was coming up. Did she go right to her home in Swindon or left into Lincolnshire? Swigging back the last of her flat white, she wondered why she had bothered pretending to debate. She had known from the moment she set off from Holmesby that she would go left.

She had stayed an extra night in her old town, unable to drive on without first going through the painstakingly gleaned archive of cuttings, notes, pictures, TV recordings and random documents on Shelley's memory stick. It was there now, an occupation force in her brain, refusing to grant her liberty. She had to dive in further, to be in it, to get the feel of it. To understand the story, because without understanding, it was all just a jumble of facts and suppositions. The girls, listed as victims of a mass murderer, were merely names, ciphers of prurient interest – and they deserved to be made real again, as they had once been.

Shelley would probably say it was Rosanna's police experience driving her. Once a detective, always a detective? But not always a police officer. Rosanna had joined the force from university, with some quixotic idea of championing the justice that her mother had been denied, but after a year serving as a detective constable with Thames Valley, she had realised that it was never going to deliver what she wanted. Her quest for truth couldn't be reconciled with the aims of the justice system, which revolved around cold calculation on the probability of conviction, shunting misery, rape, abuse, suicide onto overgrown sidings of no further action. If she couldn't come to terms with that, what could she do except quit?

But this tale, buried in the past, literally and figuratively, wasn't a matter of percentages and nice legal arguments. It was a matter of finding lost girls, and who else was doing it? Rosanna turned left.

* * *

Welsey proved to be a town like any other, not significant enough to qualify as a city, although the massive church of St Michael and All Saints, with its towering spire, could have passed as a cathedral. There were the usual industrial estates, the usual sprawl of suburbs, the usual chain stores in the centre, mingling with tokens of Edwardian civic grandeur and hints of Tudor antiquity. There was a tired-looking police station – *the* police station, presumably. There was a secondary school that none of the missing girls ever got to attend.

Buses and delivery vans clogged the High Street, but heavy through traffic had been syphoned off to the thundering by-pass skirting the town to the north.

Rosanna sat in the former marketplace, now serving

as the main car park, and studied the map on her phone, plotting the homes of the four girls who had been snatched in Welsey. Heading west along the High Street, she would come to the knot of modest suburbia that included Abbey Close, where Rachel Redbourn had lived. She'd start there.

It was a very ordinary semi-detached house, in a very ordinary neighbourhood. Why would it be otherwise? There was no pall of gloom cast over it. Judging by the basketball net on the garage and voices shouting in the back garden, it was now the home of several teenage boys. Life goes on, burying the past.

She parked up and began to walk the route Rachel would have taken, that Saturday morning twenty-seven years ago. One turn and a short stroll to the High Street, which was quiet at this end of town, thanks to the by-pass. Kind townsfolk, according to the newspaper accounts, had been quick to condemn the Redbourn parents as grossly irresponsible for leaving a little girl of only nine to cross the High Street on her own, but there seemed little danger to Rosanna. Rachel had used the pelican crossing – a woman waiting at a bus-stop had noticed her doing so. Rosanna did the same, feeling slightly guilty that she was forcing a solitary car to stop for her. A bus had stopped for Rachel and she had waved at the driver.

Another short walk to the left took Rosanna to the junction with Millfield Road, a road that had cropped up many times in the files. It was a major arterial route into town from the south and deserved serious widening, but gloomy Victorian buildings crowding around the junction hemmed it in. Satanic mills loomed over dark terraced houses, one of which, No.8, had been the home of Timothy Gittings and his mother for a couple of years. Rosanna stopped to stare at the blank windows and the peeling paint on the door. It looked like a squat. So did the houses on either side. Rubbish bags were piled up on its step. It had once been the residence of a child-killer, and it looked as if it still could be. Had Rachel run past to escape the gloom?

Rosanna walked further, only a few doors down, to the side alley that had given access in 1995 to a line of garages. It was in one of them, eventually, that Rachel's gym shoe had been found. No sign of the garages now. Everything had been demolished, levelled in preparation for a building site, though it wasn't yet clear what would replace them. If Gittings had concealed any bodies there, they would have been uncovered by the jaws of a bulldozer.

Beyond the cluster of grim Victoriana, Millfield Road crossed the river Wele. Initial police theories had suggested she'd fallen in and drowned. People didn't usually fall off bridges by accident, but Rosanna could see why the suggestion had been made. The bridge was one of the ugliest structures she had ever come across – rivetted iron girders painted a drab army green. An eyesore to most but a perfect climbing frame for daredevil children. Not for Rachel, though, surely. A polite, responsible young lady, neighbours had described her; mature for her years.

Rosanna paused to look down into the river. Further along, there were willows and a couple throwing crumbs to a swan. The water looked almost too somnolent for drowning, but anything was possible. Yes, a child could slip and drown, if playing there in twilight or at night, perhaps, but on a Saturday morning with people around, on the bridge and on the riverside walk below?

She walked on, into a stretch of bungalows and semis mingled with seventies townhouses and a few shops. No. 51 was where Mrs Vivian Quest had been waiting to escort Rachel another half mile down Millfield Road and along St Thomas's Avenue to the primary school. But Rachel and her mother hadn't turned up. Mrs Quest had hung around until any further delay would make her own daughter Wendy late for Gym Club. Then she'd taken Wendy, stayed to watch the vaults and tumbles and waited until they were safely home before phoning the Redbourns to ask why Rachel hadn't come? "*I'll never forgive myself. If only I'd phoned first.*"

If only, if only, if only. The agonised howl of every tragedy.

No point following the trail all the way to the school because Rachel hadn't even got this far. No, that alley leading to the garages was the only place where she could conceivably have been lured or grabbed without anyone noticing. What had the police been thinking?

Rosanna returned to her car and drove on down the busy length of Millfield Road. It was the same route Timothy Gittings would have driven every day to his first job in the area, at a chicken farm a few miles south. A route that took him past the Mile End estate on the southern edge of town, where Ashley Knowles had lived.

The estate was what was laughably called social housing; 1950s council houses in a series of avenues and crescents, a couple of long low-rise blocks around a square of balding grass, and a parade of shops, mostly guarded by metal grids. Ashley had lived in one of the flats, with mother Sharon. She'd gone to school, the same school attended by Rachel Redbourn. Her mother had come home from work, assuming Ashley had been at a friend's house, where she'd been invited to tea. But the invitation had had to be cancelled because of a family emergency. Ashley had hung around in the streets with friends, but none of them could remember when exactly they had parted company with her. But people did remember a screeching van. The same van, as it turned out, that resulted in the arrest of Timothy Gittings two and a half years later. Eight years old and the police had done nothing. How was it possible?

There was a sense of hopelessness hanging over the place, but it wasn't lingering grief for a child gone missing more than quarter of a century before and now forgotten. It was the hopelessness of all the children lost there. Having wandered around the dreary estate, feeling nothing but sadness, Rosanna returned to Millfield Road and drove on past the last houses of the town. Beyond lay a sprawl of flat fields and drainage ditches, featureless apart from a block of woodland, part wild, part plantation, half a mile further on. Nothing else pierced the horizon except the now distant spire of St Michael's. A sign at a turning to the left, just before the wood, pointed the way to the abattoir, Gittings' last place of employment. Except that the whole area had been his private abattoir. Rosanna shivered and turned back.

Last port of call in Welsey: Laura Wakefield's route home on the east side of town. Lacey Road Primary School was like any other school of the 1960s. There was the sweetshop where her friends left her, the crossing that had a lollipop lady on duty that day, the last person to see Laura happy and very much alive – other than Timothy Gittings, of course. He'd have had to snatch her from the main road. Where? That short stretch of lockups and workshops, perhaps, where no one would have been watching. She never made it to Kingston Avenue, just a hundred metres further on.

Rosanna took the turning for her, stopped to gaze upon the comfortable solidity of Laura's home. An elderly Indian lady was standing guard over a pushchair in the front garden while parents helped a young girl into the back seat of a people carrier. All smiles and laughter and chattering. A family making ready for an outing, completely oblivious to the tragedy associated with the house. It was the same with the whole town; scenes of horror, grief and misery eradicated by time. Rosanna had traced the past through an opaque veil of a present that had chosen to wipe it all out.

Was she achieving anything by this visit? Did it make her any better than a sightseer, hoping to get a thrill out of old bloodstains? She swallowed the doubt and chose to go on. There were a few more sights to see, if she wanted to get the whole story clear in her mind. She turned east from Kingston Avenue, out of Welsey, on the old road towards the village of

Fleetham, seven miles away. The same open country as before, vast fields, flat and featureless, straight drains, shaven hedge boundaries. Big, big sky. Rosanna wondered if this counted as the Fens? She wasn't sure. She's always imagined them as a land of water and reeds and ducks, not flat farmland and mathematically straight ditches.

Half-way to Fleetham, she almost passed through Irnby without realising it. It wasn't a village. It was barely a hamlet, nothing but a cluster of houses in total isolation. Maybe that had been its appeal to Margaret Gittings. Somewhere so easily disregarded that her son would be as good as invisible.

Rosanna slowed down, hovered, looking for No.5, the address mentioned in the Welsey Herald. There had been a grainy photo of an end of terrace house. Nothing to match it now. No.4 ended with a blank wall overlooking an empty overgrown plot, in which nothing of significance was visible except a few shattered sheets of corrugated iron, jutting up from brambles, nettles and hogweed.

The memory of the murdered girls had been smoothly erased from their old homes by time, but the last residence of Timothy Gittings had been subjected to a more dramatic eradication. Demolition. Nothing to see here.

Rosanna drove on. She passed the pictorial sign announcing Fleetham and immediately slowed again. There was a layby on her left, occupied by a couple of cars. A wide double gate gave access to a recreation ground with cricket pitch and pavilion, and a corner for swings and slides and roundabouts. This was the park where Jodie Fitzpatrick had last been seen, playing with friends after school while waiting for her parents to return from a hospital visit. "*She ran to the gates a couple of times to see if they were there yet,*" one of the parents in the park had commented. "*I thought they must have arrived and picked her up. I just didn't think for one moment.*"

She got out to look around. Intermittent hedgerows shielded the park from the road. A stream skirted the grounds, with picnic benches among the willows curtseying on its banks. A couple of mothers were pushing young children on the baby swings. A dog walker was being led round the cricket pitch by a brace of energetic dalmatians. It was all very genteel, a nice place open to the public gaze and yet how easy it must have been to snatch a child who'd slipped out for a moment through the gates. It would only have taken a moment when heads were turned the other way.

A few streets away, she turned into Piggot's Drive, a twisting road of houses and bungalows, all detached, all unique. An architect's playground. Only reasonable as Jodie's father was, or had been, a thriving architect, according to the papers. Rosanna parked up and got out, to make her obligatory pilgrimage on foot to the last house on her itinerary. It would, of course, be as barren of memories as all the others...

It wasn't. The Fitzpatrick house was all too easy to identify. It must have been a showpiece once, before decades of neglect had left it stained and shabby. Nothing had moved on here. There was a huge, faded print of Jodie Fitzpatrick plastered across the picture window. The same portrait was in a glass-fronted display board by the gate, along with a poster.

Jodie Fitzpatrick.
Disappeared 15th February 1995
Victim of Timothy Gittings.
Her body has never been found by the police.
If you have any information relating to her
disappearance, phone this number...

There was a vase with a bunch of fresh flowers below the notice board. A shrine tended for twenty-seven years? The Fitzpatricks must be still living at the same address; if Rosanna knocked on the door, she could probably speak to them.

But she couldn't do it. When she'd found their daughter, maybe, but for now, the wording of that poster gave her the shivers. Not that it said anything other than the bald truth. It was just the intensity of it, the manic obsession of parents still fixed on that one moment, refusing to believe that life could go on. She wasn't sure she could cope with it.

Was that because she recognised the same intense obsession in herself? Years on and she was refusing to let the matter of her mother's suicide go. She fixed on other deaths, other victims, because she couldn't get justice for the one who mattered most to her.

Walking back to her car, she shrugged. Yes, so what? If it made her worry at issues until she'd gnawed them to the bone, that was something positive. It was the way she was, and she might as well put it to use.

She looked at the map once more. Only one other place to visit and it meant taking the road back to

Welsey. She'd look, she'd take note, and then she'd go.

She drove back through Irnby without slowing this time.

Another mile and then… she checked the map on her sat nav. Yes, it was coming up. A sharp turn to the left, onto a narrow road. Piper's Lane. Three hundred metres to another sharp right-hand turn and then straight as an arrow, no traffic in sight, no one working in the fields around. She saw the gateway coming up and slowed to a halt. The gate where Laura Wakefield had been found, twenty-six years ago. She got out to walk the last few metres.

It came as a shock, when she reached it. There was the usual metal five-bar gate, firmly locked. Identical to a thousand other field gates in the area, except for the bouquet, wrapped in cellophane, propped by the gatepost. Flowers again. These were fading, though, petals drooping and browning, but not yet entirely dead and withered.

Rosanna bent to down to extract the card tucked into the sodden yellow ribbon. It was damp, the writing smudged but still legible.

3/10/96. Never forgotten. Never will be. Love you always, sweetheart. M, D and A.

October 3rd, 1996, the day Laura Wakefield was found on this spot. This was memory brimming with love more than obsessive rage. Rosanna felt hugely gratified that someone was still marking the anniversary, quietly, privately. But then, the Wakefields had somewhere to leave flowers. Their daughter's body had been found. The other parents didn't even have that consolation.

On impulse, Rosanna stepped back and searched the hedgerows for something, anything… late October and there were no obvious flowers to add. A string of bryony berries and a spray of haws. Would they do? She wrestled them free and placed them by the wilting bouquet. Flowers suggested promise. Fruit meant promise fulfilled. She would fulfil. She would find those girls.

It had all somehow got personal.

Unfinished Business

Rosanna settled at a computer in Welsey library. Internet research on her phone was getting tiresome. She wanted to scroll at ease.

DCI Claypole was a name that had cropped up repeatedly in the papers, concluding with a report that he was taking early retirement due to ill health. Rosanna guessed that was a euphemism for a discreet nudge to avoid scandal and embarrassment. Bringing the service into disrepute. The papers had been scathing about his investigations in the Timothy Gittings case. There was nothing more on him. Chief Superintendent Lake got a later mention, promoted to Deputy Chief Constable on the other side of the country.

Rachel's Uncle Andrew had not researched any other officers, but one had been mentioned several times in the cuttings. DI Malcolm Cannell. Was he still around?

She did a quick on-line search and immediately discovered that a Detective Superintendent Malcolm Cannell had retired from Lincolnshire police a few years back. A couple of minutes later and she found him on Facebook. His page wasn't showing much sign of use. Rosanna smiled. There was a clutch of photographs, mostly of dogs and boats, and occasional comments referred to Uncle Malcolm and Aunty Babs.

It looked very much like the page Shelley had constructed for her parents, determined to bring the older generation into the internet age, willing or no.

There was nothing much given away. He was married, retired and his location was Lincolnshire. Lincolnshire was rather large. Rosanna needed a little more to go on. She knew better than to contact Lincolnshire police and ask for the address of a retired officer, so she would have to use other means. She found one small clue on his Facebook page; he had referred to "our retirement," to which TigerWoman82 had replied "Speak for yourself!" and he had added "Yes, all right, she's still soliciting." Did that mean he was married to a sex worker? Or a solicitor? Rosanna guessed the latter was more probable. She checked the Law Society's register. Barbara Cannell was practising with a firm in Lincoln. Rosanna could contact her, posing as a client…

No, she was on an honest mission, so she would be honest. She found Barbara's professional email address on the firm's website.

* * *

Thresham was a village a few miles from Lincoln, with a couple of nice pubs, a gracious church, tea shops, riverside walk and a dog-grooming parlour. The sort of place quiet enough for comfortable retirement, without being too obviously a final resting place for the aged and infirm.

No.17 Foxley Drive was a bungalow, sitting pretty in a sizeable mature garden. The woman at the front door was middle-aged, probably not far from retirement but certainly not desperate for it.

"You'll be Miss Quillan, I imagine."

"Rosanna, yes." Rosanna shook hands.

"I'm Barbara. Come in. Through to the living room. I'll fetch him."

Rosanna was left alone for a moment to assess her surroundings. Comfortable furniture, a moderate number of books, mostly non-fiction, an antique grandfather clock that seemed rather out of place. Photographs much like the ones on his Facebook page – dogs, seascapes, plus a 1980s bride and groom looking unnaturally posed. No children. There was a trophy on the mantelpiece. She checked it out. For sailing. No mementos of a past life. No long service medal proudly framed.

She turned as Barbara followed her husband in. He was greying, bespectacled but fit for his age.

"You found us then."

"Superintendent Malcolm Cannell?"

"Not anymore," said Malcolm, wafting Rosanna to an armchair. "Just Mr. Retired for more than five years now."

"Seven," corrected Barbara.

"She counts," said Malcolm. "Now, Miss Quillan. Rosanna, is it? You told Barbara you wanted to talk about the case."

"As if there's only one," said Barbara. "If you seriously think you can get to the bottom of it, good luck. It's been hanging over us for far too long. Let's be done with it. It's why we're stuck here in our old age and not in a nice, snug little cottage in Cornwall."

"The property prices might have something to do with it," suggested her husband. He sighed at Rosanna.

"She would insist on a bungalow."

Barbara sniffed. "I don't want to be hauling you upstairs when your joints go."

"It might be your joints going first and me doing the hauling," Malcolm suggested, mildly.

"Nonsense. I'm far fitter than you. Anyway, if you're going to talk, I suppose you're expecting me to be a good little wifey and come up with tea and biscuits."

"Since it's already sitting ready in the kitchen, yes, get in there where you belong, woman."

While there was a brief bustle over the tea, Rosanna sat back, contemplating the many odd ways that couples related to each other. Malcolm and Barbara had been laughing as they spoke, but she could recall similar words spoken by her father, in a very different tone.

Malcolm set the tray down and poured. "All right then, Miss Quillan, Rosanna. Barbara tells me you claim to be a former detective constable, not a journalist. Is that the truth?"

"Yes."

"The two are not incompatible, of course. You could still be more intent on hanging us out to dry for our mishandling of the Timothy Gittings case, than on solving the riddle."

Rosanna took the cup he offered. "Was it mishandled?"

"What would *your* verdict be?"

"That it was. Grossly."

"Honesty! Good. Yes, of course it was. And I take

some of the blame for that. We never followed up on the leads we were given in the Ashley Knowles case."

"He was a DS, sent to ask questions at the school," said Barbara. "It wasn't his job to follow it all up. He's just guilt-tripping. Pay no attention."

"Thank you, darling," said Malcolm. "The fact is, if we'd given the case proper attention, we might not have saved Ashley but the next three might have been spared. I know we let Sharon down, badly."

"Sharon Knowles?" It sounded personal to Rosanna. "You knew her?"

"Only later, when it was all too late to make amends. To add insult to injury, her daughter wasn't named on the charge sheet. There was no forensic evidence to tie him to Ashley. But he took her all right. Sharon moved away, but we keep in touch, now and again. I promised…" His promise remained unexplained. "Sorry, I meant to ask. Sugar?"

"No, thanks." Rosanna remembered what Barbara had said, about there only being one case. "You still think a lot about the Timothy Gittings case?"

Barbara snorted.

Malcolm smiled. "I moved on, to Lincoln, pushed up through the ranks. Other cases intervened. You know how it is. But then, at my retirement do, my colleagues very kindly reminded me of all the great successes in my career, one being the Timothy Gittings case. A success because he was caught and the killings stopped with Laura Wakefield. But I don't see it as such a triumph." He shook his head. "The other five were never found."

"Five? I thought there were four others besides

Laura."

"Four definite, starting with the Welsh girl, Bethany, but I'm convinced there must have been another, at least one more, during his time in Essex. So I say five. Three of them in my own patch, that's what rankles. We couldn't find them."

"You looked, though?" Rosanna didn't mean it to sound like a question. Of course they'd looked.

"We looked. But trying to pinpoint likely spots was little more than a game of chance. Gittings had lived at two addresses and we took both of them apart. Rivers and drains in the area were dragged, culverts searched. Nothing. Gittings had worked as a delivery driver for Marriot Processing and it was thought he could have disposed of bodies on his journeys, just about anywhere in the Midlands. And then, of course, he was employed at Welsey Abattoir, which is enough to conjure up all manner of horrifying possibilities. Echoes of Sweeney Todd even, though he was only employed as a fork-lift driver." Malcolm shrugged. "Gittings wouldn't talk, his mother wouldn't talk, and without anything specific to go on, it was decided that we'd exhausted all reasonable avenues."

Rosanna sipped her tea, watching him over the rim of her cup. "But now you think otherwise."

"Let's say, my suspicions have crystalised since then. Since retirement... I go back occasionally."

"Every other bloody weekend!" said Barbara.

"Not true, dear. But a few times."

"It's an excuse to walk the dogs, I suppose – and gives him a chance to test his theories."

"About the wood?" suggested Rosanna.

Malcolm and Barbara exchanged glances. "What do you know about the wood?"

"Nothing specific. I've only had newspaper reports to go on, about the investigation and the trial, but I've been there and looked at all the locations. From the way he's described, I'm guessing Gittings wasn't just disposing of evidence, but hiding the girls, for himself. Owning them."

"Yes! My thoughts exactly. His sister… you know about his sister?"

"Clare? The name he kept saying in court? Was that his sister? The papers mentioned Margaret Gittings had had a daughter taken into care. Just to prove what a terrible monster she was."

"It's true the girl was taken into care. She was involved in a domestic incident, as a baby, back in the early eighties. It was the father who had inflicted the injures, slashed the child's face, but Margaret was considered unfit to keep custody of the infant. A matter of intense grievance that she probably transmitted to her son." Malcolm was quite animated now. "It was one thing we picked up on in his interview. The nearest thing to a confession. He wanted his sister back and I think the girls he snatched were stand-ins for Clare. He wanted to take them home and when they wouldn't come, his anger and frustration took over."

"There was no hint of a sexual motive."

"No. You're right. Laura Wakefield's face was cut post-mortem. I'm guessing it was done to complete her resemblance to Clare, not as some bestial act of dismemberment. He wasn't Tim the Ripper as one of the papers called him. There was no evidence of sexual interference. Strangulation, though. Twice, according to the autopsy, in Laura's case. There was a first attempt, and then he finished the job. What we concluded was that he'd had Laura in his van, unconscious but not quite dead, and while he was driving along, she came round, got the door open and jumped out. That's why he was dealing with her in the open and had to abandon her when he was interrupted."

"But you think he was intending to take her to the wood and conceal her there."

"You are talking about Hackling Wood at the end of Bartlet Lane?" Malcolm leaned forward earnestly.

"That's certainly my thought but what's your reasoning?"

Rosanna put her cup down. "He wouldn't pick an open field to hide their bodies. A wood would offer more cover. The ground wouldn't be disturbed each year. But it was the location of Laura Wakefield's body that really pointed to it. Piper's Lane. That didn't make sense."

"Yes," he agreed, cautiously.

"He worked at the abattoir. One of his possible routes home would have been along Bartlet Lane, then Piper's Lane, then onto the Fleetham Road to Irnby, missing out Welsey entirely. But if he picked up Laura Wakefield on her way home from school, he must have been taking the other route, through town, via Welsey High Street."

"Yes, yes!"

"So what reason would he have to be driving along Piper's lane, except to take her to his secret hiding place? The wood is on Bartlet Lane, just beyond the abattoir, and Millfield Road runs past it, too, which means he'd have known it well from passing it every day on his way to and from his first job at the chicken farm."

"Exactly! And it's less than a mile from Ashley Knowles' home." Malcolm sat back with a deep breath.

"You've done your homework, I see, and you've come to the same conclusion as me. But I reached it too late. I'd let it slip. Stuff happened, as they say, and it was only when I retired that I had this compulsion to go back, retrace his steps again and again, figure it out somehow or another. The woods make perfect sense. I did suggest it to the force, but have you seen Hackling Wood? I'm not sure how big it is exactly, but it must be well over a hundred acres. Don't ask me what that is in new money."

"More than forty hectares," said Barbara, helpfully. "And I can vouch for it being big. I have the scratches to prove it."

"Excuse me, I was the one engaged with that blackthorn," said Malcolm. "You just watched and laughed. Anyway, it's woodland, that's the point. Trees grow old, saplings spring up, undergrowth takes hold. A long time has passed. My hunch wasn't specific enough to justify the resources that would be needed."

"But you looked anyway," said Rosanna.

"I thought the dogs might be useful."

Barbara laughed. "Not a chance. Our boys can home in on a cowpat to roll in from a hundred yards, but they're not going to sniff out anything long dead and buried under quarter of a century of leaf mould."

"No, all right," agreed Malcolm. He turned back to Rosanna. "But you think you might do better?"

"What I'm really hoping to find is the book you suspected Margaret Gittings might be hiding for her son. A record of his killings."

"A record. Hm. Maybe. Don't pin all your hopes on that one. We discovered he was virtually illiterate. If it does still exist, I can't guarantee it will contain anything useful. I hoped we'd find it and there'd be enough in his scribbles to prove that Ashley Knowles and Bethany Davies were his victims too. And the other, somewhere in Essex, probably in the summer of '92, just before they moved to Welsey. Margaret made a habit of upping sticks and changing address or pushing her son into a new job every time a girl went missing. She'd have had a reason for quitting her cleaning job in Harlow and bringing him north. I'd like to think he did leave a record, but the general opinion was that his mother burned it along with his soiled clothes."

"You don't believe she did, though."

"I think she hid it for him. It goes with my impression of her. A very odd woman, Margaret Gittings. As disturbed as he is, in a different, besotted way. We couldn't prove that she'd taken part in any of the killings or knew of them in advance, but she did everything possible to keep him free to carry on. Totally obsessed with him and raging against everyone else in the world."

"Yes?"

"Nursing a sense of injustice that consumed her. She'd had her daughter taken from her and now we were taking her son. She'd see us all in Hell before she'd give us anything." Malcolm studied Rosanna with a frown.

"Do you think I'm lacking in sympathy? I don't have any – not for her. I reserve it all for the girls he killed and their poor parents."

"I can understand that. It's why I'm here, really."

"Not just looking for a feather in your cap? I wouldn't blame you if you were. It's okay, I don't care what your motive might be, as long as the girls are found. If it brings some closure to Sharon and Peter and Jennifer—"

"Jennifer Redbourn's dying."

Malcolm sat back, appalled. "Jenny? I knew she had health problems, but I didn't know it was that bad."

"Poor woman!" said Barbara. "Of course she needs to know."

"And I'm told she has very little time."

"Yes, yes, of course." Malcolm frowned. "Well then, what is your plan? To track down Margaret Gittings? I wish I could help you there, but, unfortunately, she slipped away from us. Another of our failures. She did return to the area; she was seen, and the locals had some idea of organising a lynching, but she eluded them and us. But the fact that she came is another reason why I think the book wasn't burned. She must have returned for something. Beyond that, I haven't found any record of employment or benefits. Not even health records. Her parents both died while she was in prison, so maybe she inherited enough to live on, under an alias.

I did make some enquiries and I was told that she'd never visited her son in Rampton but she wrote to him regularly. Endless wandering spiels of promises to be there for him always, and diatribes against the evil monsters who took him and his little sister Clare away from her, and how she'd never rest until she had them both back. Very repetitive. I don't think he ever read them and he couldn't reply anyway, because they didn't contain a return address. I wish I'd done more to follow it up now, but I'd had a bellyful of Margaret Gittings in the station. If I'd only… poor, poor Jenny. All right, Rosanna, a warning. If you are planning to go after Margaret, I'd take great care. Her son may have done the killing, but my feeling was that she was more than capable of it. She was seriously unbalanced and I imagine she'll only have got worse."

"I will take care but thank you. The more I can understand her, the better my chances of getting somewhere if I do find her. It will determine how I'll play it, since I don't fancy trying to torture the truth out of her…"

"You wouldn't succeed. She'd burn first."

"It will be a matter of winning her trust, then."

"You won't. She has no trust in anyone except her son. Like I told you, she's as damaged as he is. Two monsters together." Malcolm smiled. "But you're not deterred. Good. All I can say is, good luck."

Barbara showed her out. "If you do find anything, you will keep us informed?"

"Of course," said Rosanna.

Archaeology

As Rosanna drove home to Swindon, she wasn't sure whether to feel encouraged or depressed by her visit to Malcolm Cannell. He'd been eager to give her any information she wanted, and it was reassuring to know that at least one member of the original investigation team was still keen to see it fully resolved. But their talk had not brought her any nearer to finding Margaret. His memories of the woman were entirely negative, which of course they would be, but it didn't help.

Rosanna needed to understand the woman better than that, which meant delving deeper into her past. When she was safely back at her bedsitter, she checked out Shelley's memory stick again. The archive didn't only include newspaper cuttings. There were assorted random documents as well, gathered up by a man who was reaching for anything, however relevant. He'd acquired a clutch of birth and marriage certificates.

Birth certificate: Timothy Morris Gittings, 4th January 1973 at Abergelyn hospital. Father Anthony Gittings, labourer; mother Margaret Gittings, née Lewis; informant A.J. Gittings, The Engine, Monmouth Street, Tregarreg.

Marriage certificate: 20th October 1972, at Salem Chapel, Nantfuan, Monmouthshire. Anthony James Gittings, labourer, aged twenty-four, of the Engine, Tregarreg; father Morris Gittings, publican, to Margaret

Anne Lewis, aged seventeen, of 28 High Street, Nantfuan; father Cyril Lewis, shopkeeper.

Birth certificate: Margaret Anne Lewis to Cyril Lewis and Vera née Broderick, 29th August, 1955 in Nantfuan.

Rosanna shook her head over it. Margaret had only just turned seventeen and was seven months pregnant when she married. It wasn't a promising start. How eager had the bride been for the marriage, she wondered. To understand the woman, she needed to explore her history in the area that had formed and probably deformed her. There had been one cutting from a South Wales paper in Shelley's files – an article from 1996, after Timothy had been arrested and his name had been linked to the fate of Bethany Davies, six years earlier. There was a brief account of Bethany's disappearance in the village of Brongarn and a couple of quotes from villagers who remembered Timothy and his mother, and had, surprisingly, always thought there was something sinister about them. That was it, though. Nothing from earlier years.

Rosanna consulted maps of the area to fix the geography in her head. Tregarreg, where Margaret had lived after marriage, was a town in one of the valleys carved southwards towards Newport. Nantfuan, Margaret's birthplace, was a small village in the next valley to the west. Bethany's village Brongarn was a couple of miles further up from Nantfuan. It all seemed quite incestuously claustrophobic. Small communities, hemmed in. Rosanna knew all about them.

What had happened there? Margaret had produced another child, a daughter, Clare, who had been injured and taken into care. Rosanna searched birth records and found the reference: Clare Louise Gittings, registered second quarter 1982, Abergelyn district. Rosanna went back to the maps. Abergelyn was the sizeable town to the south where the two valleys met.

She launched into a frustrating search of online local newspapers, and finally found what she was looking for in August 1982. *Tregarreg Horror: Baby Slashed. Father arrested.*

Neighbours had heard screaming and shouting and a baby wailing, and when they'd had no reply to their knocks at no.7 Albert Street, they had broken the door down to find Tony Gittings, the father, blind drunk and standing over the crib of his baby daughter, bloody knife in hand. The baby's face had been slashed. The police were called and, after a search, the terrified mother and her nine-year-old son were found in the rain on the hillside above, soaked in blood.

Rosanna saved the article and sat back, thinking. It might explain a lot – why Margaret was obsessively protective of her son, why Timothy had slashed at least one girl's face. Not just to make her appear like his sister but acting out the crime he'd seen his father commit.

She found another account, interviewing neighbours in Albert Street. They'd had plenty to say. Both parents were heavy drinkers, always rowing. Tony Gittings was popular in some hard-bitten circles but was known to be a loud-mouthed bullyboy when drunk, a carbon copy of his father who had been a pub landlord until his licence was revoked. The family had been prone to "accidents." Tony was often belligerent, not to be messed with. Margaret was 'odd,' a recluse one moment and foul-mouthed the next.

Shouting was common enough from the Gittings house, but it was the sound of the baby's screams that caused the neighbours to step in. Tony was incapable of giving any coherent account of what had happened. Margaret later claimed her husband had been drinking while watching a football match. When the baby started to cry, the sound had enraged him and he had picked up a knife and lunged for the cot. She had been unable to hold him back and, believing her daughter to be dead, she had fled to safety with her son.

Tony was tried and convicted, still claiming he had no memory of the event. There was a mention of social services intervening with baby Clare, who was now found to have Foetal Alcohol Syndrome. Neighbours were happy that Margaret and her weird son were moved away.

Rosanna found it difficult to read the accounts without thinking of her own parents, father popular abroad but vicious at home, mother's weakness despised by neighbours. A mother so trapped that drink seemed the only escape. In her mother's case, it had ended in suicide. The consequences had been different for Margaret, but probably no better. Was it just a violent husband that had reduced her to that state? Were there any living relatives to ask? She returned to records of births, marriages and deaths. No siblings for Margaret Anne Lewis that she could find. The husband would be free by now, but as Margaret had helped to convict him, she was unlikely to be in contact with him. Still, anything was possible.

It turned out, any contact Margaret had with Anthony Gittings would have to be with psychic assistance. A quick search proved that he had died in 1994.

What else? Malcolm Cannell had mentioned that Margaret's parents had both died while she was in prison. Rosanna found the deaths registered in the fourth quarter of 1999. It wasn't that unusual for one elderly spouse to die and the other to follow shortly after. Still, it was worth looking into. She checked the local papers again for the last few months of 1999.

"Tragedy of respected lay preacher and wife." They had died together in a house fire, due to faulty wiring. Rosanna checked further copies to see if anything followed. Nothing about the fire, but several weeks after the tragedy, the paper was rejoicing in the juicy tale of a contested will, or rather the lack of one. According to the minister and congregation of Salem Chapel in Nantfuan, Cyril and Vera Lewis had declared before them all their solemn intention of leaving all their worldly goods to the chapel. Unfortunately, they had not got around to making a will to that effect.

As they had died intestate, the law consigned every last penny to their only child, Margaret Anne Gittings, currently serving a prison sentence for aiding and abetting a murderer, namely her son, child-killer Timothy Gittings.

The law had prevented them from disowning their daughter. She was condemned for failing to disown her son. Was that the definition of irony?

What sort of fortune had awaited Margaret when she was released from prison? Her parents had run a grocery shop in a run-down mining village, which had probably not brought in a fortune but even a small sum would have given her funds to start a new life somewhere where she wasn't known. But she couldn't vanish completely. There had to be a trace of her somewhere.

Born 1955: she'd be sixty-seven by now, so she should be in receipt of a state pension.

Rosanna was debating what to do with this potential lead when her phone rang. It was Malcolm Cannell.

"Rosanna, are you still intent on your quest for Margaret Gittings?"

"Oh, very much so, Superintendent."

"Malcolm, please. I hope I'm not interfering, but your visit prompted me to dig a bit more, follow up my earlier enquiries, and I contacted Rampton again. Timothy is still receiving regular letters from his mother. Still no return address, I'm afraid, but one had just arrived and they were able to tell me that the postmark was Abergelyn."

"You're kidding!"

"Does that help?"

"It must. It means she's gone home. Or at least back to the area where she was born. That is very, very helpful. I was already thinking that I'd need to visit the area, just to understand things better. Now that's decided."

"Good luck, then."

She would still need luck, but the quest was more hopeful. It was also likely to prove more expensive and she was running through her savings. Maybe it was time to turn a little more professional and contact the man for whom she was theoretically working.

Commission

"It's very good of you to come all this way." Andrew Rollinson was a man of about sixty, who looked as if he spared very little time for the gym or keeping fit, but for all that, he had clearly lost a lot of weight. Flesh hung on him. His face, otherwise pleasant, was creased with worry lines.

"Can I get you a tea, or a coffee?" asked his wife, Kate.

"I'd love a tea. Thank you," said Rosanna, letting Kate take her jacket.

"Come on through and sit down," said Andrew, ushering Rosanna through to a study, comfortable but organised. Appropriate for serious business talk, and that's what he wanted this to be. It was what she needed it to be, too.

He offered her one leather-upholstered chair, then took another, tugging his cuffs straight. Nerves. He glanced anxiously at the clock and checked it against his watch. "Shelley tells me you've found something."

Rosanna could feel the desperate hope in him. It was cruel but she was going to have to limit his expectations. "I've had a lot of help from a useful contact, and I've been doing background research. Some of it, I believe, is promising."

"You think you've tracked her down?" He was making an effort to keep his breathing steady.

"Margaret Gittings is in South Wales." Rosanna felt the sudden rush of tortured anticipation emanating from him. "That is, I think she is, but I still need to confirm it."

He nodded, calming himself. "And you'll take the case. That's good. That's good."

"I promised myself I'd find Rachel and the other girls eventually, even if it takes years."

"But Jenny doesn't have years." He put his face in his hand briefly, then took a deep breath and faced her again. "I don't know if Shelley told you…"

"That your sister doesn't have long. Yes."

"She's been moved to a hospice. She has weeks, if that. I'm afraid it might be just days. I don't know. It's bad." He shook his head. "Is there the remotest chance…"

"I am very sorry about your sister, and I promise I'll do everything I can, but I don't want to raise any false hopes. I honestly can't guarantee a time frame. I've gone as far as I can with documents, but if I'm going to take it any further, it would really help if you could cover some expenses—"

"Of course!" He jumped up, in his field of expertise at last. Money. Something positive he could do. He opened a desk drawer and took out a cheque book. "Cheque all right, or would you prefer direct transfer? Who should I make it out to? Your agency?"

"No!" Rosanna raised a hand to stop him. "I don't have an agency. If Shelley told you I was a professional private investigator or something, that's not exactly true. I was a police detective for a while, but now I'm on my own. If you're happy for me to continue, I'm very willing to carry on, but I'll be able to make better progress if I have some funds to work with."

She was sounding apologetic, which was ridiculous, but she couldn't help feeling uncomfortable at the thought of demanding payment for such a quest. She was never going to be a hard-nosed businesswoman.

She needn't apologise as far as Andrew was concerned. He didn't argue or even show a hint of disappointment. "Rosanna Quillan, is it?" He was scribbling on the cheque, ripping it out and handing it to her. "Will that cover the first month? I don't think Jenny will have that much time, but we'll all still need to know. The others will tell you. We all need to know." He glanced at the clock again. "They should have been here by now."

"Sorry?" Rosanna was looking at the cheque.

"The others."

Ten thousand pounds. Rosanna swallowed. Yes, she would need to invest some money as well as time, but this far exceeded any likely expenses. "It's too much."

He waved her objection away. "Spend whatever is required. There'll be more if you need it. We've agreed, whatever it takes. There are a lot of people desperate for you to succeed. It's killing us all. Yes!" He stepped up to the window. "Here they are, at last."

Rosanna pocketed the cheque and refocussed on what he was saying. The others? What others? The rest of his family? She hadn't been expecting to deal with anyone other than him. She stood up as Kate opened the office door and three people stalked in. A man, about the same age as Andrew; a woman maybe ten years younger; another woman, early thirties. It was impossible to assess their ages with certainty because they were all burned up, consumed by the same raging intensity. Fuelled, probably, by self-medication.

"You made it," said Andrew, pulling chairs forward for them. "Have you met… No, of course, you haven't. This is Rosanna Quillan, who is going to find our girls for us."

Did he have to be that definite? They fixed on Rosanna like hungry lions. She felt the weight of their expectation crushing her.

Andrew carried on with the introduction. "This is Ashley's mother, Sharon. And Peter Fitzpatrick, Jodie's father. And this is my niece, Amy. Rachel's sister."

What was Rosanna supposed to say as they confronted her? *Hi? How do you do? Nice weather for the time of year?*

"I will do my best, but please, you must understand, I can't promise…"

"But you'll take the money," said Sharon Knowles.

Rosanna could sense the disillusioned cynicism clogging the veins of a woman for whom hope had become a cruel joke a long time ago. "I'll take expenses, that's all."

"You'll take every penny we have, if it gets the job done," said Peter Fitzpatrick. This was the man who still, more than twenty-five years on, kept his house as a shrine, an incident room frozen in time, waiting for answers that might never come. Rosanna had fled from that house, overwhelmed by it. She wanted to flee from its owner now. A touch would scorch her.

"What have you got? What have you found?" demanded Amy Redbourn. She had been six years old when her sister went missing – gone alone to gym club because Amy had refused to go with her. She had grown up not just with the grief but with the guilt. Or had she had the chance to grow at all? Rosanna watched her nervous fingers tugging down the sleeves of her baggy sweater. Covering scars? She had the worn features of an addict.

Rosanna knew all about obsession, the driving hunger. She nursed it within herself, she understood it, but still she felt as if she were drowning in theirs.

Andrew was urging them all to sit down. He turned back to her. "Yes, now please, tell us where you've got to. You say you've traced the Gittings woman to South Wales."

Fitzpatrick jumped in. "You've found her! Where?"

Andrew raised his hands to calm things, then resumed his own seat. "Let's just hear Miss Quillan." He leaned forward, hands clasped between his knees, ready to concentrate and absorb, his eyes half shut.

"I've been through all the accounts," said Rosanna. "I've visited Welsey and Fleetham and I've spoken to the detective involved at the time—"

"Malcolm?" said Sharon, sitting back, arms folded. "He doesn't know where she is. I've asked him enough times."

"Yes, he couldn't tell me, although he's just as desperate to find them." Rosanna was playing for time, while she determined how much to tell and how much to hide. She felt that one spark too many might ignite a powder keg. "And I really don't know anything for definite." She wished now she hadn't mentioned South Wales at all. If Margaret wanted to conceal her whereabouts, she could be using some forwarding service for her letters. "I'm sorry if I gave the impression I've got further in my search than I really have. What I meant is, Margaret Gittings came from South Wales and I think my next step should be to go there, investigate further and see if I can find more definite clues than would help me pin her down."

"Nail her down, you mean," said Peter. "Nail her to the floorboards and twist the nails till she tells us what her evil son did with our girls. Kick the truth out of her!"

"Now, now, Peter," said Andrew, shaking his head.

Rosanna had to stop this. "I give you my word," she said, "that I will let you know everything I find. Every tiny detail." Yes, she would, when she had found it all, the woman, the book, the bodies, but not a moment before. Because she realised she was terrified of what they might do.

* * *

Rosanna found herself a modest B&B in Abergelyn. With the funds provided by Andrew Rollinson, she could have afforded a five-star suite in the country house hotel on the outskirts of the town, but she was determined to keep her expenses to a minimum. Her landlady was friendly but not over-inquisitive, preoccupied with a new grandchild, so Rosanna was free to consider her strategy without sociable interruptions.

Her first move, once she'd unpacked, was to drive out to see the places of significance recorded in her files. Tregarreg first, about five miles north, a small town that was having trouble picking itself up from the doldrums of the mine closures, but attempts had been made. There was a cocktail bar on Monmouth Street, which called itself The Right Place, but the bones of an old town pub were still visible and its former name, "The Engine" remained in tiles above the door. Margaret had lived in rooms above the pub when she'd married the landlord's son. It wasn't a fact The Right Place was advertising. The present bar staff hadn't even heard the name Gittings.

Albert Street, where the couple had later moved with their son, was a row of cramped terraced cottages, facing a timberyard and a neglected playground and with steep hillside rising behind. No.7 like all the others in the short row, was empty and boarded up. It was where Margaret's husband had been arrested, knife in hand, while she had fled up the hill in the rain with Timothy. What more was there to be said? There were no neighbours left to be interviewed.

And that was Tregarreg. Rosanna had to return to Abergelyn to drive up the next valley, with a string of villages, Croesowen, Nantfuan, Brongarn, all virtually identical; mining villages that had lost their mines. She headed straight through to Brongarn and found Hafod Terrace where Bethany Davies had lived. It curved down to a junction with Long Street, which ran through the village at the bottom of the valley. There was the rough ground, still neglected and littered, where the police concluded that Bethany had stopped to play, slipped and fallen in the water. The river looked little more than a stream, tamed by concrete banks, but it was fast flowing. A row of terraced houses adjoined the waste ground, their yards backing on to a riverside path. Margaret and Timothy had lived in the first one. A short way down the path, a footbridge crossed the river to a track climbing up into tangled trees. Woods. She wondered.

But it was Margaret she needed to find first. She retraced her route less than two miles back to Nantfuan and paused to look at the former grocery shop in Nantfuan's High Street, where Cyril and Vera Lewis had raised their daughter. It was now the Lotus Flower Chinese takeaway, leaving villagers to do their shopping in a Spar attached to a garage.

Directed by her sat nav, Rosanna cautiously turned up a steep side street that ended with a grim Chapel, standing stern and forbidding over the village. It was abandoned, its windows shattered, Salem engraved over its padlocked doors. Would the Lewis fortune have saved it? Probably not. It would have needed souls as much as money, and they had probably drifted away into a Godless age of consumer vice and depravity.

The house fire that had killed Cyril and Vera Lewis had happened in a street just below the chapel. It must have been severe enough to wreck the building, because there was nothing there now. The house had not been rebuilt. If Margaret had returned to the area of her childhood, she was not living in her old home, nor in her parents' retirement cottage. It was disappointing, but Rosanna would just have to find other leads.

Back in her lodgings, she checked her files again. Margaret's parents hadn't left a will, but they did have a family solicitor. Nigel Garth, LLB, of Evans, Price and

Garth in Abergelyn. He was quoted, expressing very correct shock and sorrow in the article about their deaths. Rosanna could start there – assuming that he was still alive.

He was. Just. He was very elderly, senior partner now in the firm that bore his name, but Rosanna suspected he was left to snooze quietly most days in his dusty office full of oak cabinets and paper files, while younger colleagues took on most of the work at their computers.

He was not only old but deaf and vague, which had been a problem when Rosanna had attempted to speak to him on the phone, but she decided it might actually work in her favour, now that she was face to face with him. A solicitor fully on the ball wouldn't give her the time of day if she asked about a client's affairs, but once Mr Garth had offered her tea and biscuits for the third time with the same joke about gingernuts, she guessed she could tempt him into wide-ranging reminiscences.

"I know I'm probably being cheeky," she said, "but my gran had relatives in this area and I think you knew them. Cyril and Vera Lewis."

"Ah. Yes. The Lewises. Cyril and Vera they were called. A very devout couple. Very strong in the chapel. Yes, a sad case. House fire, you know, and then, of course, the bad business with their grandson." He lowered his voice. "You know about that, do you?"

"Yes, my mum did mention it once, but she doesn't like talking about it. I'm more interested in Cyril and Vera. And their daughter, of course. Family tree research, you know, and I'd love to make connections

115

with branches of my family that we lost contact with. I know they died in a fire, which was awful. Does their daughter still live here?"

"Margaret? Ah yes, Margaret, another sorry case. It broke their hearts, you know, her marriage, the child and all. They were rather simple folk. Couldn't cope with all the horror and the scandal, but in the end... If only they'd come to me. People don't think, do they? Always postponing making a will until it's too late, and the law must take its course."

"You mean they didn't leave a will? Did they have much to leave?"

"Yes, indeed, quite a sizeable legacy as it happens. Some money, but it was mostly property. That was down to Vera's father, old Thomas Broderick. Swansea lad, made his fortune abroad. Bought the shop for his daughter when she married and put his money in other property in the area. Acquired a very respectable portfolio. There were a couple of houses in Brecon, and a cottage in the Elan Valley, I recall. And one... was it in Aberystwyth? Yes, or Aberaeron. It's all on file. Most of them, though, were round here."

"Oh, wonderful. Do you know who owns them now? Are any for sale?"

"For sale? Ah... not at present, although I have been instructed to manage the sale of a couple in the past. Or was it three? Yes, she sold one of the ones in Pontgwartheg two or three years ago."

"She? Is that Margaret? Does she live round here?"

"Well, as to that... are you sure you wouldn't like a cup of tea? We have gingernuts, although speaking for myself..."

"No, thanks, really. Margaret Gittings. You were saying?"

"Margaret, yes. I believe it's possible she lives hereabouts, but I couldn't really tell you. She was informed of her inheritance when she was... away, and I had a letter from her, from... where she was, asking me to carry on dealing with anything local. Which I have done, of course. I think most, if not all the properties were handled for her parents by Greenways. It's a letting agency here in Abergelyn, and Mrs Gittings asked me to continue the arrangement. They handle all her financial affairs, and they are the only address I have for her."

"Oh, I see. That's interesting. You say she owns a lot of properties round here. If they're not for sale, maybe there's one to rent?"

"Indeed, there would be. Seven or eight, perhaps. Now, let me see." Mr Garth hauled himself up and shuffled to a cabinet to search for the file. It took him several minutes to find the one he wanted as he was diverted by several others that sparked memories.

Rosanna sat patiently until he returned with a hefty bundle.

"Here we are. Let's see now. There's Oakgrove – no, that one's a long term let. Family's been there for ten years or more. What's their name now? Gilbert. Yes, Gilbert. And Waverley is the same. Another family there. The one on Brecon Road - that's converted to flats. Greenways can tell you if they're all occupied. Then there's the holiday lets. Llwynon – that's just out of town on the Tregarreg road. Rosewell – that's a farm cottage this side of Croesowen."

Rosanna managed to lean across, with a show of eager interest, and take a look at the properties listed.

"There are quite a few, aren't there."

"Yes, yes. Avalon. Now, that was the one at Pontgwartheg she sold recently, but I imagine the other three could still be holiday lets. I'm sure Jonathan Ramsey can tell you what's available if you are thinking of renting one. Ask at Greenways. That's your best bet."

"Yes, I'll do that. Thank you."

"Excellent. Now, about that cup of tea. We have gingernuts, you know."

* * *

Timothy Gittings' mother was probably notorious enough to be a hate figure in the area even thirty years on from her son's first murder. If she really had risked returning here, she would want to stay under the radar. Somewhere where she wouldn't attract the notice of people with long memories. She could do it because she had inherited a batch of properties and if she chose to occupy one, she'd have no rent or mortgage and the agency was probably dealing with any service bills on her behalf. The property portfolio would probably generate enough income to keep her going without having to work, and if she ran short, another one could be sold off to boost her coffers. She was here. It seemed somehow inevitable.

Mr Garth had kindly, if unintentionally, let Rosanna see the list of properties Margaret still owned. Rosanna studied the Greenways agency website and identified most of them. 45a, b and c Brecon Road, Llwynon and

Rosewell that he had mentioned, and several others whose names she had glimpsed – Y Felin, Tygwyn, Nythfa, Marlborough. Oakgrove and Waverley were not advertised, presumably because they had long-term sitting tenants. The only other property on the solicitor's list which was not on Greenway's books was a house called Cartref. Rosanna's memory for details was one of her most valuable talents. Cartref was one of the three unsold properties at a place called Pontgwartheg, along with Nythfa and Marlborough.

She checked the map for Pontgwartheg, and nearly gasped aloud. The place was two or three miles from Nantfuan by road, but as a crow flew it was less than one. It hung over the valley, nestled in a wooded cleft in the steep slope just above the place where Margaret was born. Isolated and inaccessible enough for it to escape notice by any who didn't know it.

Margaret had come home. Rosanna was sure of it.

Now it was just a question of enquiring at Greenways agency.

Friend

Marlborough. Two-bedroomed cosy holiday cottage in attractive woodland setting, available Saturdays to Saturdays, presently vacant and remarkably cheap. It was only Thursday and Rosanna was going to pick up a key in two days" time. She had Friday to spare, to make the necessary arrangements and try one more research option.

The records relating to the case of baby Clare Gittings had thrown up a link that might still be worth following. When the baby was being taken into care, Jacqueline Roberts, an old school friend of Margaret Gittings, gave a statement that Margaret was a devoted mother who had been given very little support but who would manage perfectly well if she were given more. Perhaps it was Ms Robert's intervention that had allowed Margaret to keep custody of her son, although it had failed with Clare. Was the woman still around? It would be good to talk to someone, anyone, who might be willing to see a less monstrous side of Margaret.

If she had been a schoolfriend, could she still be living in Nantfuan? Would anyone in the village know?

Nantfuan had no post office. The sole remaining pub, the Drover's Arms, seemed the best bet to ask, but it was unproductive on a wet Friday morning. Two teenagers playing bar billiards were the only customers when

Rosanna called in, and neither they nor the sleepy girl lethargically wiping the bar had anything to offer other than grunts and shrugs when she asked.

Stepping out, Rosanna saw a sign in the window of a house opposite. Mari's Curlz. A hair salon? If it was, it probably specialised in tight perms and blue tints for the older lady, the sort who would know all about everyone. Her guess was confirmed when she opened the door and breathed in the chemical fumes. A cheerful woman wrapped in a plastic apron looked up with a smile from the curlers she was applying to a grey head of hair.

"Hello, love. What can I do you for? Trim, is it?"

Rosanna smiled back. "Actually, I was hoping for some information. I'm looking for a Jacqueline Roberts? She used to live in Nantfuan. You wouldn't know her, would you?"

"Jacqueline Roberts. Mm. Can't say..." The hairdresser was shaking her head as she thought about it, but the face below the curlers scowled and tutted.

"Don't be daft. That's Jackie Griffiths, that is. You know, Jackie Roberts when she wed. Moved back to her parents' place up on the hill when she retired a couple of years back."

"Oh yes, of course! I know her, *that* Jackie. Hasn't come in here, but I've met her in the shop. Always says hello. Nice lady."

"She lives up on the hill?" asked Rosanna tentatively. The area was not short of hills.

"Yes, what's the name of the house now? Fairview, that's it. Up Chapel Lane and keep going. It's a big house. You can't miss it."

"Thank you?" said Rosanna. "I am really grateful."

* * *

Chapel Lane: the same turning she had taken before, to look at Salem Chapel. This time Rosanna continued along a narrow lane that led up past the last Victorian terraces, and out into open country, fields and moorland and woods, no sign remaining of the mines that had been Nantfuan's reason for existence. How green was my valley once more. She came at last to a detached stone house, sturdily gracious and backed by shrubs. Fairview. It offered a view across the valley that must be a lot fairer now than it had been when the house was built.

A sprightly man in his sixties or seventies was trimming a hedge and stopped to peer over his glasses as Rosanna got out of her car.

"I'm looking for a Mrs Jacqueline Roberts."

"Jackie! Someone for you!" he shouted and returned to his snipping. A woman of a similar age came round from the back of the house, peeling off gardening gloves.

"Hello?"

Rosanna introduced herself cautiously. Malcolm Cannell had understood the nature of her business before she'd arrived on his doorstep, but she was springing herself on Jackie Roberts without warning and it could go very badly. "I'm sorry if I'm disturbing you, but I'm hoping you can help me."

The woman smiled pleasantly. "Certainly, if I can."

"I believe you used to know Margaret Gittings. Or

rather, Margaret Lewis, as she was when she was young."

The smile promptly gave way to a look of shock. Jackie Roberts shut her eyes for a moment. Then she sighed. "Yes, I did know her. Why, exactly? Who are you? Because if you're a reporter…"

"No, I'm not, I promise. My name's Rosanna Quillan and I've been asked by relatives to help find the girls who—"

"Oh my God. Have they still not been found? That's too awful. But I can't help you there. I know they think Bryn Davies's girl was probably buried around here, but no one has the first idea where."

"That's all right. What I was really hoping was that you could tell me something about Margaret. Anything about her, really. Who she was, what she was and why. I found your name mentioned in the papers and I hoped you could paint a fuller picture for me."

"The reports about that poor baby, you mean? I thought I was trying to help Mags. It seemed terribly unfair, having her child taken away. But if I'd known what was to come, I don't think I'd have spoken up."

"You weren't to know, though. Not what was to come, but you did know her past and that could be really useful. If I could understand better what was going on in her head, maybe I could figure out the rest of the puzzle more easily."

Jackie winced, her eyes squeezed shut again.

Her husband lowered his shears and frowned at Rosanna. "I don't think my wife wants to dredge up some very painful—"

"Colin." Jackie stopped him. "I don't think keeping

silent is going to help me or anyone else. Maybe It's time I got things off my chest. Yes, I knew Mags as a girl. I was her friend. The very worst sort of friend."

"Now, now," said her husband, but she shook her head.

"You want to understand the puzzle? Well I was a part of it. The start of it. Maybe I really should have predicted it all, everything that happened."

"No!" said Rosanna and Mr Roberts at the same time.

Rosanna went on, calm and reasonable. "I don't believe anyone could have predicted what her son would go on to do, years later. But the relatives of the missing girls need to be able to make some vague sense of it, and if I can help them with that..."

"Yes." Jackie folded her gardening gloves over, decisively, scrutinising them for a few seconds, then she nodded and turned towards the front door. "Wouldn't we all love to make sense of it. You'd better come in and sit down, if we're going to talk."

Her husband gave her a warning glance. "Jackie."

She smiled at him. "I think I should, Colin. Lance the boil, maybe. You could make us a pot of tea?" She beckoned Rosanna to follow her in, to a comfortable sitting room. "Do please sit." She sat herself down, and then promptly got up again, going to the windowsill to shift a vase of flowers, for no obvious reason.

"Mags. Poor Margaret Lewis. I'm not supposed to call her that, am I? The world doesn't see her as poor Margaret. Quite the opposite. Those reports of Timothy's trial made her out to be vicious, uncaring, evil even, but that wasn't the girl I knew. She just seemed like a poor thing to me, back then. A sad child, that's all. If she did finish up as a monster, it's probably my fault."

She tweaked the petals of a chrysanthemum, then gazed out of the window. "I've felt horribly guilty about it all these years. Colin keeps suggesting I should have counselling, but what for? Talking won't take the guilt away or give me absolution."

Rosanna waited. It was clear Jackie didn't need prompting, if she were allowed to take her own time.

"Mags and I weren't obvious bosom pals, you know. We were only friends because we went to school together. We were in the same class, caught the same bus, but that's about all we had in common. She was one of those kids, poor thing, that everyone else made fun of, or just ignored. You know how children can be. She was always painfully the odd one out. Not remotely "with it," which is what we all wanted to be. It's probably why my parents kept nudging me to be nice to her, invite her to tea, that sort of thing. They attended the same chapel as her parents. Salem. It's just down the road. Everyone went to chapel back then. They'd drag me along, too, if I couldn't come up with a good excuse for not going. I was all for being a rebellious teenager."

Jackie smiled. "In as much as any kid could be here. It was that era, but we weren't exactly on the front line of the revolution. Some way behind, but miniskirts had reached even us. Except for Mags. Pleated skirts, never above the knee, cardigans and lace-ups. She wasn't allowed to mess around with make-up, or alcohol, or any of that wicked music and certainly not boys. Her parents were seriously religious."

"Fanatical?"

"No." Jackie turned, frowning as she thought about it. "Not Hell fire and all that. Rather sweet, really. Or at least that's how everyone saw them. Sincere. Over-protective. A bit innocent, perhaps. Maybe just a bit loopy."

She stopped, considering, and managed a laugh. "They couldn't have been that innocent, of course. Turned out, after they died in that awful fire, that they were real property tycoons. Well, maybe that's an exaggeration. Margaret's mum inherited most of it, which was just as well because they'd never have made a fortune from that shop. They refused on principle to sell the Devil's brew. Which was ironic, because when they retired and sold the business, the new owners turned it into an off-licence. Didn't last. It's a Chinese take-away now. Sorry, what was I saying?"

"That they were over-protective?"

"Yes. Protective of their only child. That's how it seemed, but I suppose, these days, you'd call it controlling. They kept her on a very tight leash. School on weekdays, Saturdays gardening and helping in the shop, Sabbath strictly chapel and Sunday School. Evenings were for prayer, improving books and knitting. The sum total of her childhood. She didn't rebel at all. Maybe it made her feel safe. Boundaries, you know. It helps some people. But I suppose the suffocation would explain her odd moments." Jackie sat down at last. "I remember her having a couple of outbursts. We could all have our moments of screaming resistance, but it seemed extra shocking with her. She was usually so quiet and passive, didn't laugh, didn't cry, didn't get upset. Didn't react to any of the bullying or mockery about not joining in or the way she dressed, but she must have bottled it all up inside. Then – it only happened once or twice – the pressure cooker would burst, and out would come a scream of rage. She'd throw things. Hit people. Go wild."

Jackie sighed. "It was an understandable response to all the repression. I don't know how they'd deal with it now, but her parents had their own ideas. It was Satan digging his claws in her. They had everyone at chapel praying over her. I can remember her sitting there, quite expressionless, while we all gathered round. It wasn't exactly an exorcism, but it was excruciatingly embarrassing, to me at least. My parents didn't approve of it at all, which is why they stopped attending Salem. They encouraged me to befriend her, to give her a refuge, I suppose, and I thought that was what I was doing. Rescuing her." She groaned. "I've felt terrible about it ever since."

"What happened?"

"I persuaded her to come out with me one evening, on some pretext or another. I think we told her parents we were going to choir practice. Something like that. If I could take one thing back in my life… I had this idea I was opening her eyes to the real world, showing her what she was missing, imprisoned behind those lace curtains, with the Lord's Prayer on her bedroom wall. Her eyes were opened all right. It was a total disaster.

"She got drunk, which was all my fault. Cider. I convinced her it wasn't real alcohol. That's what I honestly believed, being a stupid little girl myself, even though I thought I was wonderfully worldly-wise. Mags had never touched a drop of anything before, and it went straight to her head. She was all over the place, and she got herself pregnant."

Jackie got up again and headed back for the window, slapping the back of a chair as she caught her own accusing reflection in the glass. "Listen to me! No, she didn't get herself pregnant. She wasn't even fully conscious. Tony Gittings got her pregnant, by raping her.

Only we didn't call it that, in those days. We called it him getting carried away and her behaving irresponsibly when she should have known better."

"There are plenty who'd call it that still, despite Me Too."

"Yes, probably. Anyway, that was it for Mags. Trust Tony to be so fecund. I didn't know what to do. I had this idea about gin and hot baths, but that didn't work. I was almost as ignorant as her, when it came to these things. Liberation round here only went so far, back in – what was it? 1971? 72? She hadn't had much of a future ahead of her anyway. I'm not saying she would have gone to university or had a brilliant career, but she could have done O-levels at least, got a decent job, if her parents hadn't whisked her out of school at fifteen, to help out in the shop. Keeping her safe and sound from the wickedness out there. The wickedness being me, as it turned out.

"When they discovered she was up the duff, there was only one possible course of action as far as they were concerned. It wasn't 'Out and never darken my doorstep again.' It was just that if you sinned you had to pay the price, and the price in her case was to marry Tony Gittings, whether either of them wanted it or not. God knows how her father forced him into it. Cyril Lewis wasn't exactly the shotgun type, and I doubt if it would ever have occurred to any of the Gittings tribe that there was a 'right thing.' But somehow, he twisted arms. Maybe they were calculating on him having money to leave.

"I went to the… wedding doesn't seem the right word. Human sacrifice, more like. Cyril and Vera treated it as a rite of penitence rather than celebration. They didn't invite guests, but I went anyway. Bunked off school to be there.

"Tony's whole family turned up, thoroughly rowdy and improper. His parents ran a pub over in Tregarreg and I doubt if they'd ever stepped inside a chapel before. They were just itching to get back to the pub and have a booze-up. I was there, on my own, watching Mr Lewis marching poor Mags up the aisle. They'd made her wear this ghastly lilac suit. Her mother's, I think. Crimplene, awful. And her stomach was out here. She was clutching a pathetic bunch of Michaelmas daisies from the garden. I don't think she looked up once. I just wanted to cry.

"When we came out, I tried to say something to her, but it was as if she'd blocked everything out. I don't blame her. Her parents stood by her for half a minute, maybe, then her dad patted her on the arm and they both walked away. Tony's lot were too busy rowing over who got into which car to notice. I thought for a moment they might forget to take Mags with them, but then one of them dragged her along to Tony's car and that was it.

"I didn't see her again for a couple of years. The excuse I gave myself was that she was living now in Tregarreg. It's in the next valley, which meant we didn't automatically run into each other anymore. The truth is, I felt too guilty to face her. Then, I was home from university and I'd arranged to meet someone over there, and there was Mags, with Timothy in his pushchair. I couldn't just walk by, so I stopped to talk. She stank of gin, I remember that. The girl who'd never touched more than orange squash until I corrupted her. I did the talking. She hardly said a word, although she did tell me she and Tony had moved out of the pub because his mother was too interfering with the baby. It seems now, in retrospect, I should have read more into that, recognised the possessiveness. All the time I was with her, she never looked at me. She just kept her eyes fixed on Timothy, as if something might snatch him away if she blinked. I suppose he was all she had. I don't count Tony. God, I wished we'd never had to count Tony. You know about what happened?"

Rosanna nodded. "You mean the second child."

"That, yes, of course, but I meant the first thing, the accident or whatever it was, in the playground. No? That's what scarred the boy. My mother told me about it; she was working at the hospital. Everyone was telling a different version, of course. Tony and Timothy had fallen off the slide in the playground. Tony was drunk as usual and claimed it was an accident. He was just trying to teach his son to be a man because his mother was turning him into a... well, you know the sort of thing he'd have said. They'd fallen onto concrete. He had a sprained ankle, but Timothy had a broken arm and his face was all smashed up. Mags was there, like a fury, accusing Tony of trying to kill her beloved boy. I suppose she must have come across as too hysterical to be convincing. Who knows what really happened? The police wrote it off as an accident.

"I should have gone to visit her when I came back after university. I didn't, though. The only time I did see her was a few years later, not long before that awful... I was married by then and working in Cardiff, but I used to visit Mum and Dad here in Nantfuan. There was this one time, I dropped by the shop to pick up some milk and Mags came in. She was dragging a suitcase and she had Timothy with her. He'd have been eight or nine by then, I suppose, his face still scarred, and she was obviously pregnant again. She had a black eye, too. She didn't see me, just stared at her parents behind the counter. She said 'I want to come home.'"

Jackie put her hands over her face and drew a deep breath. "I still can't believe it. Mr Lewis came round from the till, and I thought he was going to hug her, but he just took her arm, very gently, nothing violent, and turned her round and led her back to the door. And Mrs Lewis said 'We've told you before, child. Go back to your husband and be a dutiful wife. You chose your path.' Can you believe it? Parents turning their back on their own daughter like that, when she was so obviously in need of help. And those words: we've told you before. How many times had she tried to get away? To come home.

"I was totally useless, yet again. I should have

131

rushed out after her, taken her home to Mum and Dad, but I was just stunned. Sickened. Praying her parents wouldn't recognise me. I stood there, head down, pretending to be choosing biscuits. That's another burden of guilt I've carried ever since, because by the time I came out of the shop, she'd gone. Back to him, it must have been, because a few months later…" Jackie stopped, unable to go on.

"The attack on the baby."

"Yes, baby Clare. It was awful. I remember bunting being out everywhere for some royal birth – Prince William, I think – and there was Margaret's baby being mutilated and… I can't bear to think about it."

Jackie paused to look out of the window again.

"Maybe I'm too scared to think about it. You know Tony was convicted. They found him standing over her, knife in his hand, but he always maintained, to his dying day, that he'd never have laid a finger on his beautiful little angel. He'd just been so drunk he couldn't remember anything that happened. There was nothing to contradict Margaret's account. I worry about that."

"She worries about all of it," said Jackie's husband, coming in with a tray of mugs. He put it down, crossed to a cupboard and poured a whisky and dry ginger. He glanced at Rosanna as he handed the glass to his wife. "I take it you're driving. Sorry, has to be tea then. I keep telling Jackie she needs to forget it all, because there's nothing she can do, but of course she doesn't listen." He turned back to his wife, handing her the glass. "Has it done any good, getting it off your chest?"

She took a sip of the whisky then tutted and put the

glass down. "Tea. And this isn't about doing me good."

She faced Rosanna. "Do you think he did it? Knowing what we came to know later, do you think it really was Tony Gittings cutting his own baby daughter? Nobody questioned it at the time. He was drunk, abusive, he was holding the knife. He was obviously guilty. Except that when Timothy was finally convicted, we all wondered. Could it have been him, not his father? Sibling jealousy or something? I know Margaret would have lied to protect him. Tony was dead by the time Timothy was caught. Liver – cirrhosis, like his father."

Rosanna smiled at Colin Roberts as she took the mug of tea he proffered. This was such a British mission. Everywhere she went, she was offered tea. "It does seem a possibility," she agreed. Sibling jealousy or sibling possessiveness? He had a mutilated face. Did he want his baby sister to have the same? A sort of twisted mutual identity?

"I'm not the only one who's felt guilty over the years," said Jackie, sitting down again. "Mum did, too, bless her, and that's hardly fair because she did at least try to help. More than I ever managed. I didn't know Mags had come back to Nantfuan. After Tony's arrest, you know, social services moved her to a flat in Newport and I thought that was where she'd stayed. The baby, Clare – it wasn't just a slashed cheek. Mags must have been drinking heavily all through the pregnancy. It was the one lesson she learned, while she and Tony were living at the pub with his parents – how to drink. The road to oblivion. Mum always suspected Timothy had Foetal Alcohol Syndrome too. It might explain a lot, don't you think? Anyway, the baby was taken into care and they nearly took Timothy too. I imagine they crucified themselves later that they didn't do it.

"That was when I stuck my oar in. I was expecting my first at the time and I couldn't think of anything worse than having a baby snatched away. It seemed too cruel, so I wrote a sort of character reference. I'd never doubted that she was a really devoted mother. In different circumstances, I'm sure she'd have been fine. I was desperate to make amends for letting her down before. I don't know if I made any difference. Mags was allowed to keep Tim, as long as she gave up drinking.

"That was the last I heard. As I said, I was living in Cardiff by then and Mum didn't tell me, not at the time, but Mags turned up again in Nantfuan, with Tim in tow. Her parents were still refusing to have her back and Mum found her huddled in the bus shelter, with nowhere to go. She said she wasn't going back to Newport because Timothy was being bullied at school, so Mum brought them here for the night. She suggested Mags could look in the paper for a job and she found an advert for a clerk at a depot up the valley. Next morning, after breakfast, she slipped out without a word and took Timmy off to Brongarn.

"Well, of course, Mum was a bit annoyed that Mags had gone without even saying thank you, but she didn't think anything more about it. Didn't think it worth mentioning to me. When Bethany Davies went missing in Brongarn – that was several years later – no one suggested there was any connection. It was put down as an accidental drowning, not a murder. But then, dear God, when Timothy was arrested and it all came out, Mum was beside herself. If she hadn't sent Mags after that job in Brongarn…"

"That's where you get it from," said Colin. "Guilt-ridden women all around me. What you need to remember is that Timothy Gittings did what he did. No one else, and no one made him do it."

Jackie shrugged, with a smile. "If you say so, dear. Besides, I don't know if anything I've said has been of any use to… sorry, I forgot your name."

"Rosanna."

"Yes. It doesn't help you find his victims, does it?"

"No, but maybe it helps me find his mother."

"I can't see how. She won't be anywhere round here. She wouldn't dare show her face in Nantfuan again, surely. If I were her, I think I'd have emigrated to the other side of the world. Somewhere no one would even have heard of me."

"I expect you're probably right," said Rosanna. "But thank you for all you've been willing to share."

□

Part 4: TREACHERY

Pontgwartheg

Rosanna had booked out of her guesthouse after breakfast on the Friday morning. That night, after a hasty shopping trip to Newport, she took a room instead at a Travelodge. She needed somewhere anonymous for her next move. Somewhere where reception staff probably wouldn't notice who arrived and who left.

Setting her bags on the bed, she unpacked her purchases, and stood there, staring down at them and debating. Was she really going to do this? It seemed a perfectly logical idea if she wanted to be coldly calculating about it. But if she wanted to be plain human, wasn't it too cruel? The woman was trapped in obsession for her missing children. How could it be justified to deceive her with a snippet of hope, to win her confidence and then shatter it all?

Rosanna's laptop was in the same bag. She pulled it out, thinking to search for some other less distasteful means, but as she opened it, four faces immediately looked at her from the screen. Four little girls, school photographs, some beaming broadly, some shy. Lost girls. It was for them she was going to do this. For them and their suffering families. Picking up the hair bleaching kit and the packet from the fancy dress shop, she marched into the bathroom.

* * *

"Marlborough. Here are the directions. I hope you have a nice stay, Ms Craven." The girl in Greenways letting agency handed over a set of keys with a fixed smile, as if she doubted her hopes would be fulfilled.

"Thanks. I will." Rosanna took the keys and a print-out and returned to the carpark in the centre of Abergelyn. As she settled back into the driver's seat, she paused to look at herself in the mirror. Her reflection still disturbed her, both because it was wrong and because it wasn't her. She smiled at memories of Shelley trying to concoct imaginative terms for the colour of Rosanna's hair. Hazelnut had been one. Dusky Dust had been less appealing. Rosanna had been happy to settle for mid-brown. It was a part of her, and the pale gold of her reflection was simply not Rosanna Quillan. Any more than the scar on her cheek, dabbed gently with makeup, but still visible.

But then she wasn't Rosanna Quillan now. From this moment she was Lisa Craven, from Winchester. If she found herself engaging in anything directly criminal, it might help to keep her own record clean.

Taking a deep breath, she started up and headed once more for Nantfuan. The lane she wanted veered off just before the village. It was a minor road, fair enough for quarter of a mile, but after passing a couple of bungalows, tender loving care gave out. Grass was sprouting from its centre as it turned sharply to climb along the course of a stream chattering its way down to the river below. She approached each bend cautiously, in case she met someone head-on, because the single track wouldn't allow much manoeuvring space. As she passed an old stone bridge that carried a farm track over the gulley, her sat nav told her it was less than a mile now. The road dipped a little and then started a steady steep climb.

There they were. A string of four dour, Victorian cottages, opening straight onto the road that separated them from the stream, the wooded valley sides rising high on both sides. Under grey clouds promising rain, it looked like the gloomiest spot on earth. But maybe it was her guilt colouring the scene, casting its own funereal shadow.

She stopped, the engine still running, picked up the print-out from the agency and studied the photograph of a sparkling holiday let. Golden stonework, green door and gay curtains. She compared it to the four grim cottages. They faced almost due north and it was unlikely that they were ever bathed in sunlight. Grey stone. Either the letting agency had relied on the miracles of Photoshop, or it had managed to catch the briefest of sunny windows on June 21st. It was the end of October now, late afternoon, and the place was already half-way into night.

The third one along. That was hers. The slate nameplate was unreadable in the gloom, but it had the same front door as in the photograph, though it looked more brown than green in real life. *Marlborough;* it sounded quite grand. The reality was anything but.

The first cottage that she had passed, Avalon, the

best kept and recently modernised by the look of it, had a track at the side, room for a car although it was currently vacant. The other three had no possible parking space. The last cottage, Cartref, to the right of Marlborough, abutted a rocky spur that thrust out from the valley side and dropped to the road as an almost sheer cliff. Nothing for it but to park where she was, and hope nothing came along the lane. She got out and opened the khaki front door, studiously avoiding any glance at Cartref. She had seen enough to confirm that it wasn't derelict. Thick lace curtains covered the windows. Someone was definitely living there.

Marlborough's door opened onto a chill gloom. Holiday lettings in October, even at half-term, were obviously few and far between, despite its cheapness. She had taken it for a week, on the understanding that she could renew the tenancy for another week and probably as many as she wanted. She doubted if it ever had many takers. Maybe the resident next door preferred it that way.

She flicked the electricity on, as instructed, in the fuse box high up on the wall and looked around. It was clean enough at least – Rosanna could detect the smell of bleach mingled with the aroma of damp – but that was the best that could be said of it. A black vinyl sofa, a slightly battered Ercol armchair, 1960s Formica-topped table with matching chairs. The kitchen, two steps up, behind, had the necessary basic fixtures and fittings, even if they didn't match. A range of aluminium pans and assorted Tupperware were stacked in the cupboards. Tucked onto the back was a bathroom with an avocado suite. Someone had been busy at house clearance sales.

It didn't matter. It wasn't as if Rosanna really intended a holiday. She ran the tap in the kitchen. After a brief gurgle, the water came through clear. She filled the plastic kettle, put it on, waiting to make sure it was working, then returned to the front room, to switch on the two-bar electric heater. The cottage had storage heaters, but they would probably take a day or two to warm the place up. She went out to the car for her luggage, dumped a carrier in the front room and carted her laptop, suitcase and hold-all up the steep stairs. Two bedrooms, furnished in the same eclectic style, double bed and a wardrobe in the front one, bunk beds in the back, assorted chests of drawers in both.

The back room did have the benefit of a window facing southwards, up the steep back garden, which might catch any sun going. Possibly the cheeriest room in the house. It would do as an office. She dragged a small table through from the front bedroom and went down to grab one of the dining chairs.

She nearly slipped on the stair as a loud honking suddenly blasted through the house from the road. Rosanna opened the front door to see a grimy Land Rover, its passage blocked by her car. She stepped out as the driver, a wild and woolly bearded man, poked his head out of his window. Not hostile, angry or impatient, just questioning.

"Sorry," she shouted. "I was just unloading. I couldn't find anywhere to park the car."

He grinned, pointing back over his shoulder. "There's a place just round the bend. I'll reverse."

He did too, with a trailer full of manure, something

she wouldn't have dared attempt on a narrow winding road on the brink of a stream. She got back in her car and followed him round past the crag of jutting rock. As he had promised, there was a parking space, or turning area, gouged into the steep slope like a miniature quarry. Space enough to put a couple of cars safely out of the way. Safe as long as boulders or trees didn't crash down onto them from above.

He wasn't in a hurry to get past her now, despite the previous hooting. He leaned on his open window, waiting as she locked her car.

"Don't tell me you're on holiday, here."

"Yes, I suppose. In a way." She had her cover story ready. "Taking a break for a month or so."

"Month or two! Jonathan will be over the moon. Jonathan Ramsey? The agency?"

"Oh. Greenways."

"Last tenant early August, I think. Does it meet your expectations?"

She could see him laughing silently in anticipation of her reply. "It was cheap."

"I bet."

"Seriously. It will do me fine. It's all I can afford. Doubt if I'll find anywhere that doesn't cost twice as much." Rosanna was summing him up as she spoke. Not bad, despite the beard. Early to mid-thirties. Friendly. Curious – maybe too curious, but a local, which was useful. He had a Welsh accent but toned down, more Anthony Hopkins than Gavin and Stacey. "I've managed to find a kettle that works. Would you like to come in for a coffee?"

He gave the briefest glance at his watch. "Yeah,

why not? Thank you." He opened the door and leaped out, holding out his hand. "I'm Gethin Matthews."

"Lisa Craven." Rosanna could feel herself blushing as she said it. She glanced at the tractor. "Where are you going to park that thing? There's not enough room to tuck it in by mine."

"No worry. I'll leave it here. No one else is going to come along and if they do, they'll shout." He followed her back to the house, grimacing as he looked around. "They haven't exactly made an effort with the place, have they?"

She laughed. "It will do me." She unearthed two mugs from the cupboards, checked that they were clean, and rummaged in her carrier for the coffee and milk she'd brought. "Hope you don't take sugar."

"I'll take it as it comes. Thanks. So you're here for an autumn break."

"Yes, sort of. Taking time out."

He laughed. "Pontgwartheg's the place for that. Time hasn't happened here since 1926."

"Pontgwartheg. That's the village? Where is it? Further up the valley?"

His grin widened. "This is it. Pont Gwartheg is the bridge half a mile downstream. Not what you'd call a village, more of an address. These four cottages, and a couple of farms – Rhoshelyg up there, and mine over the bridge, Hendy. And maybe a couple of bungalows down at the bottom of the road, although, come to think of it, they're probably listed as Nantfuan. That's it. Most of the houses are empty. Rhoshelyg is farmed by a guy with another place over at Blaenllafni, one of the bungalows is up for sale, and these cottages... Well, these two in the middle are holiday lets, such as they are. A couple called Pike bought the one at the far end a couple of years ago, but they only use it for occasional weekend visits. I think they work in Birmingham. And that's it: me and my Dad at Hendy, Sue Phillips at Skokholm, and your neighbour, Mad Annie, next door—"

"Mad Annie?" Rosanna wasn't expecting that.

"That's what we call her. Shouldn't really, should we? Very uncharitable. Her real name is Vera Broderick, but—"

"Sorry, what?"

"Vera Broderick. But I'm ashamed to say Mad Annie suits her better. Not that she's wild-eyed and dangerous, just a bit of a recluse. Not one for an idle chat…"

Rosanna's momentary panic that she had got the wrong woman faded, as connections snapped into place. Vera Broderick. It was the maiden name of Margaret Gittings' mother, although not many people in the area, if any, would remember that. It made sense., and it fitted Rosanna's idea of Margaret as obsessive, desperate, disturbed, but not overly imaginative. She tuned into what Gethin was saying again.

"Anyway, total population four, six if you count the Pikes. And now there's you, at least for a month, which is great news. Always good to have a new face around."

"Thank you." Rosanna handed him his coffee. "So you're a farmer."

"What gave me away? Don't say it was the trailerful

143

of cow muck. I hoped you hadn't noticed." He sniffed the sleeve of his overalls.

She laughed.

Gethin shrugged. "Okay, nothing as grand as serious farming. It's Dad's place, but he's getting past doing much now. I was in programming, in Cambridge, but then I decided it was time to come home, get back to nature. Spiritual recharging, renewable energy, organic veg and honest labour." He grinned again. "I'm sure I'll grow out of it soon."

Not married, she concluded. No wife in his list of residents. Rosanna needed to fill in a few gaps for him. Best to get them out of the way.

"I live in Winchester. Thirty. Been working in a bank but they've just closed the branch, which means I'm currently unemployed. Thought I'd pause for a while and consider my options."

"Well, if you fancy a pause in your pausing, there's a more or less decent pub in Nantfuan, down the valley."

"With food?"

"Not what you'd call a gastropub, but if you're happy with cod and chips…"

"Cod and chips sounds great. I've got coffee, milk, bread and cereal. I didn't think about dinner."

"Seven o'clock?"

"It's a… Fine. Seven it is."

Bryn

Rosanna watched Gethin go, then she went up to her new office and switched on her laptop. No internet hub in the cottage, so she'd have to rely on her phone for that. She checked it. No signal. Bugger. One bar appeared as she frowned at it, then disappeared again. There was no landline in the cottage, either. It was a discomforting thought. It had seemed like providence that a cottage was available right next door to the woman she suspected of being Margaret Gittings. But she had assumed there would be other neighbours around. It was one thing trying not to call too much attention to herself from the wrong quarters, but quite another to realise there were no other quarters. Gethin Matthews, living a mile away, was probably her nearest neighbour apart from a woman locally known as Mad Annie. Gethin had said she wasn't dangerous but he didn't know her true identity or what Rosanna was planning to do.

Rosanna put her phone down and gazed out of the window. Marlborough's garden, if it could be called that, featured a few slabs of stone laid unevenly at the back door, with a rusting barbecue and a couple of plastic chairs, but the rest of the land, rising steeply up the hillside, was just a jungle of long grass and a couple of moss-encrusted fruit trees. The garden next door was a complete contrast, a neat stair of terraced vegetable beds, with bean canes, huge cabbages and currant bushes. It reminded her of an intricately embroidered sampler. The embroiderer was an old woman, working in one of the beds now, digging, bending. Rosanna stood watching, her pulse racing as the woman straightened, hands pressing the small of her back before she picked up her tools, and carried them down the path to the house.

Rosanna willed her to raise her head. The woman's face was hidden by the brim of a canvas hat, her figure concealed within an oversized gaberdine. Mad Annie. Vera Broderick.

Or Margaret Gittings.

Before reaching her back door, the woman raised her head, maybe to gaze at the clouds, and caught sight of Rosanna at the bedroom window. She stopped short.

Rosanna remembered herself enough to unfreeze and flash a warm, friendly smile. It was met by a glare of anger, as if by looking out of her window, Rosanna had invaded her territory. She dismissed her with an indignant shake of the head and bustled into her house. Rosanna could hear the back door slamming shut.

Rosanna had nothing to go on but grainy newspaper prints of a police mugshot taken over twenty-five years ago, but that brief glimpse of the angry face was enough to convince her. It was Margaret Gittings and this was surely the time to make contact, since it had already happened unintentionally. Rosanna went down, out onto the road, and knocked on her neighbour's door.

Nothing had been done to update Cartref since its

nineteenth century construction, but it looked immaculately clean, even down to the polished brass knob on the door. The nets in the window were starched and spotless.

Rosanna waited. Listened. It might have been her imagination, but the house seemed to fall utterly silent. Not that it had been noisy before. No radio blaring, or vacuum cleaner moaning. But every house had its soft breathing, and that ceased entirely.

She tried a second rap. Still no response, except that a light, somewhere in the back, went out. She hadn't realised it was on until its faint gleam through the lace curtains suddenly vanished. Mad Annie was in there and pretending that she wasn't.

Rosanna bent down and pushed the letterbox open, calling through it. "Hello? Hello, It's only me, your new neighbour from next door. Lisa. Lisa Craven."

She waited, listening, her ear to the letterbox. Still nothing.

"I only wanted to introduce myself, just to let you know if there's anything I can do—"

"There isn't!" The reply, when it came, was much closer than she had expected. Only a door's thickness away. Rosanna jumped back, imagining Margaret Gittings standing there, knife in homicidal hand.

"I don't need anything. Go away!" A thick curtain was twitched violently across the door. Through its folds, Rosanna could hear, muffled, "Leave me alone."

No point in pressing it now, Rosanna told herself, stepping back to her own front door with relief. The next day, maybe. Best to wait. Besides, she needed to prepare for an evening at the pub.

* * *

Gethin Matthews pulled up in the narrow car park behind the Drover's Arms in Nantfuan, and Rosanna was out of the Land Rover before he had time to come round and open the door for her. She wasn't entirely sure if his invitation had been a purely friendly gesture or an attempt at flirtation. He was quite an attractive guy, in a hirsute sort of way, but her mind was primarily on food. She was starving.

"Allow me." He made a point of swinging the pub door open for her and she accepted the slightly inane chivalry. No point getting into a feminist argument on an empty stomach. The Drover's was a lot livelier on a Saturday evening that it had been on the Friday morning. No drowsy girl at the bar now but a plump and wheezy landlady, who greeted Gethin like a long-lost friend.

He leaned on the bar. "How you doing, Mandy? Business okay? This is Lisa, by the way. She's staying in one of the cottages at Pontgwartheg for a few weeks."

"A few weeks?" Mandy beamed her pleasure at the prospect of a new regular.

Rosanna smiled and said nothing. If she found what she'd come for, it might only be a few days. Thinking of those dark cottages and the lack of signal, and Mad Annie's voice through the door, she prayed that it would be only a few hours.

"I told her a trip to the Drover's would be the cultural highlight of her stay," said Gethin.

"That's right. Karaoke night on Thursdays, if you

fancy it."

"And Saturday darts, Mand. Don't do the place down."

Mandy slapped his arm, tutting. Then she winked. "Mind you, a bit old for you, isn't she? Likes them very young, does Gethin."

Rosanna turned to him, ready to reappraise him in a more negative light, but he was already laughing, wincing with embarrassment. "Shut up, Mandy!"

"What was her name now?"

"Chelsea!" He shook his head, catching Rosanna's expression. "No, no. She's kidding. We rent out a cottage on the farm and this couple came to stay in the summer, with their daughter, Chelsea. She was fourteen. They were into long country walks and she wasn't. Bored as hell and, you know, a teenage girl – she was ready to latch onto anyone under seventy for the duration. I spent the week sneaking around the farm, trying to find routes where she wouldn't see me. Came knocking on my door once. Ashamed to say, I hid, singing loudly, pretending I was in the bath."

"Poor girl," said Rosanna, soberly.

"Oh, she was all right," said Mandy, resting comfortably on the bar. "Found her way to our Barry before the week was out, and Gethin was right out of the running."

There was a laugh from the other end of the room, where a gang of young men were gathered for the weekly darts match. One of them, the James Dean of the group, turned to them with a sheepish grin. Our Barry, presumably.

"Well then, what can I get you?" asked Mandy.

They ordered cod and chips and took their drinks to a table by the window, adorned with a sticker from the Good Beer Guide 1987. With her back to the glass, Rosanna could look round the room at her leisure – lurcher slumbering by an empty grate; grainy photos of miners and a rugby team; large TV screen on the wall, but blank on this occasion. A scattering of inscrutable locals in flat caps gave her cautious nods if she caught their eye. One, propped on a table nearby, was nodding over an empty glass, eyes half shut in a querying frown, not asleep so much as dead drunk. There was a young girl with the boys at the end, but it was definitely a traditional man's pub, a point that seemed to dawn on Gethin as he raised his hand to an acquaintance for the sixth time.

"It's out of season," he said, in explanation. "Only the Welsh half-term now."

"Oh?"

"Last week there were English families, couples, teachers, looking for a bit of Celtic magic before the winter closes in. The Welsh don't bother looking for magic in a Welsh mining valley."

"No mining, now."

"No anything much, unless you like the great outdoors."

Rosanna smiled. "Unlike Chelsea. And speaking of hiding from visitors…"

Gethin put his pint glass down sharply. "You do understand…"

"Yes, yes, of course I do. Never mind Chelsea. I was thinking of my neighbour. Mad Annie. Vera, is it?"

"Vera Broderick. Yes, have you tried tackling her?

I'll be very surprised if you managed to get the time of day out of her."

"I didn't. I did try, though. I thought I should introduce myself, but she wouldn't even open the door. She shouted at me to go away."

"She does that. Either won't say a word, or she shouts. I've tried stopping to chat but she won't have it. Sorry about that, with her being your only close neighbour. But you can always come to me if you have problems. I promise I won't hide in the bath if you knock."

"Unlike Mrs Broderick. I think she was doing just that."

"Vera Broderick," said the drunk, near them. He had been stirring while they talked, as if he thought they were talking to him and he was being asked to clamber out of his drunken haze. He spoke now, grabbing at random words, a triumphant declaration that he was back in the land of the living. "Mother. That was her. Fire."

"Evening, Bryn," said Gethin.

He stared at them for a moment, red eyes swimming in and out of focus. Then he gave up on connecting the dots, hauled himself to his feet and walked to the bar. Didn't stagger, but walked as if all his consciousness was required to keep him upright. "'Nother pint, Mandy."

"Maybe not too much more," said Mandy, filling a fresh glass. "Eh, Bryn? Time to go home after this one, I reckon."

He grunted in reply.

"Bryn Davies," explained Gethin. "Comes here

because he's been banned from the pubs in Brongarn. Quite harmless. Don't mind him."

Rosanna took a sip of her beer, trying not to glance too overtly at the man. He was still propping up the bar as he swigged half the glass back. "Bryn Davies? Seems rather sad." There could be dozens of Bryn Davies in the area. Was it the same Bryn Davies on her list of bereaved parents?

"Yes, sad all right. He's had a pretty tragic life. Lost their only child, then he lost his wife – overdose. Some people think it was suicide. Then he went to pieces and lost his job. Now, he just drinks."

Lost a child. It had to be the same one. He was here on her doorstep, the last thing Rosanna needed, with all the complications it might create, but she could only pity him. "That is tragic. How will he get home? He doesn't drive, does he?"

"Hell, no," said Gethin. "Lost his licence way back. Don't worry, someone usually gives him a lift up the valley."

"I expect you know everything about everyone round here, despite having lived in Cambridge."

"Well, I grew up in these parts. Dad passed me all the local gossip even when I was quaffing Chardonnay in the intellectual hub of the universe."

"Oh yes, Gethin's still got family, haven't you, love?" Mandy was hovering over them with cutlery and sauce bottles. "Very nice for us. He's got a cousin in the police. Always good to have useful contacts. Nudge, nudge. He keeps them at bay if we get up to no good."

"I don't do any nudging," said Gethin. "And you

152

never do get up to no good, apart from ignoring opening hours and serving the odd under-age teenager."

"There you go, then."

Gethin raised his eyes to the ceiling as Mandy went to fetch their dishes. "You do appreciate there hasn't been a sighting of any policeman in Nantfuan for about thirty years, and my very distant cousin is with the North Wales police, so he's not remotely interested in the opening hours of a pub in Nantfuan."

Rosanna laughed. "If she thinks you're the local mafia boss, paying off the rozzers, I'd go with it, if I were you."

He pulled a face. "She doesn't even call me Godfather."

While they were talking, Bryn Davies had returned to his table, and slumped onto a chair nearer to Rosanna, staring at her as if trying to place her in the swirling confusion of the evening.

"Vera Broderick," he said again.

She really didn't want him focussing on that name.

"No," she said, clearly, carefully. "I am Lisa Craven."

Gethin butted in. "She's staying in one of the old miner's cottages in Pontgwartheg, Bryn. You know them? Past my place, on the way up to Rhoshelyg?"

Bryn grunted in reply and turned his attention back to his beer.

Rosanna tried to move the conversation on. "Tell me about all the other eccentrics in the area."

"Don't know that there are any others." He mulled over his beer. "Nope. Just Vera. And there isn't even much to tell about her. A genuine hermit. I've never seen her in Nantfuan, though I caught her once posting a letter down the valley in Croesowen. She plods down there occasionally to catch the Newport bus for groceries – won't accept a lift, although I've tried offering. Never talks to anyone. Never has any visitors. She's lived there for as long as I can remember. And that's about it. We're a boring lot, aren't we?"

"Except for the black sheep who escaped to Cambridge."

"Ah, but I came home with my tail between my legs." Gethin bleated pathetically. "So what about you. Tell me you're going to add a bit of eccentricity to our community. No one sane rents a miner's cottage in Pontgwartheg for autumn recreation. So come on, what's your dark secret? Truth time. What are you really doing here? Yoga? Prayer and meditation? Or plotting murder?"

Rosanna was grateful for the interruption of cod and chips as two plates descended on their table. "Thank you, Mandy."

"Enjoy," said the landlady, waddling away.

Rosanna considered the choice of condiments, conscious that Gethin was still watching her. "All right. If you insist. I'm writing a book."

"Ah! Mystery explained. So you're a writer. Have I...?"

"No you haven't read anything I've written, because I haven't written it yet. Don't laugh."

"Hey, I'm not laughing. You have a dream, you go for it. You're taking the plunge. Good for you. Go on, tell me, what's it about?"

"Look, I'd rather not talk about it until I've got a better grasp on what I'm doing. You know, how personal to make it. It probably won't work, anyway, but what the hell. My job came to an end and I thought, when will I have another chance to sit down and write? But I need to get more of it out of me, before I can face sharing it. Okay? How about you?" She changed the subject with relief. "You decided to go for your dream too. Organic turnips. Was it the endless supply of manure that lured you back, or just the thought of home sweet home?"

He laughed. "Both. Manure and home. As good a reason as any. My father's here, so I can keep an eye on him. But it's his Scrabble night tonight with Sue, so no problems." He waved at Mandy for a top-up from the bar. "What about you? Family, I mean. Boyfriend kicking his heels till you return?"

"No boyfriend at the moment." Was that a mistake? Maybe she should have invented one, because Gethin looked inordinately pleased.

"Live alone or are you stuck with Mum and Dad?"

She had created mythical parents for Lisa Craven, living happily in Eastbourne, but now she couldn't bring herself to claim them. She shrugged. "I don't see nearly as much of my mother as I wish I did." That at least wasn't a lie.

"Maybe now you can move nearer to her?"

"That's certainly a thought."

"Pontgwartheg," said Bryn Davies, suddenly. He had shifted closer to them without Rosanna noticing.

"That's right," said Gethin, cheerily. "Lisa's staying just up the road from me. Next door to Vera Broderick,

155

if you… No, you probably won't know her, come to think of it. Total hermit. Mad Annie, we call her. Right. Cod and chips. Can't beat "em."

Rosanna concentrated on her food, while her brain worked. Even if Bryn Davies still lived up the road in Brongarn and drank here regularly in Nantfuan, it was perfectly possible that he hadn't come across the recluse hiding out of the way at Pontgwartheg, never coming into the village. But he was probably the one person in the district who would latch onto the name Vera Broderick. He'd had little else to do for quarter of a century other than to think about his daughter and the family responsible for her disappearance. Even drunk as a skunk he could probably make the connection, but was he too drunk to be able to remember it in the morning?

She'd have to pray he wouldn't. Anyway, there was nothing she could about it now. She finished her cod and chips, and insisted on paying for her own meal, although Gethin rolled his eyes. As they left, she saw Bryn Davies staring after them, that semi-conscious frown still on his unshaven face.

Gethin

Rosanna usually had no trouble sleeping in a strange bed, but tension roused her early. It wasn't as easy to relax as she had hoped, knowing that a very hostile Margaret Gittings was close. But somehow, today, she was going to have to worm her way into the woman's confidence and win her over with the most unforgiveable of deceptions. She didn't want to do it.

She kept telling herself that she was here for those families, let down so unforgivably by the police. But after listening to Jackie Robert's painful account, Rosanna could only think that Margaret had been let down all her life, by the whole world. Where did any of the blame start or finish?

No, no, no. She wasn't there to put Margaret's hurts to rights. No one could do that. All she could do was try to find the girls and to do it, if humanly possible, before Jennifer Redbourn died. So just get on with it.

Six a.m. Not the right time to knock on the door with a feeble excuse about borrowing some sugar or something. She'd have to wait till a reasonable hour, hover maybe until the woman appeared in her garden and… well, wait and see what opportunities might arise.

Rosanna removed a large spider from the bathroom and showered. The flow was feeble but it would have to do. She dressed and sat down to a coffee and a bowl of cereal, stirring the flakes around until they turned soggy, while she debated, argued, justified, accused… She left her breakfast half eaten, and went up to the rear bedroom, to look again through her files and keep an eye on the garden next door.

It was just after eight when there was a loud rap on her own front door. She jumped up, took a second to steady herself, checked herself in the spotted mirror, then went downstairs to answer. It would be Margaret Gittings. It had to be. There was no one else it could be. The other houses in the row were all empty. Taking a deep breath, she opened the door.

"Morning," said Gethin. "Not hung over?"

"God, no." Rosanna stepped back, deflated but also relieved. "You're up and about early. Where's the Land Rover?"

"Back at the farm. I walked. Thought you might like to join me for a Sunday hike, let me show you the area. That's what we do round here, by way of a good time. None of your nightclub and theatre rubbish. Just good healthy strides across the hills that leave you knackered for the rest of the week. Don't suppose you brought walking boots?"

"I did, but I am supposed to be working on my book, remember."

"Walking gives you inspiration. Give yourself time to get things in perspective. And then maybe, I thought, come back to Hendy for lunch? Meet my dad, while he's having a good day. Sue's with him, from down the road, so they'll have cooked something up."

Rosanna held up her hands in defeat. "An offer I can't refuse, seeing as I have no food in the house. I'll fetch my boots." She went up to fetch them from her hold-all and sat on the bed to pull them on, thinking. Was this just an excuse to prevaricate? No, of course not. It was surely best to mingle, rather than seem suspiciously stand-offish. Besides, he was quite nice. Very nice, to be honest.

* * *

"Call this dinner time?" said Mr Matthews senior, replacing one book on the packed shelves in the cluttered farm living room and selecting another.

"No, I call it lunch time, 'cos I'm posh," said Gethin, peeling off his coat and hanging it on the back of a chair.

"Anyway, it's barely gone half two. That is lunchtime in the real world. If you two have scoffed the lot, I'll make something else for us."

"No, you won't," called the old lady from the kitchen. "We saved you some of the roast, don't you worry. You stop teasing them, Henry Matthews."

She had been introduced as Sue Phillips, their neighbour from Skokholm, one of the bungalows on the road up from Nantfuan. Neighbour meant living anywhere within a couple of miles.

Gethin's father gestured to Rosanna to come to the fire. "Warm yourself up, girl. I expect you're frozen to death if he dragged you all the way up Moel Walch. Didn't have a donkey with you, I hope, or he'll have talked the hind leg off it."

Rosanna settled into an armchair and wiggled her toes, her boots discarded in the porch. "He was informative."

Gethin pulled a face. It was true he had talked. He might be strong, but he wasn't the silent type. He had pointed out towns, valleys, and the sites of former mines, from the vast panorama their hike opened up, holding forth like Wikipedia on medieval lordships, the coming of industrialisation, the decline of industrialisation, Aberfan, the miner's strike, Nye Bevan, the limitations of highspeed broadband coverage, the effects of Brexit on science, Covid 19, revival of the Welsh language, the problems of tunnelling under Stonehenge and likely advances in AI.

Rosanna hadn't objected. It was quite agreeable being with someone who had intelligent things to say, though she had wondered, occasionally, how he managed to draw breath, especially during the more strenuous sections of the climb.

"He's short of company," said his father. "I hear him lecturing the sheep sometimes."

"I do not," said Gethin. "Don't listen to him."

"You should be back in your thing, business place, boy. You don't need to be baby-sitting me. We can manage, can't we, Sue? Knees might not be what they were but I can still drive the quad."

"Of course you can," said Gethin, exchanging meaningful looks with Sue, as she emerged from the kitchen with a large tray. He jumped up to take it from her and set it on the table.

"Off you go, Phoebe. Get a hot meal inside yourself," said his father, settling into an armchair.

"Lisa," corrected Gethin.

"That's what I said. Wash your ears out. Off you go,

Lisa."

"Sunday dinner," explained Gethin. "Always served at twelve thirty on the dot. We don't break with traditions here, so as we are two hours late, the sky will probably fall." He set out plates of roast meat with all the trimmings. "Lamb plucked from our very own fields this morning, and slaughtered in the yard. Sue's a dab hand with the cleaver."

Sue tutted at him. "A joint from Morrisons up the valley. They don't slaughter anything here."

"Is it just sheep on your farm?" asked Rosanna, coming to the table.

"Farm!" scoffed his father. "Only a smallholding to keep me busy in retirement. No one else in the family wanted it, so I might as well have it. I don't need that boy here just to deal with a score of lambs."

"What did you do before you retired?"

"Conveyed the gift of enlightenment to young minds."

"He was Sir at Brongarn Primary," added Gethin. "Head. Before he got power-mad, he was plain teacher. Newport, then Tredegar. Henry Matthews the globe trotter."

"Ha! Just because you went to... that place."

"Cambridge," said Gethin, softly.

"That's what I said."

"The dinner is very welcome," said Rosanna. "I haven't had a proper roast dinner for I can't remember how long." She was trying to judge how old Henry Matthews was. Brongarn Primary School. He'd probably taken up his post there long after Bethany Davies went missing. Long after Timothy Gittings was

161

named, by common consent if not by law, as her murderer? "Do you miss your old job?"

"No," said Henry.

"Yes, he does," said Gethin.

"He doesn't want to be coping with dozens of screaming kids at his time of life," said Sue, producing a large teapot as Gethin handed down mugs to her from the dresser. "We want peace and quiet at our age. The odd game of Scrabble is quite enough excitement."

"Was it a big school?" asked Rosanna.

"No, not really," said Henry, folding his hands together over his belly. "Only kept going because they closed the one in Nantfuan."

"So not too exciting, then."

"Not by my time there, no." His eyes were closing.

Gethin opened his mouth to add something, but when Sue discreetly shook her head, he took the hint.

"So you're writing a book, Lisa," said Sue, cheerily changing the subject.

"Trying to," said Rosanna. "I would be working on it today, but this strange man dragged me off to climb a hill."

"You have to be firm with him," said Sue.

* * *

Gethin started the engine as Rosanna buckled her seatbelt. "Alzheimer's?" she suggested.

"Early stages. But yes." He turned out of the yard.

"Most days you'd never know. Most days."

"I'm sorry. That's why you came back here, from Cambridge, isn't it? Nothing to do with getting back to nature."

"I don't know about that. Well, yes, maybe. Can't leave it all to Sue. I'm the baby of the family. Mum died a couple of years ago and my brother and sister are both married, busy raising kids, so…"

"You made the noble sacrifice."

He laughed shortly. "Sacrifice? Crap. I can carry on working here, you know. And it's not exactly a burden. Not at the moment, anyway. His memory just slips occasionally. But there are the odd days when it has a stronger grip on him, and it's upsetting. For him as much as anyone."

"And you don't want him getting distressed. Sue didn't want you talking about the school, did she? Did something happen there to upset him?"

Gethin wrinkled his nose as they bumped down the farm track. "You could say something that upset a lot of people, but it was before he took over. Girl went missing. It was Bryn Davies's daughter, actually. Official verdict at the time was that she must have drowned, but a few years later they discovered she was the victim of a serial killer. Timothy Gittings. Heard of him?"

"The name rings a bell. How awful."

"Yeah. We were living in Tredegar at the time, but the grandparents had this place back then, and they were very distressed about the whole thing. Especially when Bryn's wife died. That really upset Nan. She knew Debbie Davies. Sleeping pills. No one's sure if it was accidental or deliberate, but it kept the wound raw. Parents were paranoid about their children when Dad took over at the school. There was still a lot of

163

rage. Just as well Gittings family connections were all gone from the area or I think there might have been some pretty stupid things done."

"I can imagine. It must have been a terrible time."

"Yeah. Well." The Land Rover rumbled over the old stone bridge and Gethin turned right onto the lane up to the cottages without looking to see if anything would be coming. Nothing would be coming. It was a lane to nowhere.

"Tell me, now we've shared a Sunday roast, are we intimate enough for me to ask how you came by that?" He touched Rosanna's cheek. "That mark."

"What? The scar? A car crash, apparently. I was only a baby. I don't remember anything about it. I forget it's there most days."

"Sorry. Big foot. It's hardly noticeable."

Was that him being chivalrous or telling the truth? She needed it to be noticeable, that was the trouble. At the same time, she wished it wasn't there at all. She was still wondering how to respond as they came to the cottages. "Oh! Is that…?"

"Bryn Davies," said Gethin, coming to a halt and pulling on the brake. "Talk of the Devil. What's he doing here?" He jumped out. "Hello, Bryn. Where are you heading? Want a lift back down?"

Bryn Davies looked old, stooping, but not drunk. He'd just been standing there, on the road, staring at the cottages. Now he looked at Gethin, shook his head and took a step back. "Heading up to Rhoshelyg."

"Okay." Gethin watched him plod on up the lane, then he turned back to Rosanna. "If he's looking for work with Gwynfor, he won't get any. Right, then, you've got the loot?"

Rosanna held up the carrier of groceries Sue Phillips had given her, to save her starving to death or resorting to the nearest supermarket. "Should keep me going for a month or two."

Gethin grinned. "Got a tin opener?"

"Yes. Not much else, but definitely a tin opener."

"Right. Well, then. I'll see you. Tomorrow, maybe?"

The part of her that was Rosanna Quillan, unemployed and unattached, really wanted to invite him in for coffee. Or, more precisely, something more than coffee. But she was Lisa Craven, shameless deceiver with a mission that took priority over everything else.

She was decidedly thrown by the presence of one of the grieving parents, possibly hovering just round the corner. Gethin was an additional distraction that she needed to put aside.

"Not tomorrow," she said, firmly. "I want at least one day to knuckle down and have something to show for my sabbatical. If I don't start now, I never will."

"Fair play," he said, graciously admitting defeat.

"Day after tomorrow it is, then."

Rosanna went in and shut the door. She heard Gethin drive off, then she sat down to think. Sunday had been an agreeable interlude, but as day two of her campaign it was wasted. The evening gloom was already settling, though it was still late afternoon, and she didn't want to go calling on her neighbour in twilight. It would seem too sinister. Besides, she didn't want to advertise Margaret's address while Bryn Davies was still lurking in the shadows. He could only have been here for one reason. Until now, he'd known nothing about the secretive Mad Annie, hiding in her hermitage. Until now.

Rosanna thought of the other desperate relatives she had met at Andrew Rollinson's house. People who had sat in court and witnessed Margaret Gittings' callous indifference to their pain. Bryn Davies might be as bent on revenge as them, and she couldn't blame any of them, but it wouldn't help her mission. With a sigh, she decided to leave her quest for the day, keep her door shut and start afresh in the morning.

Cartref

Rosanna slept well, this time. The long walk saw to that. Still, she woke at a reasonable time, although it was later than she'd imagined on first opening her eyes. The cottage was gloomy, the sky above the deep valley grey. There was drizzle in the air as she peered out of the window. Never mind, she had work to do. With a cup of tea to stir her into action, she set about making herself respectable.

She hadn't thought about it enough the day before, dressing in her usual sweatshirt and jeans, which, as it turned out, had been fortunate, since a hike up to the ridge wouldn't have suited a skirt and heels. But she should be more formal today. As formal as her packing allowed. No dress, but she had included a skirt, and a couple of blouses and... no, not a jacket. That would make her look like a council official. She wanted to look like the nice girl next door. Someone who would be no possible threat.

It proved futile. Margaret wasn't interested in nice girls next door. Twice, during the day, Rosanna knocked on her door and still she wouldn't answer. A third attempt would seem too much like stalking. Which was exactly what it was.

Rosanna resorted to other ploys. She'd take an occasional stroll up the lane, waving at Margaret's windows with a broad smile, not sure if she looked like a jolly hiker or a demented idiot. Either way, Margaret refused to respond. Rosanna made a show of tackling the wilderness of her back garden, hacking down the brambles that threatened to overwhelm the fence between them and throwing out cheerful comments about the weather, whenever Margaret ventured out to tend her vegetable beds. All she achieved was to send Margaret scurrying back to the house with a scowl, slamming the back door.

Two futile days passed and she had nothing to show for it but a second pub meal with Gethin, fending off enquiries about her non-existent book. So much for gradually gaining Margaret's confidence. Gaining a single grunt of recognition would be a major achievement. Rosanna was growing desperate. She couldn't afford to waste more time getting nowhere.

On the Wednesday, woken by rain splattering on the bedroom window, she hit on a new plan. A medical emergency. If she fell ill and called on her neighbour for help, would that do the trick? Surely the woman would feel obliged to respond.

Rosanna was still debating whether to go for incipient pneumonia or actual bloodshed when she heard a front door slam. She rushed to the window and looked out. Margaret Gittings, swamped in mackintosh and hat, and armed with two shopping bags and an umbrella, had emerged from Cartref and was heading down the lane. Rosanna almost rapped on her bedroom window, then changed her mind and raced down the narrow stairs, flinging open her own front door. Margaret had already passed. Rosanna ran after her.

"Hi. Wait. Hello. It's just me, your neighbour, Lisa. I saw you passing. I'm going out myself. Can I give you a lift?"

The woman strode on, head half-turned but not looking at Rosanna. "No. I don't need a lift."

"It would be no trouble."

"I said no."

Rosanna might have kept following, persisting until she forced a concession, but she was getting soaked and she hadn't got as far as putting shoes on. The wet gritty tarmac was biting into her soles. "You're sure?" she called, but the woman didn't reply.

Another chance missed. But maybe not. With two empty bags, Margaret must be off on a shopping trip and, according to Gethin, she always walked down the valley to catch the Newport bus, rather than use the garage store in the village. She was heading for an anonymous supermarket well away from local faces, from people with long memories.

Wherever she went, to Abergelyn or all the way to Newport, she'd be gone for a good while, leaving Cartref deserted. There was some benefit, after all, in having no other neighbours around. It was a perfect time for a bit of burglary.

Rosanna dried her hair and changed into dry sweater and jeans. That allowed enough time to be confident that the rain hadn't induced Margaret to change her mind about shopping. She pulled on a cagoule, raised the hood, then she stepped out into the lane, armed with a cluster of lock picks she'd acquired from Amazon. It seemed that lock picks were a perfectly legitimate purchase. The trouble was, possessing a set didn't make Rosanna a competent lock picker. Margaret's front door was not fitted with a normal Yale lock like Marlborough, just an old-fashioned keyhole. She hadn't received a proper criminal training and the lock refused to respond to her fumbling. She was painfully conscious that she was standing in the road, in full view of anyone who might pass. There was always the possibility that Gethin might come by in search of more manure from the farm higher up. Or Bryn Davies might return. The back door would be a safer option.

No chance of getting around the side of Cartref. Its end wall virtually adjoined the buttress of sheer rock thrusting out from the hillside. An undernourished cat might manage it, but not Rosanna. She returned to her own cottage and went out into the back yard, to assess the situation.

She had already cleared a route through the undergrowth to the wooden fence between the gardens. It was topped with rusting barbed wire, but it wasn't so high that Rosanna couldn't climb over. She fetched a rug from the living room and laid it over the wire to avoid the perils of accidental tetanus, then she slid over, into the neat terraced vegetable patches that marched down from the brick-built shed at the top of Cartref's garden. The beds were still well stocked with winter vegetables, though the bean canes were bare. Rosanna approached the back door of the house cautiously, ears pricked for any sound from the lane. Nothing.

She fished out her lock picks and applied herself to the keyhole in the plank door. This time it wasn't that she simply lacked the knack. She couldn't get in at any mechanism. Margaret had locked the door from the inside and left the key in place. Possibly with superglue, because no amount of poking and jiggling would shift it.

After a few frustrating attempts, Rosanna gave up, stood back and considered her options. The windows might be a better bet. Not the kitchen window, nor the bathroom one. Both were firmly jammed, painted shut, with no crack to slide a knife in. Margaret clearly didn't believe in letting fresh air in or steam out. That left the bedroom sash above. It might be better, but Rosanna couldn't reach it without a ladder.

She ran back up the garden to the shed, nearly breaking her neck on the steps, the wet slate slippery as ice. The shed was padlocked. This time, the lock picks worked, after some clumsy fiddling. Even with latex gloves, Rosanna's fingers were numb with nerves and cold rain.

It would make sense to search the shed as well as the house, and Margaret had made that easy. The interior was desperately neat, with garden tools clean and in their racks, scrubbed trays and flowerpots, strings of onions, crates of carrots, parsnips and swedes, sacks of potatoes. A chest of drawers was full of seeds, twine, labels and other bits and pieces, nothing precious. No sign of a book of any description, concealed or otherwise.

There was a long ladder, but it was roped to the cross beams of the roof, with knots Rosanna would never be able to retie if she tried to put it back. That left a stepladder hanging on hooks on the wall, along with aprons and sieves. It wouldn't be tall enough, but it would have to do. She carried it down to the house and opened it. It came far short of the bedroom window, but it would, just about, allow her to scramble onto the roof of the single-storey bathroom, and from there, if she kept her balance, she could, just about, reach.

She clambered up onto the slates, teetering, but she managed to edge along, enough to study the window. This one wasn't painted into place, and it was shut with a simple catch that could easily be slipped open with a knife. Easily if it didn't involve balancing on a slippery slate roof and clinging on for dear life. She was able to push the upper sash down, get a grip, perch on the windowsill and haul herself up and in, slithering through into a bedroom that immediately had her hair standing up on the nape of her neck.

It was a bedroom, but it was also a shrine, which dispelled any lingering doubt that Mad Annie was Margaret Gittings. There was a cot and a bed, both neatly made, never used. Unopened toys – Scalextric, Lego, a Barbie Doll, a teddy bear, all still in their wrappers, waiting for the children who were to open them.

The walls were papered with photographs. A solemn-faced toddler; a tiny school snap of a boy, left side of his face contorted; a teenager, eyes averted, long hair draped down to cover his scars. A baby wrapped in a crocheted shawl. All that Margaret had left of her precious son and daughter.

Those pictures seemed professional compared with the rest, which were snap shots, sometimes out of focus, sometimes askew or mis-aimed, half a face, or a pair of feet. Trees. Bucket. Kitchen table. A snarling cat. And Margaret. Margaret caught in the act of turning or bending. Margaret's face tight with nerves. Margaret's face slack, clearly drunk. The work of a boy who hadn't quite got the hang of his camera. Some were torn, stained by damp, damaged where they had stuck together, but they were all arranged with devotion around the walls.

The thought that Timothy Gittings had been the photographer gave the pictures a sinister aspect to Rosanna. His mother clearly thought otherwise. Had they been left scattered in the ransacked house in Irnby while Margaret was in prison? The house she had returned to, briefly, on her release. Supposing she had gone there to reclaim these sad snaps and not his secret book? That was a deeply depressing thought.

But working on the assumption that she did have the book, where would she have hidden it? This shrine would be the obvious place. The toys were arranged on a chest of drawers. Wiping her gloved hands on her sleeves, Rosanna took a step forward, squelching. She glanced down at the damp patches spreading around her on the floorboards. Not good. She untied her trainers and slipped them off, pushing them under the bed. Her cagoule followed, and then her jeans. That would have to do.

Tugging her sweater down, she crossed to the chest of drawers and removed each drawer in turn, checking through its contents – clothing still in shop wrappings for boys and girls. Did Margaret realise that even her daughter would now be a grown woman, and Timothy was a middle-aged man? Not in her twisted mind, which had restored both to some age that comforted her. The woman lived marooned between sour reality and delusion. Sane enough, though, to keep her defences up and her treasures hidden. Very well hidden. Rosanna felt for anything taped to the back or base of each drawer. Nothing. She raised the mattress, flipped up the carpet, reached up through the tiny fireplace to grope for hidden ledges. Nothing.

No better luck in the front room, Margaret's. There were pots of pins and hair clips and a few pieces of antique jewellery in a china dish on the dressing table.

A fusty array of skirts and coats and dressers in the wardrobe. Drawers full of underwear, nightgowns and jumpers, nothing else. Nothing in the chimney. Nothing behind the two pictures of highland cattle on the wall. An alarm clock by the bed, hairbrush and comb. Folded nightdress under the pillow. A roll of banknotes, bound by an elastic band, thrust into an old stocking and hidden under the mattress. Fifty-pound notes among them. Rosanna didn't count them all, but she guessed that had she been a conventional burglar, they would have made the visit more than worthwhile. Rosanna tucked the money back. She wasn't after swag, just a book that might have been reduced to ashes twenty-six years ago.

She made sure everything was left exactly as it had been, then she went downstairs and searched the living room, sifting through the contents of the sideboard, flipping carpets, lifting cushions, checking behind the few innocuous books on the shelves by the chimney breast. There was no way to search up the fireplace because it was blocked by a fitted electric fire.

The kitchen was a more formidable task. While the one in Rosanna's cottage had been gutted and tiled to make way for cheap fitted cupboards, the kitchen in Cartref was almost as it must have been a hundred years earlier. The wide fireplace remained, with a heavy wooden surround and brass rail along the high mantelpiece, although the range that had once occupied it had been replaced by an electric cooker and a seriously retro spin dryer. The chimney was blocked.

Panelled pine doors opened onto cupboards on either side, shelves full of jars and tins – not just sealed food storage, but stone jars and old biscuit tins, any of which could contain valuables. But none of them did. It took Rosanna over an hour working through them, replacing each one exactly where she'd found it. The same care with the painted dresser on the opposite wall. She searched under the sink and in the oven, checked the quarry tiles of the floor for any that might be loose. Nothing. She searched in the bathroom, even wrenching the side off the bath to look, spending half an hour prising it back again.

And at the end of it all, she had nothing to show for any of it. If Margaret did have her son's book, Rosanna wasn't going to find it by means of burglary. Which left persuasion, and she had no idea how she was going to break through with that.

Returning to the back bedroom, she extracted her sodden clothes and pulled them on, shivering. The floor under the window was still damp, but with any luck it would have dried out before Margaret next came that side of the bed. Rosanna adjusted a rug to

175

absorb some of it. She couldn't leave doors unlocked, so her only option was to go out by the same route she came in, through the bedroom window. Theoretically simple; in practice, anything but. She was reasonably agile, but even a gymnast would have been challenged.

Wriggling out onto a narrow window ledge was far more difficult than wriggling in onto a bedroom floor. She tried it three different ways before succeeding and stepping onto the slates of the bathroom roof. Then she had to reach back to pull the window shut. It resisted. She tugged harder. It slid up with a jerk, she lost her balance and found herself flying, two metres down. If she hadn't just missed the stepladder, she would probably have broken something. As it was, her sprawl onto cracked concrete was painful enough. Her shoulder jarred as she rolled, and she felt her knees graze, but after a moment or two of frozen shock, she tentatively tried to move and decided that she was more or less intact. Soaked again, though. The rain was still pouring down.

She picked herself up, wincing with the pain from her shoulder, but at least she hadn't twisted an ankle. The shoulder was bad enough, though, when it came to hauling the ladder back to the shed. She hung it back on its hook, then paused to check once more for any hiding places she had missed amidst the gardening gear. Nothing. She clicked the padlock back into place, hurried back down to the rug over the fence and climbed into her own garden.

As she did so, she caught a sound, faint but metallic. A key in a lock? A faint light glowed suddenly in Cartref's kitchen window. Rosanna tugged the rug free, leaving tufts of fibre on the barbed wire, and rushed to her own back door. Once safely inside, she switched on the light and groaned aloud.

* * *

Rosanna showered, primarily to warm herself up, and tended the grazes on her knees. Her shoulder was all right, she decided, as long as she didn't move her arm too violently. She was still drying her hair when Gethin knocked on the door. He was standing in the lane quite indifferent to the rain that was showing no sign of abating.

"How's the writing going? Getting your teeth into it?"

Rosanna beckoned him in. "I think I've made a good start. Probably rubbish, but that's what the delete button is for. I wonder how Dickens and Austen and all the rest would have got on with a laptop instead of a pen?"

Gethin laughed. "Speaking as a computer geek, I hope they'd have embraced the potentials of a new age. Can I read it yet?"

"No! Not yet. And didn't I say—"

"To leave you to get on with your work in the daytime? Yeah, I know. But I was thinking, this place is gloomy enough in good weather. With this rain looking to be setting in for the duration, you can't find it at all inspiring. Or even comfortable. Cold and damp?"

"Oh, I don't know." Yes, she did. Cold and damp described Marlborough perfectly.

"I was thinking – well, I had this idea of inviting you

to stay with us."

She opened her mouth to object, but he got in first. "But I thought, that was really pushing it. Didn't want you to get the wrong idea, and I know you need to be left in peace to write. But like I told you, we've got a holiday cottage of our own on the farm. Stone barn conversion, very nicely done, comfortable, quiet, wood-burning stove to warm your toes, and we don't have any bookings for it until December. You'd be much better off there than in this…" He hesitated over the right phrase.

"It's not that bad." The allure of a wood-burning stove was seriously tempting, but Rosanna couldn't even afford to think about it. It would ruin everything. "If your place is that nice, I'd never be able to afford it. This was the best I could manage."

"Hell, we weren't going to charge you. It's standing empty. Much better for us to have someone in it, keeping it warm."

She pulled a pained face, pretending to give it serious thought, and desperately wishing she could accept the offer. "It's really kind of you, honestly, but I'm immersed in the flow at the moment and if I break off now, I don't know that I'll be able to hang onto the spark. Can you give me a couple of days to think about it?"

He shrugged, grinning. "Sure. I get it. I'll leave you to it."

"Thank you, though. Really."

For a moment, Rosanna thought he was going to shake hands. Instead, he leaned forward to kiss her. Just a friendly peck, not a rush of romantic passion, but it was deeply worrying – mainly because a part of her wished it would go further. Quite a lot further.

Had she flinched? "You don't mind?" he asked.

"No. It was an interesting experience, the beard. I'll write it up."

"You'd prefer it if I shaved it of?"

"No, you're all right, Gethin, exactly as you are. Don't change a thing."

She smiled as she saw him out. Then she shut the door and sighed. She could not afford this and, more to the point, she didn't want to hurt Gethin. He was altogether too nice. She didn't want him falling for a friendly but slightly intriguing novelist, only to find she was nothing of the sort.

How had she got herself into this?

Mad Annie

The rain was easing off a little, but no chance of any sunlight flooding the valley to cheer the place up. It probably never did. Marlborough would always be cold and damp. In November, a grey gloom was the best that could be hoped for. Rosanna massaged her shoulder, considering her next step. She had run out of ideas to make Margaret Gittings even look at her, let alone speak.

Determined cheerfulness had achieved nothing. A peace offering, perhaps. Dosing herself up with paracetamol, Rosanna pulled on a dry jacket and went for her car. There were lights on in Cartref. Margaret was home and dry, shopping done. She wouldn't be going anywhere soon.

A quick consultation with the sat nav and then Rosanna headed for the covered market in Abergelyn. Sue Phillips had mentioned it, and it had exactly what she was looking for: a WI stall, or something like it. It might have started the day laden with sponges, fruit loaves, Welsh cakes and jars of home-made jam, but, mid-afternoon, stocks were running down. Still, she was able to buy half a dozen impressively fat scones. Then she headed for the nearest supermarket to stock up on general supplies, including a bag of flour in case she needed to make it look more convincing.

By the time Rosanna was back at Marlborough,

darkness was descending. Her plan would have to keep until tomorrow.

In the morning, despite the chill, she waited for a glimpse of Margaret in the garden. No point putting on a performance if the woman stayed in bed, out of earshot. Margaret appeared at last, clumping up to a vegetable bed and pulling a leek. She'd be in the kitchen then, preparing her lunch. Rosanna hurried down and flung open her own kitchen window to let sound carry, then made a point of clattering pans, while the oven warmed. It was just as well she wasn't planning on serious baking, because after half an hour, the oven was still only mildly warm. But for her purposes, that would serve. She gave the scones a few minutes to warm through, then she piled them on a plate, slipped it into a plastic bag and carried it to the door of Cartref.

She knocked.

No reply.

She knocked again. Still nothing and the rain, which had abated overnight, was starting up again, with gusts of wind driving it sideways. One more go. Rosanna bent down to call through the letterbox.

"Hello? Mrs Broderick? It's me, Lisa, your neighbour. I've just made some scones and I thought—

That voice again, from the other side of the door. "Go away. I don't want anything."

"I just thought you might like—"

"I'm not interested. Go away."

With a sigh of frustration, Rosanna gave in and stepped away. Turning, she found herself staring at a man. Bryn Davies again. He was only a couple of dozen yards away, on the road, by the first of the cottages. Whatever his intention had been, he'd stopped short at sight of Rosanna. Keep him there. She didn't want him coming further, so she marched down the road to join him.

"Hello," she said. "Remember me? We met the other night." She wanted to command his full attention. Now that she was close, she could smell the whisky on his breath, but he wasn't totally inebriated.

His sad, bleary eyes narrowed as he tried to place her.

"I saw you."

"That's right. I'm Lisa. I was at the Drovers, with Gethin. Remember?"

"Gethin Matthews."

"Yes."

"Good man, Gethin,"

"Yes, he is. I've been baking. Too much for me. Here are some scones." She held out the bag. "Why don't you take them home and have them for your tea, yes? I think you should be heading home, Mr Davies. You're going to get drenched through, standing here in the rain. It looks like it's coming on again and only going to get worse."

He was struggling with his thoughts. At last, to her relief, he turned and wandered back down the road, the way he had come. Rosanna watched until he was out of sight, then she hurried indoors.

Drying herself off, Rosanna prowled around Marlborough, trying to come up with another scheme. She couldn't let another day drift away, with nothing gained. She listened to the wind whipping up again. It was turning into quite a gale. Through the seething grey rain, she watched the thrashing branches of trees above the steep rear gardens, the swirl of the last sodden leaves of autumn ripped free. An idea… Might it work? Nothing else had, so why not try it?

She hadn't given much heed to Marlborough's garden other than as an access to Margaret's, but she had made a subconscious note of three large roof slates, mossy and caked in dirt, stacked by the back door. She stepped out to retrieve one, ran it clean under the kitchen tap, until it was gleaming purple, then carried it upstairs. She dragged a chair to her bedroom window, then climbed on it and lowered the upper sash. The wind whistled in furious gusts as she raised the slate with both hands as high as she could, her bruised shoulder complaining. The wind quietened. She waited. Another gust came. She could hear it rumbling down the valley like a juggernaut. As it reached the cottages, she let the slate slide out of the window.

She heard its satisfactory smash on the road. Jumping down from the chair, she raced downstairs and out, making a show of standing over the shattered shards, glancing up at the roof, only the gutter of which was visible from the doorway. She crossed the lane to stand on the bank of the stream, churning at twice its former size now, and almost filling its deep gulley. She turned her back on the grey surging foam and looked up at the roofs of Marlborough and Cartref, searching for any place where a slate might have broken loose.

It worked, at least to the point of inducing Margaret Gittings to open her door. She stood staring angrily at the broken tile.

"I can't see where it came from," called Rosanna, stepping closer. "I thought, from that crash, the whole roof had come down."

"It didn't. Just a slate," said Margaret, sounding more irritated than aggressive.

"You are all right, are you? No other damage?"

Rosanna was standing right in front of her now, and for the first time Margaret looked at her. There was a moment, just a brief moment of hesitation. Rosanna couldn't waste it. She turned her head slightly to ensure that her faux scar was clearly visible. "I don't know who you go to round here for roof repairs. My foster father was a roofer, back home, but—"

"Foster."

"Yes. He used to mend roofs before he retired."

Margaret reached out a hand to touch Rosanna's cheek, lightly as if stroking a ghost. "Where d'you get that?"

Rosanna forced herself not to flinch. "What? Oh, this scar. It happened when I was a baby. An accident, I've been told. I don't remember anything about it." She beamed. "It was before I was fostered."

Margaret stared at her. Rosanna kept smiling, wishing herself a thousand leagues under the sea. She shouldn't be doing this. But if it were the only way…

Margaret turned back into the house. "I had a daughter."

"Oh?" Rosanna followed her in, her pulse racing.

"Clare. Clare Louise. My baby. They took her from me."

"That's sad. How awful for you. Was she your only

child?"

"And my boy. *My* boy."

"Oh, you had a son, too. I'd have loved to have had a brother."

"They took him, too. Bastards."

"Oh dear."

Rosanna had followed her through to the kitchen. Margaret was absentmindedly putting crockery and cutlery away, her lunch already prepared, eaten and washed up. One last pan in hand, she turned back to face Rosanna. That intense stare again, seeing and unseeing, her hand reaching out to stroke Rosanna's fair hair, her scarred cheek.

Rosanna held herself steady, though her stomach was rebelling. "Tell me about them, your children. Your girl and boy."

"She was fair. Yellow hair. Like him."

Rosanna had seen enough pictures of Timothy Gittings to know that his lank hair was light brown, if not actually blond.

"Like yours," said Margaret. She touched Rosanna's cheek again, almost in a trance. "Scar."

"Yes? It was just an accident, like I said."

"Yes!" Margaret was suddenly fierce. "Not his, though! Wasn't an accident. It was that brute, pushing him off." She talked like a woman who spoke so rarely she'd almost forgotten how to string a sentence together.

"Smashed his face. Joked about it. Said he wasn't a man without scars, just a namby-pamby mother's boy. My boy! Bastard! Hurting my boy."

"Oh dear."

"Different with her. My Clare. My little princess. That's what he called her. My princess. She wasn't his. Not his. You were mine. Beautiful darling, he said. Bastard. Not like that great ugly mug of a boy. So I…"

Margaret's eyes wandered away into some dark realm of forbidden memory.

Rosanna began to wonder. What was she saying? Was it possible that…

"They took you!" Margaret was staring again, at her or through her, now totally in the grip of delusion, and Rosanna had to fight the urge to get out of there, to run. But she had started this, deliberately. This was precisely what she had planned, this sick trick. She had thought to build on the deception bit by bit, a smile one day, a few words the next, one or two confidences and hints dropped here and there, sowing suspicions and possibilities, in the hope that Margaret would eventually break and confide all. But she hadn't been prepared for this instant, explosive crumbling of defences. It was shocking, chilling, trespassing on a woman's mental derangement, but she had to go through with it.

"And your son?" she asked, weakly.

"He wanted you. He just wanted his sister back, that's all. But they'd never come. I saw her, in the street, going to school. I pointed her out. That Davies woman always boasting about her, her golden girl, her little sweetheart. Where was mine, though? My Clare. You. I told him, you'd be eight now, just like her."

Rosanna said nothing.

"He didn't understand. He tried to bring you home. No. Not you. Her. She wasn't you. I said, she wasn't really you. She didn't have the scar. He thought, if he gave her a scar, she'd be you. But she wasn't. She wouldn't move. He didn't mean it. I had to help him get rid of her. Keep her safe, I said. All he wanted was his sister back. They never understood that. Never understood him. I understood him. Mine. My son. They had no right to take him away. But I'll be here, here for him when he comes out. I've kept it all safe. Everything. When he comes out."

It happened. The unconscious reveal. Rosanna held her breath, watching as Margaret still muttering and mumbling, laid a hand on the wide panelling surrounding the fireplace. Held it there a moment, as if touching a sacred relic, her other hand groping at the chain around her neck. What was the pendant on it? Small, like a cross. Rosanna only caught a flash on it, briefly tugged from Margaret's knitted top. Not a cross, a key. She dropped her hands, and Rosanna noticed, in the panel, what had seemed no more than a chip, a crack. A keyhole. How had she missed it? Easily. Anyone would miss it.

She must have started or even gasped, because Margaret was staring at her again, brows knitting, suspicion building as the spell shattered.

"Who are you? I don't know you. I want you to go now."

"I'm sorry?"

"Get out of my house. You have no right to be here."

"Oh. All right." Rosanna was backing to the front door, all too ready to escape. "If you're sure there's no damage…"

"Get out!"

Rosanna was out, as Margaret slammed the door on her, almost sending her flying. If she could fly, she would. She hurried back to Marlborough, went through to the kitchen and gulped down a glass of water. Her hand was shaking. Why did she feel this awful? She'd done what she'd needed to do: she'd discovered where Margaret kept her treasures. She should be rejoicing at the ease with which she'd finally done it, but she couldn't. She just felt dirty.

She'd known that the woman must be disturbed, but she hadn't realised quite how much. Mad Annie really was mad. Always had been, probably. Had been when her parents had the chapel congregation praying over her. Had been when she was marched into a doomed marriage to her rapist. Had been when a knife was used on baby Clare. It excused nothing that Margaret Gittings had done, it didn't ease any of the pain caused by her silence over the years or undone any of the damage. But still Rosanna felt soiled in the part she was playing.

She just wanted it to be over, now. Over, so that she could stop the lying.

Book

It was dark. Not yet night but the clouds overhead were black, veiled by sheets of rain that sounded as if they would beat their way through wood and stone and bring the house down around her.

Rosanna stood at the window of her temporary office, looking out into the gloom. She was still trying to recover her equilibrium. As Margaret was unlikely to leave her house again for days, what was to be done now? A night-time break-in while Margaret slept? If she did sleep. More likely, she'd wake and cut Rosanna's throat while she was still picking the lock.

Suddenly the whole scene outside – her wilderness, Margaret's garden and shed, the thrashing trees climbing the steep hillside – everything was bathed in livid light. Three seconds of gloom again and then the thunder rolled over, and over, rumbling and cracking. The windowpanes rattled.

Rosanna stepped back. The lightning had woken her up to reality, telling her she needed to stop this mad adventure and be sensible. The woman was hiding a book that could finally close four, or maybe five, unresolved cases. It was something for the police to deal with. Not an ex-detective constable on a private mission, but officers armed with the proper authority to search. If her phone were functioning, she'd have called them then and there. But as it wasn't, she'd better go and find a signal.

She hurried into the front bedroom and started stuffing her clothes and other things into her case and bag. Laptop, toiletries – anything else could stay. She pulled on her cagoule and headed out into the storm, the rain whipping her face with icy needles.

A lace curtain twitched in the window of Cartref as she passed, but she didn't turn to look. She made it to her car as another flash of lightning illuminated the narrow valley with ghoulish light. Thunder rumbled again and small stones skittered down from the rock face next to the car. She started the engine hastily.

Where? She could go down the valley, to Gethin's farm, with its promise of safe, warm accommodation, but she didn't feel capable of facing him, of having to explain how she was a complete fraud, from start to finish. All she needed, right now, was to get a signal for her phone. On their walk, Gethin had led her up the lane, as far as the entrance to Rhoshelyg farm, where they had turned off on a footpath, but the lane had continued on, zigzagging up the ridge. If she drove high enough, out of this deep blind spot, she would surely be fine.

Passing the farm gate, she wished she had chosen the other direction. This higher section of the roadway looked as if it hadn't been visited by the highways department in the last fifty years, its narrow strip of patched tarmac cracked and crumbling as it steepened, trees close on either side, their branches whipping the car as she edged past. She peered into rain that was defeating her windscreen wipers. At last she was out of the woods, onto the open ridge, and she parked up on a gravel verge with relief.

She pulled out her phone. Yes! A signal. Her thumbs paused on the keys. Shouldn't she figure out precisely what to say? Another flash of lightning urged her on. *I think... I believe... I have strong reason to believe that the old lady next door is Margaret Gittings who is concealing a book that should... that will reveal the whereabouts of missing bodies.* She could imagine the police response. If she had Andrew Rollinson to back her up, to explain what she had been hired to do, they might be more inclined to listen. She should keep him informed, anyway. She pressed his number.

"Miss Quillan!" His response was very prompt.

"You've got news? You've got it?"

"No. But I think I know where it is. In her house, Cartref. I'm living next door to her in Pontgwartheg. It's north of Newport and—"

"Yes, yes, they're there. Please, you can get it, yes?"

"Wait! I need—"

"You must get it. We can't wait. She's on her way out. Jen. I don't think she can hold out any longer. Please! Do anything."

"Yes. Yes, all right." She could tell he was in such a state he wouldn't be able to understand what she was asking of him. "I'll get it."

She rang off and her thumbs hovered over the keys again. If she did call the police, what then? They wouldn't come storming up from Abergelyn or wherever and batter Margaret's door down on her say-so. Not to follow up a decades-old case. No, they'd call Rosanna in and demand a full explanation. They'd have a conference, assess the productivity of using up

191

precious police resources and then apply for a warrant. It would probably take far too long for Andrew Rollinson's sister. It was no good. She'd have to do it herself.

Reluctantly, she switched the engine on again, turned the car round and headed back down the lane, into the woods. Parking up in her usual place, she had to force herself to get out into the storm. The roar of the wind and the rain were answered by the thunder of the water in full flood. She was hauling her bags out of the car when a groan stopped her and she spun round, half expecting Margaret to be standing there.

No one in sight. Another groan, a creak, and she realised what it was. The creaking and groaning built up as a heavy branch on the far side of the stream began to tear loose, twisted by wind. She watched as the last splinter ripped from the tree and the branch plunged into the water. Another lightning flash captured its passage, tossed and tortured, and a thorny bush, undercut by the torrent, followed it into the flood.

Nature was collapsing around her, reminding her of the urgency of her task. She grabbed the remainder of her luggage and headed back to her cottage. The curtain of Cartref did more than twitch this time. It was flung back and Margaret Gittings was standing there, staring at her as she passed. Rosanna didn't pause but fumbled with her house key and pushed her way into Marlborough. She leaned back against the door as it shut.

"Shit! Shit! Shit!"

What now? She had no choice. There was nothing

else for it but to revert to plan A – wait for Margaret to fall asleep and then break in. Risk a cut throat. If the storm kept up, it would at least drown any noise she created.

She rummaged in her case, pulled out her darkest jeans and fleece, changed quickly, then tried to settle with a mug of tea in the kitchen. Not yet six o'clock. Was that all? It was seriously dark now. She had to be calm. No point rushing. This could take hours. Just settle down and prepare to wait. She checked her watch again. Quarter past six. She rolled up the rug ready to lay over the barbed wire. Switched the kitchen light off because somehow it would bring the night on sooner. Stupid. She sat in the dark for five minutes, ridiculing herself. Then, just as she was about to switch the light on again, she caught a faint flash out in the dark.

Hearts really could miss a beat. Rosanna's did. Her breathing stopped. There it was again, a torch beam, in Cartref's garden. Margaret was heading up the garden in the rain? Why? A flash of lightning, and there was the woman, bent into the wind, in her gaberdine, climbing the steps between terraces.

For one second, Rosanna hesitated, then she leaped up, grabbed the rug and headed out, kicking aside the brambles again to get at the fence. As she threw the rug over the wire, a light came on in Margaret's shed. Now or never. Rosanna raced for the kitchen door. It was open. The light was on. She pushed aside chair and table to get at the panel by the fireplace. A minute or two, that might be all it would take.

Rosanna could see the tiny gap that was the

keyhole, obvious now. She tried the lock picks. Useless. She was no good at this. Too close to panic, probably. She hammered on the wood. It was only a panel, wasn't it? She looked around, opened the side cupboard, found what she had seen before – a tray of kitchen implements.

A rolling pin, old and heavy. She smashed it into the panel. It bowed. She smashed again, heard wood splinter. Again. This time a crack appeared. She thwacked at it until the panel began to fall apart. Enough. She wrenched chunks out, until there was room to grope within. Something… a picture frame. A tin. Grope again. There! Her fingers closed on a cord. A book – no, an album. An album! Of course!

As she began to withdraw her hand, she heard the squelch of footsteps approaching the back door. She couldn't stop now. She had it, the album, safe in her grasp as Margaret Gittings appeared on the threshold.

For a moment, Margaret stood there, frozen in shock. So did Rosanna, but for a second less. Any pretence of innocence was utterly pointless. As Margaret's expression changed from bewildered astonishment to an inhuman rage, Rosanna said, "I'm just going."

She stepped away from the fireplace, her chin raised in a vain attempt to suggest she was unafraid. What could Margaret do? She was a frail old lady, unsteady on her feet, her joints cracking up, and there was no one she could call on for aid. They were stranded in this house, alone in this valley. It should have been Margaret who was terrified. Any other old lady would be, screaming, quivering in a corner for fear of what

Rosanna would do.

But Margaret Gittings wasn't any other old lady. Her eyes seemed to double in size as they bored into Rosanna, before dropping to the album in her hand. The rage within her doubled, filling the room. If spontaneous combustion were a reality, it would surely happen now.

"Give that back!" she hissed, coming at Rosanna.

The shifted table was between them. She circled it as her quarry circled the other way. All Rosanna needed was a clear passage to the back door. Margaret realised it, retreated, stood between her and escape, as Rosanna ran for it.

"Give it back!" One hand was grabbing at the album as the other punched Rosanna, catching her on the breast and making her squeal with pain. But Rosanna clung on.

"You will never take that. I'll kill you first. I'll kill you! Give it to me!"

Rosanna managed to wrench the album out of her grip, and held it aloft, pushing her away, but Margaret was scrabbling at her arm, nails digging into her flesh, kicking at her.

It was a matter of self-defence. Margaret would be true to her word; she was going to kill Rosanna. Rosanna kicked back, reached for a jug on the cupboard and hit her with it, desperate just to get away. The blow caught the side of Margaret's head but she had warded off the worst of it by raising an arm in time. The arm came down, nails raking Rosanna's face, ripping the fake scar loose. She had the album again, or rather Rosanna's hand gripping onto it for dear life. She sank her teeth into the fingers, a wildcat, hissing with a bestial fury. There was nothing for it but to be a wildcat in return. Rosanna hit her again, with more effect. She reeled and an almighty push sent her staggering back. Rosanna prayed that she would topple, giving her time to run. She didn't, not quite, grabbing at cupboards to save herself, moaning and screaming at the same time, spitting foul obscenities.

Rosanna took her chance anyway and bolted for the back door, which was still ajar, turning just long enough to see Margaret lunging for a kitchen knife. She ran, skidding on the wet concrete. The storm hadn't eased off in the least. The rain was lashing down again in torrents that threatened to flatten Rosanna to the ground, but she kept going. She had no defence against a knife and Margaret was following, hissing, her invectives one with the howling wind and hissing rain. Rosanna hurdled over the fence and flung herself across her yard, scrabbling for the door handle. Margaret was following, faster, nimbler than arthritic knees could possibly allow. It must be demon wings bearing her along.

The door opened and Rosanna was through, panting like a dog. Slamming it shut again, she groped for the bolts and pushed them home. Then she leaned back against the planks, feeling her knees giving way.

Panic was still surging through her veins, unwilling to let go. With reason. She felt, rather than heard, the blows against the locked door. Margaret was beating on it, hacking at it, shrieking still.

"Give it back! Give it back!"

"No!"

The thudding stopped. Hugging the album to her, Rosanna took a deep breath, choking on it, daring to think that perhaps she was safe. Then, with an almighty crash, the windowpane smashed, showering the kitchen with glass. A chimney pot lay on the floor. Maybe it had come down in the storm or it had just been lying around as discarded rubble, like the old slates, but Margaret had found it, lifted it, hurled it. What diabolic power was in her? Brushing off flakes of glass, Rosanna pushed the album into her fleece, picked up the chimney pot and heaved it back through the shattered window.

Maybe it found its target. Rosanna heard a grunt. But no, Margaret was back at the window, scarcely recognisable. Her face was white, skeletal. The driving rain had flattened her greying hair to a blackened cap. Her eyes were staring, mad. A thin arm, the hand clutching the knife like a dagger, reached through the broken glass, stabbing wildly.

Rosanna was out of reach, which was as well, because she couldn't move.

"Give it to me! You bitch! You bitch! Give it me! I'll kill you! It's mine!" Margaret was screaming.

And then Rosanna was screaming back. Screaming about mothers and justice and children and evil and truth and God knows what. They screamed and screamed at each, the wind and the rain screaming with them, flinging threats and pleas and accusations, till neither could scream any longer, both hoarse and drained. The arm with its knife pulled back. The white tormented skull face vanished. Rosanna was half expecting Margaret to come leaping through the window, snapping the bars, like the infernal monster she was, but no. Rosanna's terror had been quenched by her own rage, and she staggered to the window to stare out. Rain still drove down like rods of steel, but Margaret was there, crouching on the stones, rocking herself in agony, her face contorted now by sobs that convulsed through her.

There couldn't be a more pitiful spectacle. Rosanna should have felt pity, but it was only rage keeping her going now. She watched the old woman crawl back to her own yard, the knife abandoned, her saturated frame convulsed with the sobs that wouldn't stop.

Rosanna remained standing at the sink, gripping it for support, feeling her breath steady, her pulse begin to slow. She wiped a trickle of blood from her cheek, sucked at scratches on her fingers, and pulled herself into the bathroom. She peered into the mirror, tugging the remains of the scar away. There were a couple of shards of glass glinting in her hair. She extracted them, wiped her face with a flannel and dabbed at cuts. Nothing serious. Nothing that mattered, compared to what was in her fleece. She took a deep breath and drew the album out.

She had it. That was all that mattered. She had what she had come for.

She carried it back through the kitchen, upstairs to her bedroom, which felt safer, switched on the light and sat on the bed to look at her prize.

There were empty pages at the end but most of it was jammed full of photos, pasted in unevenly, overlapping. Groups of children running past. Children in crowded playgrounds. Children chattering on buses.

And then, gradually, individual children, girls, all similar, all fair, all aged about eight, interspersed with words in crayon or pencil. *Clar. My sista. Princes. Cler Loos.*

Rosanna turned a page with shaking fingers, and there was a close-up. Unmistakable. Bethany Davies, recognisable although her face was turning away, as if she were running. Pink bobbles on her knitted bonnet.

Worse. Infinitely worse. Bethany again, in shadow, on a stone floor, eyes closed, mouth open, cheek cut and seeping blood.

A photograph of trees on a steep slope, in near darkness, a crayoned cross heavily scored beneath one.

Swallowing bile, Rosanna turned the page. Another girl. A girl she didn't recognise. Grubbier, thinner, but fair hair, just like the others. Eyes puzzled. Fearful. Another crayoned cross beneath trees. How many more victims were there? Rosanna had seen more than enough. Horrifying though the pictures were, they were more than she could have hoped for. Not just illiterate scrawls but photographic evidence of murders and sites of concealment. She didn't need to torture herself with the rest. It was time to get out of there, and hand it over to the police. She'd explain once they had it. They could take their time deciding what to charge her with, but there was the evidence for them to act on immediately and find the missing girls.

Just go. Except that it would mean leaving the relative safety of the house and walking past Cartref to reach her car. She stepped into the back bedroom to peer out into the gloom. It was too dark to make out much. At least there was no sign of Margaret in

Marlborough's back yard. Was she back in her own house, nursing her grief, or waiting to spring out of the front door, wielding her knife as Rosanna ran past.

Suddenly, movement. Or was it? Yes, definitely movement among the terraces next door. Rosanna pushed the bedroom door shut, to block out any light and peered harder into the night, letting her eyes get accustomed to the dark. It was her, Margaret. No torch this time, but she was making her way up to the shed again. Stumbling. Crawling.

Rosanna's anger had died down now. Detached instinct urged her to help the woman. She must be in pain, physically and mentally. But no, Rosanna's first task had to be to hand the album over. Safely delivered, she'd come back, with an ambulance maybe. While Margaret was out there, climbing the steps, it would surely be safe to run for the car.

Rosanna slid down the stairs, gathered up her luggage, still stacked in the hall, and raced back to the narrow layby where her car was waiting. Somewhere far up the lane a dim light gleamed. A car's interior, maybe.

Perhaps the farmer who owned Rhoshelyg had come to check on things. It would have been a relief to know there was someone else around, earlier, but she didn't need reinforcements now. She just needed to go. She groped for her keys, in her pockets, in her bag, in the clothes she had worn earlier, beginning to swear at her stupidity until she realised she had left them in the ignition. At that moment, she would have given anything for a stiff drink. Just as well she didn't have any to hand, because she'd be tempted to down the bottle.

    She started the engine and drove.

Valley of the Shadow

Rosanna turned onto the lane and steered cautiously round the buttress of rock. No Margaret in the road. The car was past Cartref. Past Marlborough. Past the third and the fourth cottage. Only then could she feel safe from pursuit. Unless… Supposing Margaret had climbed into the back of her car! She adjusted the mirror in a moment of panic, to check. Ridiculous. Hadn't she just seen Margaret heading for her shed? The momentary loss of concentration had her swerving dangerous close to the edge of the road and the steep drop into the stream. Except that it wasn't much of a drop anymore. The foaming, surging water was almost at road level. Concentrate.

She was safely round a bend and the cottages were out of sight now. As the road wound on, her pulse began to slow. Just a couple of hundred metres and she would pass the turning over the bridge to Gethin's farm. Gethin, a beacon of safety. She rounded the last bend before the bridge and… She slowed, blinking in disbelief as her headlights flashed on gleaming, churning silver. No!

She had forgotten that the lane dipped down almost to the level of the stream this side of the bridge. Way below the level of the stream now. The boiling water had spread out across the entire valley, drowning the roadway. She could make out the parapet of the bridge beyond a great heap of debris that was blocking the channel.

How deep was it? Could she risk it? She would have to try. Carefully, she edged forward, her door ajar to see how far up the wheels the water was coming. Too far. She realised that, slamming the door shut hastily as she felt the force of the water beginning to tug at the car. How stupid could she be? Another inch and the car would be dragged in, washed away with her in it, smashed into the debris at the bridge.

She put it into reverse and began to edge backwards. Was the car moving? In which direction? The water was threatening to prove stronger than her engine. She wasn't sure what progress, if any, she was making, and she couldn't make out a damned thing. She might be reversing off the road altogether. The wheels were spinning as she tried to adjust, veering to the inner bank, and she felt rock scrape against metal. Adjusting again; she had to keep trying. She couldn't get out of the car; the water would sweep her off her feet in seconds. Keep going. Finally, finally, she felt the pull of the water give up its grip. It was still splashing noisily under the wheels, but she was getting clear. She was out. Another metre or so to be sure. Another crunch of stone on metal. She stopped, switched off, leaning on the steering wheel to recover. This was a bloody nightmare.

She got out, clambering round the car to see if she could figure out what to do now. No possibility of turning the car where she was, jammed between the water and the steep slope above. She walked back along the lane, searching. Yes, there was a place, fifty metres back, maybe – a bit of a grassy verge that might give her turning room. Maybe. She could reverse that far, surely. She climbed back in and switched on. The engine spluttered and died. Swearing, she tried again. Another cough, a splutter and then nothing.

Margaret Gittings was a witch, that was it. She was in league with the Devil and *she* was doing this, sending her curses after Rosanna. What next? Would it be an earthquake, ripping the ground apart to swallow her up?

Get a grip! She sat there, waiting, counting. She tried the engine again. Another splutter, but did it almost catch? Don't flood it. Wait. Just wait. She counted again, slowly, to one hundred. Better make it two hundred.

Finally, she switched on, one splutter, and the engine fired. It didn't sound happy, but she didn't blame it. She wasn't feeling happy either.

Keep calm. She started reversing, her rear lights useless in illuminating the way. Better to suffer the scratches and scrapes of stone to the possibility of slipping into the flood.

She crawled back in jerks, hugging the rocks, her aching shoulder screaming as she wrenched herself round to see. At last, there it was, the widened verge. It might take a twenty-seven-point turn but she could do it. Back. Turn. Forward. Back, till she bumped into something. Turn, turn, forward. Back again, forward, nearly there, and then, bump, into a rut. Turned, and the rear wheels were just spinning in mud. The more she tried to pull forward, the more they spun. She got out to look. It was mud she had created, turning the car back and forth, and any attempt to try again was only going to dig deeper unless she could give the wheels something to grip on.

She rummaged in her bags, pulled out random bits of clothing and crawled down to shove them as best she could into the mud under the wheels. Not enough. No good spoiling it by trying too soon and making it worse.

She grabbed some more, crawled again, working on both sides. Caked in mud, she climbed back in, shut her eyes, praying to any god willing to help, and started the engine. Got into gear. Released the clutch, foot hovering on the accelerator. The car strained, and... hallelujah. It edged forward. No more manoeuvring; she would have to risk slipping into the stream. She swung hard round and she was safely on the lane, heading back for the cottages.

There was nothing for it but to keep going, up the lane as she had done earlier in search of a signal. On her previous drive up there, she had reached the top of the ridge, more or less, and the road had still continued. It must go on down the other side, into the next valley. It was the only way out.

Her stomach tightened as the cottages came into view. She stopped, nerving herself to go on, to drive past them. She wouldn't look, because the sight of Margaret Gittings staring out at her would finish her. And yet, as she passed Cartref, she couldn't help herself. She looked. She braked. Cartref's door was open. Hanging open, almost off its hinges. It had been forced. Lights were on inside. Furniture was overturned. What the hell had happened? Was this

Margaret's madness at work, wrecking her own home in her fury? Would she really have broken down her own door?

Something was wrong, badly wrong, and Rosanna couldn't just ignore it. She had left Margaret to her misery last time, but not now. Somewhere deep inside, she still felt obliged to uphold something – civilisation, if not the law. She hesitated. If someone else had broken in and ransacked the property, maybe hurting Margaret in the process, it was no more than Rosanna had already done. Was it hypocrisy or irony that she should respond to this second wave of lawbreaking like a police officer reborn?

She reminded herself that Margaret had been out to kill her or at least do her serious injury. Self-preservation demanded that she start up again and drive on. But she couldn't do it. Anyone who could break down a door could do a lot worse to an old woman. Rosanna pushed the precious album into the glove compartment and locked it. Then she braced herself and got out. It felt like a day and a night had passed since she had attempted to drive away, but it had been less than an hour. Not much less, thanks to her hapless manoeuvring. In that time the storm had begun to abate. The rain still came but in half-hearted flurries and rents in the clouds gave a hint of moonlight. Just enough to make the valley seem even more nightmarish.

"Hello?" She paused on the doorstep, calling in. Nothing stirred in reply. The living room was wrecked, more by destructive rage, it seemed, than by larcenous intent.

"Margaret?"

Silence.

"Bryn?" Who else had been anywhere near the cottages today?

Still no answer. No. It couldn't have been Bryn, creating this havoc. She had sent him on his way back down the valley that morning and if he'd returned, surely she'd have seen him. Or would she? But no, not Bryn. He was a sad man plaintively groping for answers in the wilderness of his mind, not a spirit of vicious retribution.

But who else… she recalled the glow from a vehicle up the lane. Who else?

"Hello?" she repeated, pausing again at the bottom of the stairs. Still not a sound. Cautiously, she opened the door to the kitchen. Was she mad to be doing this?

The kitchen was in chaos too, but it had been when Rosanna had fought her way out of it. The splintered panel by the fireplace had been further demolished. Rosanna looked inside. There had been more in there when she had grabbed the album, but it was empty now. A small framed photo had been smashed on the floor, stamped on by the looks of it. She flipped it over. A very young woman, a mere girl, holding a baby. Margaret and her precious son, in a world where he was all she had.

Rosanna stared at it. Someone had been here for vengeance, nothing else. Looking out, she realised that the light was on in the shed, up at the top of the garden. A torch lay abandoned on the kitchen floor. Rosanna switched it on and stepped out into the dark. She climbed carefully. The bean poles had been pushed aside and toppled. Leeks and cabbages had been kicked and trampled. She could pick out footmarks in the muddy soil. Different sizes. More than one person. She climbed on. Still no sound, except dripping from trees and the whistle of the wind, no longer a gale.

The shed door was ajar, just. Rosanna gave it a push and stood back, ready to run. "Hello?"

Nothing.

Fists clenched, she stepped in. She stood there, staring. Seeing, and not wanting to see. Not capable of believing. No.

The long ladder had been untied from its high perch, and had been laid neatly to one side, the stepladder beside it. The rope that had attached it to the cross beams was serving another purpose. Margaret Gittings was hanging by it.

Was she dead, or was this some sort of demonic joke? No joke. Her bulging eyes were staring straight at Rosanna, just as they had stared before. The darkened features were splattered with blood, smeared around her mouth, dribbling from her lips. Gouts of it had dripped into the pool of urine on the floor. Her hands were tightly knotted together.

Rosanna stepped back to the door, gasping for air. This was a lynching, pure murder. If the blood on her mouth and the bound hands weren't enough to prove it, there was evidence elsewhere to make it crystal clear. GUILTY GUILTY BURN IN HELL BITCH. Someone had dug out a can of paint and had written it on the wall in large dripping letters.

Rosanna sank down on the step of the shed and put

her head in her hands. Distantly, she fancied she heard an engine start up. A vehicle driving away? She couldn't be sure in the dying gusts of the storm. The wind was creeping into the shed, setting the rope creaking as it slowly turned. Rosanna was going to be sick.

"They are there." That was what Andrew Rollinson had said, when she'd phoned him, only she hadn't paid attention to that. Who were where? What did he mean? The vigilante relations she had met at his house? They'd had the rage that poor Bryn lacked. She'd told them she was heading for the valleys. They could have followed her there. She had given Andrew the precise address just a few hours ago. If he'd passed it on, they could have come racing over the top from the adjoining valley, broken in, ransacked the place in search of answers that were no longer there, tried to beat the truth out of Margaret and then, when that failed, taken their revenge by passing on her the judgement they had wanted the courts to make.

It was cruel, it was pointless… no, it wasn't. She understood it perfectly, the desire for payment for all the pain and grief of years and years and years, the damaged and crippled lives. The lost children. Who was she to condemn them for what they had done?

Then it struck her, like a punch in the gut. It wouldn't be them condemned. Who suspected they were here? When confronted by Margaret's murdered body, in this isolated valley with the road flooded, who would be blamed except the stranger, Lisa Craven, who had taken up unexpected residence next door and then had fled the scene. If she called the police and stayed, she would be taken straight into custody. Margaret probably had Rosanna's skin under her fingernails. Rosanna had Margaret's bite mark on her hand, and ample evidence of having been involved in a fight. If she gave the full story, with no other suspect to hand, who would believe her?

She got up and forced herself to face the dangling corpse again. Could she make it pass for a suicide? Untie the hands? Tip the stepladder over beneath the gallows? That wouldn't explain the bloody mouth, or the words emblazoned on the wall.

She tried to clear her head. Margaret was beyond saving, and the only thing that mattered was the album. She couldn't take it to the police, not now. Any explanation she gave would merely bring them straight to the scene of Margaret's murder and that would be their primary focus. No, the police would have to wait. Somehow, she would have to use her prize to find those missing children before Jennifer Redbourn died. Then the police could be involved and she would face whatever followed. The children had to come first.

The trouble was her brain was switching off. Think. Whatever she did, she had to get out, get away. She staggered back down the garden, and out through the house, propping the battered door back into position, as if to shut in the horror of what had happened there. It was already locked into her imagination. Margaret, bloody, bound, blue, twisting on that rope. She ran back to her car. Driving like an automaton, she headed up the narrow, shattered lane, out of the woods, to the open slope where she had stopped before. She got out her phone, her fingers beginning to tremble so much she dropped it. Groped for it between the pedals, found the number she wanted and rang it.

It rang and rang, before it was answered.

"Superintendent Cannell," she said. "I'm going to need your help."

Part 5: TRUTH

One Man and his Dogs. And Wife.

"Malcolm, you're not going anywhere without breakfast," said Barbara, switching on the kitchen light and opening the fridge.

Malcolm groaned at the thought of a cooked breakfast. Not yet six a.m., pitch dark outside, and besides, his stomach was tight with tension. "All right, a bit of toast, if you insist, but no more than that, please."

"Two slices. And I'm joining you, so don't try feeding it to the dogs."

The two Labradors raised their heads, eyes all innocent in case they were being accused of something, but ready to respond to any more positive suggestion.

"Hush." Malcolm winked at them. "You can have the crusts," he whispered.

Tails thumped enthusiastically.

Barbara's head appeared round the kitchen door. "And you might as well take your coat off. It won't be here for another hour yet."

Malcolm sighed and obeyed. He'd been out once, taking the car to the all-night petrol station to ensure the tank was full. He just wanted to be on his way now, but she was right, of course. He had no choice but to wait. He shrugged his sheepskin coat off and walked to the window, gazing out on the blurs of light from the streetlamps, idly tapping a rhythm on the pane.

Barbara brought him a mug of coffee. "Toast ready in a minute." She laid a hand on his arm. "Malcolm, don't invest too much in this. It could still come to nothing."

"I know. I know. But if there's the slightest chance that I can find—"

"We can find. You don't think I'm letting you go off on your own, do you?"

"I'll have the dogs."

"Ha. You'll have me, too, so lump it." She returned to the kitchen, and a minute later came back with two plates of toast and marmalade. "Eat," she ordered.

Malcolm did his best. He'd just managed one slice when he caught the faint sound of an engine. He looked up and met Barbara's eyes. Yes, it was definitely approaching. He peered out just as a single beam from a headlight turned in at their drive. "This is it. It's here."

The dogs were up. "Sit!" Barbara ordered them, as Malcolm headed for the front door. He opened it as a motorcyclist dismounted and opened a courier case. Like all bikers clad in black leather, with black helmet and darkened visor, he could have passed for a Martian dropping by, but he took his helmet off to reveal a shock of ginger hair and a freckled nose, very human.

"Malcolm Cannell?"

"Yes. I was expecting you. Come in."

Ginger shook his head with a grin. "It's okay. I was

just instructed to hand you this." He held out a package.

"Let me at least make you a coffee," said Barbara, coming to Malcolm's side. "You must have driven through the night."

"That's the job. You're okay."

"Thank you," said Malcolm, eyes fixed on the packet in his hand, before looking up. "Wait. How was she? The woman who gave you this?"

"Oh." He shrugged. "Okay, I think." He raised a hand in a farewell salute, donned his helmet again and was off, into the dark.

Malcolm turned to face his wife.

"Go on," she said. "Open it."

Malcolm ripped the package open and drew out the contents. That was it, then. An album. "Of course! Photographs. I should have guessed. We knew he had an instamatic." He flipped through the pages, realising the contents, shutting it again, quickly. "You don't want to see this."

"Malcolm, I've lived with this for how long now? Do you really think I haven't imagined every possible scenario?"

"I know. Sorry." Malcolm took the album back to the living room, needing to sit down. He took a deep breath and opened it again, frowning as he took time to study each page more closely. He looked up at Barbara. "It's all here, better than I dared to hope. The girls, all of them, even the one we can't name. I knew there'd be another. He's marked the exact spot where he put them. Look. St Michael's spire, visible in the distance." He showed her an open page. "It's Hackling

Wood all right." He flipped back a page. "There's the stile from Millfield Road in this one."

Barbara nodded, pursing her lips. "And that's Jodie Fitzpatrick, isn't it?"

"Yes." Malcolm's sense of triumph died down. "And Rachel Redbourn, Ashley Knowles, Bethany Davies…"

He opened another page, with just two photographs. "And this is our mystery girl. Essex, it has to be, before he moved to Welsey. Who was she? Why was she never reported missing? That's what I can't understand. Only one shot of her, but he's marked the spot where he put her. Trees again. Always among trees."

"The others." Barbara cautiously turned back a page. "All cut on the cheek, but just that."

"Yes, thank God, just that. And probably done after death. That is something to be grateful for, I suppose. But five missing girls. Five."

"It's the Welsey girls we have to worry about," said Barbara, turning away to gather up coats and a bag of walking boots. "Rachel Redbourn first, for the sake of that poor dying woman, so let's get it done. Come on, dogs. Walkies!"

* * *

It was a half-hour journey down to Welsey. Barbara drove, while Malcolm studied an ordnance survey map, comparing it as best he could to the photographs in the album marked with heavy crosses. Not much sign of sun but it was daylight by the time they turned off the bypass, heading for the town centre.

"Millfield Road?" she suggested.

"Head for the layby just beyond the woods."

She nodded. The town was waking, delivery vans busily unloading, traffic already building up on Millfield Road coming up into town from the south. Every marker along the road was etched on Malcolm's brain – the seedy house where Timothy Gittings had first lived, the girder bridge over the Wele, the turning on the right into the Mile End estate, houses petering out until the turning on the left into Bartlet Lane towards the abattoir… and then the wood.

They drove past it in silence. A short way beyond the last few trees, Barbara pulled into an empty layby and switched off.

Silence. The occasion was too momentous for words. Then Barbara stirred. "Right. Come on. Boots on."

There was the usual palaver of dressing up, sorting out the dogs, just as if they were embarking on a perfectly normal outing. Hackling Wood was a favourite spot for dog-walking. No one would glance twice at them. Barbara picked up the backpack she had prepared. The usual contents: gloves, phone, dog biscuits, poo bags, flask. The less usual contents: two trowels, pruning knife, bin bag and a roll of clingfilm.

"Come on, boys."

The dogs knew the way without waiting to be told, back down the road, past the first part of the wood, a wedge of conifer plantation, to the stile. Beyond it stretched a well-used footpath into deciduous woodland, almost bare now. A helpful noticeboard listed the flora and fauna that might be observed.

Into the privacy of the woods, Malcolm persuaded the dogs to curb their enthusiasm. He opened the album to the page devoted to Jodie Fitzpatrick. It distinctly showed the stile they had just climbed over, seen in the distance between the trunks of tightly packed fir trees. Barbara leaned in to study it with him.

"That way," she said, and set off, away from the open path, into the plantation. It took them quarter of an hour, churning up fallen needles, shielding their faces from the scratches of dead branches, to pinpoint the position from which the photograph had been taken. The dogs, taking on board the notion that they were searching for something, were only too eager to help, sniffing around every tree and scrabbling in the compost.

Malcolm and Barbara stood side by side, the album held out before them as they compared the scene, inch by inch. The trees had not changed greatly over the decades, just grown that little bit taller. There was a gap between two, where a tree had fallen, its upturned roots almost rotted away, but still identifiable as the remains of the huge disc in the photograph. Withered weeds had taken hold in its place, making the most of the stronger light from above, although the branches of the surrounding trees had expanding into the vacant space.

Barbara leaned down to seize a handful of brittle stalks.

"She's here."

"Yes, but leave it. If we've managed to find it, an official search will do the same."

"You don't want to dig?"

"Not here. It has to be Rachel's grave. The last before Laura Wakefield. We can't expect them to believe he'd have stowed his album with an earlier victim."

"No. Of course." Barbara took the book from him and turned the page. Rachel's page. "We need a site with the church spire in view. That looks like a horse chestnut, if that helps."

"Let's see."

Urging the dogs on, they worked their way free of the conifers, back to the path, covering their tracks as best they could. A hundred yards into the woods the path divided, branches leading through to two separate entrances on Bartlet Lane. They plodded diligently along one to a kissing gate, came back and tried the other. The distant spire came into view several times, but never exactly as it appeared in the photograph.

Malcolm stood gazing at it for a while, shaking his head. "He won't have picked a spot anywhere along the open paths, will he? Stands to reason. He'll have chosen somewhere where he couldn't be seen by random strollers.

"Of course." Barbara stood, hands on hips, ignoring the straining of the dogs on their leashes, as she surveyed the woods to either side. "That way?" She pointed. Beyond a bank of holly, the ground dipped slightly.

It proved to be a fine and private place, well shielded from prying eyes, but the spire of St Michael's was entirely hidden from view. Not there, then, but they ploughed on, leaving all trace of paths behind. They searched for more than half an hour, with

Malcolm growing quietly desperate, before Barbara, ahead of him, gave a shout of triumph. The dogs barked in happy accompaniment.

Malcolm hurried to join her and instantly knew this was the spot. The trees were not identical – a couple of saplings were threatening to block the view – but between two mature trunks the distant spire was visible, against a faint rising skyline exactly as the photograph depicted. He hurried forward. Trees were not his speciality, but he knew conkers when he trod on them, spiked casings split open, nuts littering the freshly fallen leaves.

There was a bit of a bank below the horse chestnut, stones jutting from it, much as they did in the photo, though the earth had shifted a bit since. Barbara was vigorously sweeping aside leaves and weeds.

"Here. This is it. His marker." Gittings had scrawled his crayon cross on a flat stone that he must have prised loose from the bank. The crumbled earth where he had extracted it was visible in the photo, though nature had smoothed it over and filled it in in the intervening years. But the stone was still where he had placed it, embedding itself in the ground.

With an effort, Malcolm prized it free from the grip of the soil. He took the trowel that Barbara proffered and began to dig. She dropped on her knees beside him to do the same, which was all the encouragement the dogs needed. For once, they were not reprimanded for scrabbling gleefully and sending soil flying. They were creating quite a pit.

"How far down do you think we need to go?" asked Barbara, pausing to look at the results of their efforts.

They'd dug about two feet down. "He wouldn't have gone the full six feet, would he?"

"I hope not. Although he probably used a spade, not a trowel. A bit more."

Only a bit more. "Stop!" said Malcolm. Tails wagged as he sat back on his heels. Something was visible in the bottom of their excavation. Something blue.

"Cloth?" said Barbara. Her voice was steady, but only with an effort.

"She was wearing a blue anorak," said Malcolm, staring down at it. "Nylon, I suppose. Takes forever to decompose. Terrible for the environment, but on this occasion…" He leaned in to clear more of the earth away. Yes, it was undoubtedly nylon, cold, wet, stained, quilted. He ran his hand over it, gripping its folds, then sat back again.

"Bone underneath. Shoulder blade, I think."

Barbara managed a nod, then turned away, shaking.

Malcolm groped in his pocket and fished out a handkerchief. "Here."

She wiped her eyes, then blew her nose loudly. "Well then. Do we dig on?"

"No. We leave it for forensics now. All we've done, remember, is find the book."

"Because of the dogs."

"Yes." Malcolm looked at the Labradors. They were completely unaware of what it was all about but only too ready to play their part. "I ask you, is anyone going to believe these daft buggers would be capable of finding anything?"

"Can't we just tell them the truth?"

"I'd like to, Barbara, but you didn't hear Rosanna Quillan on the phone. She sounded seriously stressed. I don't want her to have to confess to housebreaking and, anyway, complicated explanations would only create delays that I gather Jennifer Redbourn can't afford."

"Yes, of course I understand that. In which case, you're going to have to come up with a believable story. One they won't think of questioning."

"They'll have human remains on their hands. That will be their priority. The questions might come later, of course, but for now, we just look shocked and innocent and let the boys hog the limelight."

The boys sat up, ready for a photoshoot.

"Here." Barbara threw them a biscuit each, then turned her attention to the album. She stared at the open page once more, then shut it firmly. "Does it need treating, do you think?"

Malcolm considered it, frowning. "I don't know where she had it, but It's already spotted and aged. No, leave it as it is."

She nodded, then got to work wrapping it tightly in clingfilm, pressing it flat, before slipping it into the bin bag, folding it round as the final casing of the mummy. She opened the flask – not the usual coffee but cold water from their rain butt. Malcolm watched her pour it over the cocoon, then he took if from her, stood it in the hole They'd dug and backfilled it, pressing earth into every plastic fold, until only one corner was left exposed. "What's the time?" He glanced at his watch. Well past nine. "I think you can call Jill now."

"Give me a moment." Barbara shut her eyes,

breathing deeply, then she took out her phone and tapped the keys. Her voice changed to bright and breezy. "Jilly! It's Barbara – Oh yes, fine. Not too early for you, am I? – Good. Listen, Malcolm and I are heading down your way. How do you fancy meeting for lunch at the Crown? Time for a catch-up? – That's great. Make it twelvish? We'll take the dogs for a walk first, use up some of their surplus energy so they don't show us up – Perfect. We'll see you there. Love to Gerry. Bye."

She pocketed the phone and looked at her husband. "Now we dig it up again."

* * *

Jill Brown edged her way back to their table in the Crown, the classy old coaching inn in the centre of Welsey, dropping her phone back into her handbag.

Her husband Gerald looked up, frowning. "Did you get through?" He glanced at the clock over the bar. Nearly one o'clock. "They did say twelve, didn't they?"

"Well!" Jill sat down, brimming with excitement. "Such a to-do! Barbara apologised, profusely, but they can't join us after all. They're at the police station, giving statements!"

"Why? What have they done?"

"Oh, nothing bad. It sounds as if Malcolm's managed it at last."

"Got a new boat? Don't tell me he nicked it."

"No, no! He's done it, found them. The missing girls. Or a body, at any rate. In Hackling wood."

"Good God. That's what he always suspected,

wasn't it? So those police cars and vans we saw, heading down Millfield Road—"

"Exactly!"

"Well, well. What a turn up, eh. Shall we order, then?"

"Oh yes, why not. As long as we're home in time for six. It's bound to make the news."

Clearance

Gethin Matthews herded the sheep through the open gate into a slightly less water-logged field. They immediately gathered in the shelter of the hedge, muttering in a disgruntled manner, the lingering drizzle glistening on their fleeces, but they perked up wonderfully as he hoisted the sack of sheep nuts from the quad.

"Cupboard love, that's what it is," he said as they pressed around him. "You look at me and see a food machine. Mind you, I look at you and see lamb chops."

They ignored the jibe and he left them munching, shutting the gate behind him. Back on the quad, he paused, standing up to survey the land for damage done by the previous night's storm. Not too bad. A branch was down on one of the oaks and an empty plastic drum had escaped from its store and was wedged in the hedgerow, but roofs were intact and chimney pots in place. Further down, though, there might be more of a problem. The water was very high; he could see it glinting through the trees. The bridge was probably blocked again, which meant he'd have to get the tractor out.

He was heading back into the yard when he caught a glimpse of a figure, black in the grey twilight of early morning, disappearing down the track on the far side. A figure that stopped, started, stopped again.

"Dad?" Gethin leaped down. "Dad. Stop there. Don't wander away. Stay there!" The wind was still strong. There was no knowing if his father could hear him or understand even if he could. Gethin raced after him, swearing at himself for leaving the back door unlocked. Thunderstorms had always disturbed Henry and this one must have jogged him into more than usual confusion.

"Dad!"

His father turned towards him, distress deepening in the effort of putting a name to a face.

"Where are you going, Dad?" He corrected himself.

"Henry, where are you going?" There were odd days when he couldn't remember he had a son, but he usually remembered his own name.

Henry peered around, uncertain, the soft rain flattening his grey hair. "I'm going to chapel."

Gethin opened his mouth to argue, to remind him that he hadn't been near a chapel for twelve years, since he'd declared, out of the blue, that all religion was balderdash, but there'd be no point in that. "Okay, but let's go back to the house first, and get you a coat and hat. You'll get soaked through, otherwise. Don't want you catching your death of cold, do we?"

"I'm going to chapel," insisted Henry, resisting. His mind might be cracking up, but his body was still fighting fit. When he chose to dig his heels in, it took all Gethin's strength to restrain him. Persuasion was always better.

"The chapel's this way, remember? Just up the hill a bit."

"I know!" Henry scowled. "You think I don't know

225

where the chapel is?"

Hebron Chapel was along the valley at Brongarn. Best not give him time to remember that. "I'll come with you."

"Why?"

"To sing hymns. Always like a good sing song. Come on, let's sing!" Step by step edging him back towards the house.

"O! fy Iesu bendigedig, unig gwmni f"enaid gwan…"

His father joined in, automatically, with relish, his rich baritone recovering all its old strength, until Gethin launched into the next verse. Henry struck his arm, scowling angrily. "Why are you singing that nonsense? I don't believe in that rubbish. Where's my coat?"

"In the house, Dad. Let's go and get it, shall we?"

"I'm wet. I told you I didn't want a bath. You never listen!"

"Okay, okay, no bath. Let's get into the house and you can dry off by the fire. Yes?"

"I don't know why you made me go to chapel. I don't believe in all that."

"No, Dad. My mistake."

Gethin had just got him back into the house when the phone rang. Gethin guided his father back to his chair by the Rayburn and answered it.

"Gethin?" It was Sue Phillips. "How is everything with you? Henry all right? I was coming up to check on you, but I saw the bridge was almost under water and I didn't dare risk it."

"I thought it must be. Dad's been having a walkabout in the rain, I'm afraid, but as soon as I've got him dried off and warmed up, I'll go down and clear the bridge. How are things at your place? Any damage?"

"No, all fine here, love, but I know how Henry feels about thunder. Let me know when you've done and I'll come over to sit with him."

"Please! I'd really like to go and check on Lisa, as soon as I get a chance, but I can't risk leaving Dad too long."

"Right you are, Gethin. Just let me know."

Gethin managed with an effort to remove his father's wet cardigan. He switched the kettle on and went to fetch a couple of warm towels from the bathroom. His father did not take kindly to being dried.

"What are you doing, boy? Leave me alone."

"All right." The kettle had boiled and Gethin hastily made a mug of tea. "Here you are, to warm you through. And here's your library book. You sit there and keep warm while I take the tractor down to clear the stream. Okay?"

The chapel was forgotten. Henry, still cocooned in towels, seemed happy to settle with his book, and Gethin left him to it, taking care, this time, to lock both doors. He didn't like doing it, trapping his father inside, but when Henry's mind was having a day off, he wasn't safe to be left. Starting up their elderly tractor, Gethin trundled down to the bridge.

It was blocked all right. Hardly surprising after that storm. The dip in the road up towards Lisa's cottage was submerged. The sooner he cleared the tangled flotsam that was damming the flow the better. It was a cold, wet and messy job, wading in and attaching ropes and chains to jutting branches. What was that he'd said to Lisa about wanting to get back to nature? Right now he could only think with longing of getting back to Cambridge. Still, this was a job that had to be done, and quickly.

Back in the tractor, he let it take the strain, a great mass of debris sucking free of the swirling water and following him up the slope. He dragged it further along and off the lane, before reversing back to check. It had done the trick. The penned-up water was now thundering through the low arch. It would take a while to clear, though, and he couldn't stand and watch while his father was left locked up at home. Satisfied that the flood would soon drain, he returned to the house, unlocked the door and went in, to find, to his relief, that his father was now nodding and snoring gently in his chair. Gethin picked up the phone and called Sue.

She pulled up in the yard ten minutes later and bustled into the house. "Hello, Henry. What's all this about you wandering out in the rain, and catching your death of cold?"

"We've been to chapel," said Henry, looking pleased with himself. "He wouldn't let me wear a coat."

She and Gethin raised their eyes, then smiled.

"I'll take care of him now," said Sue. "You go off and check on that girl of yours."

"Sue, she's just a friend, that's all. Not my girl."

"Of course not, love. You tell yourself that. Now, Henry Matthews. What's it to be? Scrabble or Monopoly?"

Over his father's head, Gethin clasped his hands in thanks. Mostly he managed fine, but without his ever-helpful neighbour, he suspected he would probably have gone crazy by now. Sue had endless patience – or maybe, with her husband dead and her children gone, she was just keen to find another mission. Whatever her motives, Gethin was grateful.

Steering the Land Rover down to the bridge, he paused to check that the blockage hadn't reformed. The stream was still roaring, but the level had gone down. The lane up the narrow valley was now clear of water, although it was littered with sodden debris. Good enough. He turned up towards the cottages, noting where the bank was giving way or trees were looking unsafe. Nothing that needed urgent attention.

He rounded the bend and the cottages came into view. God, what a dreary place. He really needed to get Lisa out of there and into their holiday cottage. Or into the farmhouse… That would probably be pushing his luck.

No lights on in Marlborough. He stopped in the lane, jumped out and banged on the door. Waited. Knocked again. Silence. Frowning, he drove on to the turning area. It was empty, Lisa's car gone. If she'd left, it couldn't have been this morning. The undisturbed mat of saturated muck across the road told him his tractor was the first vehicle on the road since he'd unblocked the bridge. She must have gone the previous night, before the flood trapped her in, and then she'd been unable to drive back. She was probably holed up in the Drover's Arms, God help her, or the Travelodge down the valley.

Instinctively, he reached for the phone that lived in his pocket out of old habit. No signal. Of course there wasn't. There never was, and besides, he didn't know her number because they hadn't bothered exchanging. There would have been no point in that signal blackspot.

He groped in his other pocket. A nearly exhausted biro and a couple of scraps of paper – old receipts. He wrote on the back on one. "You can't stay here. Pack up and come to the farm. We'll be expec…" The pen gave up.

It would have to do. Gethin folded the paper neatly, then walked back, intending to slip it through her letterbox. But he didn't make it that far. He had driven by Cartref without giving it a second glance, but now, passing it on foot, he couldn't avoid noticing the state of the door, battered, a panel broken, a hinge loose.

His first thought, as he stopped short, was that the storm must have done it. Or the flood. Had the blockage of the bridge really caused the brook to break its banks this far upstream? He should have gone out in the night to check. He should have cleared it sooner. At least Lisa had been safe from it all.

He turned his gaze back to Marlborough. Its door was undamaged. And the lane, now he looked at it, was barred with ripples of mud washed down from the bank, but it wasn't littered with the detritus of flooding. No, it wasn't the stream that had battered and broken Cartref's door.

He looked at it again, a chill creeping down his spine. The blows that had cracked the panels and loosened the hinge had been struck at chest height.

Struck ferociously by something heavy and full of intent. He hesitated. There was no hope of calling the police, but he couldn't just drive away. There was nothing for it but to investigate for himself. He pushed the door and it swung inwards on its intact hinge. Propping it in place, he peered into the gloom of the house, at upturned furniture, scattered books and papers, smashed china. What the hell had been going on?

"Vera? Hello? Mrs Broderick, are you there? It's me, Gethin Matthews, from Hendy." His words echoed into silence. Not a sound responded.

He opened the door to the kitchen, and stared at the chaos within, everything pulled apart and wrecked, every cupboard and drawer emptied, glass and crockery shattered in a mess of milk and jam and flour. This was vandalism on an utterly insane scale. He couldn't begin to understand it.

But what really mattered was that Mad Annie wasn't lying in this mess. He tiptoed through it to check the bathroom. A mirror was smashed but there was little else to damage and she wasn't there. He raced upstairs, tried both bedrooms. The same chaos, furniture tipped, linen scattered, and in the back room, photographs ripped and shredded by a fury that was surely demonic. Gethin wasn't religious but he felt as if he were wading in the wake of something let loose from Hell.

He went back down, muscles rigid to stop himself trembling. Where was Vera Broderick? The woman couldn't have survived an assault like this, so had she escaped? Where? He looked out of the back window, up the storm-battered garden to the shed at the top.

Was there a light on, up there? It was faint in daylight but yes, the window was not a blank. He heaved a sigh of relief. She must be up there, hiding from whoever had done this.

Going back down, he waded again through the pigswill of the kitchen, and out into the yard. "Vera?" he called as he strode up the steps from terrace to terrace.

"Mrs Broderick!"

Not surprising that she wasn't replying. She must be terrified. That would be it. He was probably making it worse by calling. Reaching the shed door, he knocked gently.

"Mrs Broderick? Nothing to worry about. It's only me, Gethin Matthews, come to help."

Silence.

He cautiously tried the door. It opened. He looked inside. Looked. Turned his back on it and leaned against the door jamb to get his head straight. Turned back. Looked again.

"Jesus." He crossed to the dangling corpse and reached out, hesitating before touching the bound hands. Cold as ice. One glance had been enough. He couldn't bring himself to look again at the mottled, bloodied face. She was dead. Murdered. There was nothing he could do. He would have to contact the police...

Lisa! Panic seized him. Was this why she had fled? Had her cottage been attacked too? Maybe the attacker had taken her car and she was lying somewhere...

He ran back down, all too eager to get away from the shed. There was a rug flung over the fence into the garden next door. He hadn't noticed it before. Someone had climbed over. He vaulted over and hurried to the back door. It was bolted but the kitchen window was smashed. He put his shoulder to the door and heaved. Rammed it again and again, until it finally burst open. There was glass across the kitchen floor, but no other destruction. He raced through the house, checking every room. Nothing seemed disturbed. There was no sign of Lisa. No laptop, no clothes, no anything. What... where... Could she have...

He paused to collect himself. Lisa was gone and there was no blood, no sign of struggle. It was the murder of Vera Broderick he had to deal with, first and foremost. He ran back to his Land Rover, jumped in and headed wildly back to Hendy, screeching to a halt in the yard.

His father and Sue were sitting at the table, engrossed in a game of Scrabble. Sue looked up with a smile as Gethin flung the door open, then her expression turned to anxiety, one hand reaching out to Henry's to calm him, as his puzzlement gave way to recognition.

"Gethin."

Just need to make a phone call," said Gethin, grabbing the phone and retreating to the parlour he'd adopted as his workplace.

It was several minutes before he re-emerged and put the phone back in its cradle.

"Everything all right, love?" Sue had gone to make a pot of tea.

"All this rushing around," sniffed his father. "You'll do yourself damage if you don't take care. Sit down, boy, and stop fidgeting."

"I'll help Sue with the tea, first." Gethin joined her in the back kitchen.

She was hovering over the tea tray, waiting for his explanation. "What's happened?" she asked in a low voice.

"There's been a… an incident," he said, in a half-whisper, realising that his hand was shaking.

"Yes. What sort of incident."

"A death. Mad An… Vera Broderick."

"Oh, poor woman! Accident or heart attack or what?"

"No. No, it was, um…" He had to say it. "Murder."

Sue gave a gasp, nearly dropping the teapot.

TV crime shows had it all wrong, Gethin thought. Women wouldn't really burst into a bloodcurdling fit of hysterical screaming in the face of murder. Maybe he should mention this to Alex, a university friend now working with a production company… He shook his head, realising that he was just trying to wipe out that image of Vera Broderick. "Make that tea strong, will you?"

Sue nodded. "You phoned the police?"

"Yes, they're on their way."

"Not a word to your father just yet."

"No, quite."

"We'll break it gently. He's just settling back down after that storm." She stirred the pot and put the lid on.

"Oh, and Lisa? Is she all right? She must be in a terrible state."

"She's gone. I think she went before it happened. Because of the storm."

"Yes," said Sue, doubtfully. "I expect so."

Gethin studiously shut his mind to any alternative. "Okay. Let me have a quick swig of that, and then I'll got back to the cottage and wait for the police. You can keep Dad occupied for a bit longer?"

"Of course. You take care, bach."

* * *

Considering the narrow winding roads they had to travel, the police arrived remarkably quickly. Of course they would. It was a murder. A brief blare of a siren and then a police car appeared, blue light flashing. It pulled up and two officers got out. One turned straight to Gethin, who was waiting at the door of Marlborough.

"Mr Gethin Matthews?"

Gethin nodded. Now was not the time to explain about parking arrangements.

"Sergeant Howells. You say you've already been in the house?"

He nodded again, with a sigh. "Yes, and probably contaminated everything. Sorry."

"Mm. You didn't just see the damage to the door and call the police then and there?"

"I would have done, if there were any signal here. I had to wait until I got back to the farm. I thought the most important thing was find Mrs Broderick. She could have been lying injured. I had to find her first."

"Yes, of course. It's a pity but can't be helped. You say she's hanging in the barn behind the house."

"Yes." Gethin winced.

"You reported it as murder. You didn't consider suicide?"

"No! Go and look at the place. Look what someone's done. And… well, look at her, go up there. It was more than just murder. It was an execution."

"You think so?"

"You'll see for yourself."

"We will. Are you all right, sir? You look a bit queasy."

"So would you."

"I'm sure. All right, if you're up to it, I'd like you to wait in the car while I examine the scene for myself."

"Sure."

Feeling nauseous, Gethin climbed into the back seat, while Sgt Howells struggled into protective gear. His mate was already taping off the lane in both directions. Gethin shut his eyes and leaned back, listening to the crackle of police radios and the slamming of doors as another vehicle arrived. Then another. Shouts and instructions. He opened his eyes as Howells climbed back in.

"Right, sir. I can understand your reference to an execution. While we're waiting for the doctor and CID, I'd like you to talk me through it all."

"Fine. Yes. Where do you want me to start?"

"How about you tell me, for starters, what you were doing here. Do you live in one of these houses?"

"No. Hendy. It's a farm, just a mile down. A small holding really. There's a bridge over the stream. It was blocked in the storm and the road flooded. I cleared the blockage and then I came up here to check that everyone was all right. After the storm, you know."

"Can you tell me the name of the other residents here?"

"Only Vera Broderick. She lives alone and the other houses are all empty."

"Ah. You said you intended to check on everyone."

"Yes, Mrs Broderick and Lisa. Lisa Craven. She was renting Marlborough, the cottage next door. But she'd already gone."

"Gone where?"

"Home, I expect. It was only a short-term visit."

"And where would that home be?"

"Winchester, I think she said. I don't know the address."

"I see. Right, moving on, you came here to check on the cottages and you found what?"

"Vera's door had been smashed open. I didn't do that."

"Mm-hmm." Howells, taking notes, was noncommittal. "You looked inside."

"I could see someone had gone berserk in there. I thought they must have attacked Vera, so I went looking for her. I saw there was a light up in the shed and I... I saw. Jesus! Why would anyone do a thing like that to an old woman?"

"That's what we'll want to find out. What did you do next?"

"I checked next door, in case... The kitchen window has been smashed, but there was nothing else. The place was deserted."

"No sign of this Lisa Craven."

"No. She'd packed up and gone before any of this happened."

Howell's eyebrows shot up, "But you didn't know that, since you were intending to check on her and her neighbour?" Fortunately, he was diverted by the arrival of another car. "If you could just wait a little longer, sir."

"Sure."

"Then I'm afraid we'll be needing you to come to the station."

"I can give a statement here."

"But we'll also be needing your clothing, fingerprints, DNA sample. Just for elimination, you understand."

"Yes, I understand," said Gethin. "I am entitled to a phone call, aren't I?"

"Of course, sir. As many as you like. You're not under arrest."

"I need to warn Sue. Our neighbour. She's sitting with my father. He gets confused. I'd be grateful if you didn't do anything to alarm him."

"We'll do our best, sir."

Discovery

Malcolm Cannell was back in the station where he had worked all those years ago, before promotion had wafted him on to pastures new. It had received a lick of paint since his time, and other changes were predictable: fewer personnel and more technology. The main difference was that he was here now on the other side of the desk. A member of the public, going about his private business but keen to do his civic duty.

It wasn't quite like that, of course. He could be a suspect, just as much as an innocent passer-by and, considering the story he had concocted, it wouldn't surprise him if he were treated as such, although Detective Inspector Willis was all smiles and bonhomie. Malcolm remembered Sam Willis as a cocky young PC, bright enough but not entirely dependable. The years had matured him.

"Superintendent.

"Mr Cannell will do. Or Malcolm if you like."

"All right then, Malcolm. You've returned to the hunt yet again. I'm told you've had a theory about Hackling Wood and you've been haunting the place since your retirement."

"Hardly haunting. I did think the wood was a likely place for Gittings to have buried his bodies, so yes, I have been back to Welsey a few times, but mostly to visit old friends and colleagues, and the wood is a good place to walk the dogs while I'm here."

"And this time you struck gold. Isn't it lucky for us how many times dog walkers turn up murder victims? Doing our work for us."

Malcolm smiled ruefully. "I'd love to say my keen-nosed hounds sniffed out the body for me, but they are quite useless in that department. It was a sheer fluke, that's all. Otherwise I'm sure I would have struck gold, as you put it, on previous occasions. All Barbara and I were intending was to get some surplus canine energy used up before we met Jill and Gerry Brown. Gerry's Barbara's accountant."

"Yes, Gerald Brown. You'd arranged to meet him for lunch, is that right?"

"At the Crown."

"And you decided to walk the dogs in Hackling Wood first."

"That's right. We headed off along the path but Solly tugged free while I was rummaging in my pack. I expect he'd spotted a squirrel. He was off into the trees before I could grab the lead back. We had to follow him and we caught up with him eventually, when his leash caught on a rock. He was barking at a tree and in his excitement, the rock must have come loose. Tomtom started scrabbling at the earth, while I was busy catching Solly, and Barbara noticed something, just a piece of plastic, where the rock had been dislodged. It was a bit of a surprise. Not what you expect to find buried under an old mossy stone."

"And you naturally decided to dig it out."

"The dogs did most of the digging. The moment I realised it was a package, I finished the job. I have to admit, it sent shivers down my spine. I'd always suspected there was a book, and that's what it felt like. It seemed too much to hope for. But it was a hope, just that. Blind hope, not a real expectation until I took it from the bag it was wrapped in. I was tempted to rip off the tight binding, to see, but the dogs were still busy scrabbling, and Barbara shouted that there was something else there, buried deeper. Blue cloth. I could make out the blue and I knew one of the girls had been wearing a blue jacket. I stopped at that point and we pulled the dogs clear before they could do any more damage. Then I called the station. I didn't want to risk any further contamination."

"Thanks for that. Forensics have extracted the book. You're quite right. No doubt about it being Gittings" record of his kills. Photographs."

"Ah! Goodness. That's more than I was hoping for."

Willis smiled disingenuously. "Like I said, you struck gold."

"It has actual photographs of his victims?"

"Oh yes."

"Does it include Ashley Knowles?"

"It does, and two before her."

"Two!"

"One we didn't know about."

"But we always suspected there might be more." Malcolm heaved a sigh. "I'm guessing we've found one of the bodies."

"You found Rachel Redbourn. Or at least we're assuming it's her. Positive DNA identification will be needed, of course, once the remains have been fully exhumed, but there's not much doubt, is there? Gittings must have hidden his book with each victim in turn. An odd thing to do, don't you think?"

"Yes, but Gittings was odd, so nothing surprises me. I suppose he didn't get the chance to reclaim it after killing Laura Wakefield, which is why it was still with his previous victim. What about the earlier ones? Any chance of finding them too?"

"I should think so. A second site has already been identified from the photographs. We've got the cadaver dogs in, and they're digging now. We think It's Jodie Fitzpatrick."

"What about Ashley?"

"Still looking for that one. Some trees… well, one tree looks like another to me, but we've got an expert in to identify the species from the photographs. That should narrow the search."

"Thank God!"

"Luck, eh?" Willis's smile was so broad it was threatening to crack his face.

"No," said Malcolm. "Luck would have been finding them twenty-five years ago."

"But you can be satisfied you've achieved your goal at last. A fitting finale to your career. The press is already onto it, of course, gathering with their tongues hanging out. Once you've given us a formal statement, you can face the cameras, if you're up to it."

"What I'd rather have, first, is a bit of quiet privacy," said Malcolm. "You'd think an old hand would take it in his stride, but to be honest, I think the shock is beginning to get to me."

He was given his moment of quiet privacy, but it wasn't shock he had to deal with. Rosanna Quillan had given him the number. He needed to make an urgent phone call.

* * *

Andrew Rollinson looked down on his sister, withered and worn, her head engulfed in the pillow, her eyes shut, deep in blue shadows.

"Am I too late?"

The nurse patted his hand reassuringly. "No, she's still with us. She's just sleeping. The painkillers make her drowsy, that's all."

He nodded and took the seat beside the bed, gently stroking his sister's fingers. "Jen?"

Her eyes flickered open, focussing slowly on him.

"Drew?" Her voice was a whisper.

"Luke will be here very shortly. He's bringing Alan."

There was a flicker of response at her son's name, but none to her husband's. The marriage had never legally ended; it had merely ceased to exist. Alan had dwindled into a silent inadequate ghost in the corner.

"I've phoned Amy too, and she says she's on her way." Best not to tell her the state Amy was in when he spoke to her. "Because, Jenny, I've got some news for you." He squeezed her skeletal fingers. "The very best possible news." The words stuck in his throat. They had come to this: final confirmation of his niece's death was to be treated as a source of joy. "They've found where he put her, Jen. They found your Rachel. She's coming home."

He watched the lips twitch into a smile, even as tears rolled down her cheeks.

Thorne Moore

Suspicions

The police driver let Gethin out by the bridge as he requested. No need to alarm his father with the sight of a police car pulling up in the yard. The walk up the muddy lane gave him the chance to inhale some much-needed fresh air, though it did nothing for the bottoms of his trousers. He slipped his muddy shoes off in the porch, and cautiously entered the house.

"Ah, there he is," said Sue, brightly, coming forward to hug him. She whispered in his ear. "I've told him there was an accident and a death and you saw it, which is why you had to go and tell the police."

"Accident, my foot," said Henry, whose wits and hearing were clearly now in good form again. "Who was it, then? Who do they think Gethin murdered?"

"Oh now, what nonsense, Henry Matthews!" Sue scolded him, indignantly. "Look at your son, so smart and respectable. As if anyone would suspect him of murdering anyone."

A police officer had called at the farm to pick up a change of clothes for Gethin, since he'd had to surrender most of what he'd been wearing, and Sue had picked out his one good suit, because one must look one's best when being questioned by the police. Gethin had hardly ever worn it in Cambridge. He'd never worn it here. He looked down at his muddied hems and forced a laugh. Inside, he was just thanking a

God he didn't believe in that he had barely set foot in Vera's shed, and only touched her dead hand for a second. Her house would be covered with his fingerprints but there would be no trace of her on his clothing. Or any trace of him on her.

"Don't worry, Dad," he said. "They're not accusing me of anything. But I found... I discovered a body."

"Yes, yes, but who was it?" asked his father, impatiently.

There was no point in keeping him in ignorance now. "It was Vera Broderick."

"Ah," said Henry, not at all surprised. "Margaret Gittings."

"No, love," said Sue, hastily. "Mrs Broderick, the old lady up the valley."

"Margaret Gittings," repeated Henry, obstinately.

Sue shook her head at Gethin. "It's the latest bee he's got in his bonnet. Now never mind that. Come and sit down and tell me, was it very bad? The police, I mean."

"The police? No. It was fine. They were just very thorough. Didn't want to miss anything and it all took time."

"Well, never mind. You're home now. I'll put the kettle on." She bustled off.

Henry sat back, surveying his son. "So she was murdered, was she?"

"Yes, Dad."

"Some would say she had it coming."

"Oh, come on!"

"Well. Just saying."

Gethin changed the subject. "Enough of that. How

about you? What have you been doing all day?"

"Checked on the sheep. There's a bit of fence going to need fixing in the top field."

"I'll see to it tomorrow." Conversation moved on to farming matters, which was fine by Gethin.

"Supper will be ready in half an hour," said Sue.

Supper was dippy egg and soldiers for her and Henry, but she had saved some shepherd's pie and cabbage from the dinner that she and Henry insisted on eating at lunch time. She was a resolute champion of good solid nursery food and although Gethin's preference would have been for a nice hot Thai curry or some seafood linguine, he never considered holding her back. If he and Henry were replacement chicks for her empty nest, he could only consider it a blessing.

He was still convincing Sue that the police had offered him a very ample BLT lunch and he was too full to finish off with stewed apples and custard, when a knock on the door stopped him in mid-flow. Locals never knocked. They just walked in.

Gethin got up and opened the door. DS Armstrong, the detective who had taken charge of him at the station, was standing there, stamping against the chill.

"Evening, sir. I'm sorry to be disturbing you yet again, after that tedious session you've already gone through, but our investigations are throwing up some interesting queries and I wonder if you wouldn't mind filling in a few more details for us."

"Yes. Sure. Er, come in. Didn't I go over everything earlier?"

"About your involvement, yes, sir. We're rather more interested now in the young lady who was living next door to the victim. Lisa Craven, of 23 Fletcher's Lane, Winchester?"

"Lisa, yes. I don't know about the address, but I'm sure she said Winchester."

"A very nice girl," added Sue.

"That's the address she gave the letting agency," said Armstrong, "where she paid a week's rent in cash. We're having a spot of trouble tracing her. Could you describe her, perhaps? Age, for instance?"

"Er. Well, late twenties? Thirtyish? Not really a girl."

"Colour of hair? Height? Build? Any distinguishing features?

"Fair hair, sort of shoulder length. Not sure about height. She was quite a bit shorter than me."

"Taller than me, though," said Sue, who was already busy making the inevitable pot of tea.

"And you are... Five four?" suggested Armstrong, peering round the door at her with a practiced eye.

Sue laughed. "I used to be, but nearer to five three now."

"Right. Okay, let's say somewhere between five-five and six foot." With a sigh, Armstrong noted it down."

"Five six or seven, by my reckoning," interjected Henry, from round his winged armchair.

Gethin shrugged. "Maybe," he mouthed.

"Colour of eyes?"

"Um. Not blue. Not brown really, either. Sort of hazel? Yes, hazel. Oh, and she has a scar." Gethin touched his cheek. "Just a slight mark. But why? Is it important? She'd already left the area before anything happened."

"You know this for certain, do you? You saw her

go?"

"I..." Gethin was going to have to face unpalatable possibilities soon, but he really didn't want to discuss them with Armstrong. "I didn't see but I think I heard a car."

"When would this have been?"

"Oh, about two, three..." He had no idea when Vera had been murdered, but hopefully long after that.

"Rubbish. Couldn't have heard anything in that storm," said Henry.

Gethin turned a meaningful look on his father, which made no impression.

"But you didn't see her go," repeated Armstrong.

"No. All right, no I didn't see her go."

"Which means she could have left any time in the night?"

"Except that the road was flooded. Like I told you at the station, the bridge was blocked."

"Yes. But the lane does lead over to Blaenllafni. She could have gone that way."

"Well, yes, I suppose, but what are you suggesting? That a novelist, having a quiet writing retreat, would suddenly go berserk and viciously murder her neighbour, a woman she barely knew. I don't think she'd even spoken to Vera Broderick."

"Margaret Gittings," said Henry.

"Now, Dad," pleaded Gethin. "Don't go confusing things again. You're getting it mixed up." He turned back to Armstrong. "He does that, I'm afraid. Gets mixed up. Margaret Gittings, that was an old case. It's the mention of murder, I suppose. Her son murdered a girl, but she moved away. Years ago, that was, before my father took over the school in Brongarn."

"And you never associated the two, Vera Broderick and Margaret Gittings?" Armstrong stepped around him and helped himself to a chair near Henry. "But you did, Mr Matthews."

Henry nodded, satisfied. "Margaret Gittings. Born just down the road in Nantfuan."

"Dad, please," said Gethin.

Armstrong held a hand up to silence him. "The fact is, the woman you know as Vera Broderick was indeed the same Margaret Gittings."

"Good God." Gethin exchanged startled glances with Sue, who had come, open-mouthed, to the kitchen door.

"You're kidding."

"No. The agent who dealt with her properties confirmed her identity." Armstrong turned back to Henry. "It was common knowledge in the area, was it? You all knew who she was?"

"Ha. You think we'd have left her there, sitting quiet, if we'd known?"

"How come you did know, Dad?" asked Gethin.

"Bryn figured it out, didn't he?"

"Bryn Davies? Oh shit. He was at the pub with us. How long has he known?"

"Figured it out a couple of days back. I saw him in the lane yesterday, had him in for a cuppa. He had a bag of scones, God help us. Don't know what he was going to do with them. He didn't seem to know, himself. That's Bryn. Doesn't know what way's up or down half the time, poor bugger. But he knew who she was. Margaret Gittings."

Detective Armstrong had started to take notes, but he'd stopped to sit back instead, eyes narrowing. "Bryn Davies. This would be—"

"No-one," said Gethin, hastily. "Just a drunk, does odd jobs here and there. Quite harmless."

"Bryn Davies whose daughter Bethany was Timothy Gittings' first victim."

"Terrible business," said Henry.

Sue, white-faced, had come to sit with them. "That poor girl," she whispered.

"And he knew the mother was living in one the cottages up the lane," persisted Armstrong. He frowned at Gethin. "You mentioned meeting him in the pub."

"Yes, I was chatting with Lisa about Mad Annie. Sorry, that was what we called her."

"But you never called her Margaret Gittings?

"Good God, no! I had no idea. Are you sure? Bryn was drunk. Yes, he seemed to be taken by the name, Vera Broderick, but why would that—"

"Margaret Gittings' mother's maiden name was Vera Broderick."

"Are you sure?"

"Quite sure. As soon as we discovered her real identity, we reopened the files on the Gittings case. Her parents ran a shop in Nantfuan. They were well known in their time, although probably forgotten now. We've been checking on possible links in the area, Bryn Davies being the most obvious one. He still lives in Brongarn, up the valley. One of our officers is calling on him right now."

"Won't find him in," said Henry. "Not till the pubs close."

"Maybe." Armstrong had shut his book. He rose to his feet. "Well, thank you. That was very useful. We are still interested, however, in contacting Lisa Craven. If that is really her name."

"Of course it is. Why wouldn't it be?"

"The address she gave the agency is a bit of a problem. The family living there have never heard of her."

"Well… well, the agency must have written it down wrong. Or something."

"But the fact remains that we do urgently need to speak to her and her whereabouts, at this moment, is unknown, so—"

"Has it occurred to you?" Gethin grabbed a handful of his hair, pacing. "Whoever killed Vera, or Margaret, or whoever she was – they could have attacked Lisa too.

Her kitchen window was broken. They could have kidnapped her."

"That is one possibility, and a very good reason why we need to find her. She had a car, I understand, but it's not there now."

"They could have taken it, too."

"Make? Colour?"

"Kia. Picanto, I think. Red."

"We found scrapings of red paint on rocks down the lane from the cottages. And various items of women's clothing in the mud. It does look as if someone had a lot of trouble turning the car there. You say the lane was flooded by the bridge."

"Yes. Look, you need to get out and find her!"

"We certainly aim to." Armstrong smiled, in what

was presumably intended to be a reassuring manner. "In the meantime, if she does contact you at all, I hope you'll let us know. And let her know that we are very anxious to speak to her."

"Yes, yes, of course."

Gethin shut the door on the detective and turned back.

"He thinks she did it," said Henry.

"That's ridiculous!"

"Of course it is," said Sue, soothingly. "Such a nice girl."

"Well, it had to be her or Bryn Davies, now, didn't it?" insisted Henry.

Gethin swore silently. Why did his father's grasp on logic have to reassert itself now?

"And ask yourself, what do you really know about her?" said Henry.

"Enough to know she wouldn't murder anyone!"

"Bamboozled by a pretty face, that's your trouble. Psychopaths don't have to look like wild-eyed monsters, you know."

"She is not a psychopath!"

"Lied about her address."

"They misheard. That doesn't mean anything. It certainly doesn't make her a psychopath."

"It makes her a liar. And think about it, boy. If not her, it must have been Bryn. You think he's capable of murder, poor bugger?"

"He'd have reason enough."

"I don't think it would have been anyone from round here," said Sue.

Henry laughed. "Margaret Gittings? I could name

twenty locals who'd happily do her in."

"Stop it," said Gethin. "Just stop it, will you. I saw her. Believe me, there was nothing happy about it." He headed up to his own room and stood staring out into the dark. Remembering the body, twisting on its rope, eyes bulging, mouth bloody, the angry words scrawled on the walls. He shut it out. Whatever had happened there, it was done. What mattered now was Lisa. Where the hell was she?

Doubts

Despite Sue's prediction that he would sleep like a log after all that trauma, Gethin hardly slept at all. He was out early, in the dark, on the excuse of seeing to the sheep and checking on the fence his father had mentioned. He just wanted chill fresh air to wash away the overheated thoughts that had kept him tossing and turning all night.

Where was Lisa?

Hooking broken wire back into place as a makeshift repair before he fetched the proper tools, Gethin mocked himself for trying to hold two contradictory notions at the same time. He wanted the police to find Lisa, because she might be kidnapped, injured, scared. He wanted the police to stop looking for Lisa, because she had nothing to do with all this. And all the while, he was doing his level best to avoid a third scenario, one he couldn't bear to contemplate. But there were the facts: only two people had been in those cottages up the lane, Mad Annie and Lisa. One had been brutally murdered and the other had vanished without a word. What was the obvious explanation?

He could concoct some Gothic alternatives, with homicidal strangers roaming the hills, but this wasn't Hammer House of Horrors fiction. It was worse than that; it was reality. Vera Broderick was really Margaret Gittings, an obvious target for revenge, and Lisa

Craven, her neighbour, was… who exactly?

Gethin leaned back against a fence post, folded his arms and faced it. What did he really know about her? Nothing. She hadn't been particularly forthcoming about anything, apart from claiming that she was writing a book, which she hadn't permitted him to see. Would an aspiring author seriously choose a cottage at Pontgwartheg as a writing retreat? Would anyone seriously choose Pontgwartheg for anything? Yes, someone who wanted to hunt down Margaret Gittings and beat her secrets out of her. Someone untraceable because she wasn't really who she said she was. Someone who had been playing him all along.

No, no, no, that was all too depressing.

If she were one of the bereaved relatives, it would make some sort of sense, maybe. The Gittings case wasn't something Gethin knew much about, except that it had still been a source of grief and anger in the area when his father had taken over at the school in Brongarn. He had been looking forward to moving on to the secondary school in Abergelyn and more concerned about the ribbing he was getting for being the son of the new head at primary school. He remembered the funeral of Debbie Davies, the missing girl's mother, partly because his nan had been upset and partly because a punch-up had broken out afterwards in a debate about whether her death had been accidental or suicide. He remembered his father intervening, much to his own embarrassment.

Bethany Davies had never been found. That was the issue. Everyone knew who'd done it but no one knew where he'd put her. Except his mother? Was that why there had always been such ill feeling erupting to the surface whenever Margaret Gittings' name had cropped up? She was the keeper of his secrets, so naturally all the grieving relatives would be keen to get the truth out of her.

Oh God, it was such a mess. Give him computer coding any day.

He stomped back to the house and found Sue waiting for him at the door, her expression both distressed and excited.

"Gethin! Have you heard?"

His pulse quickened. "Heard what?"

"They've arrested Bryn Davies! That poor man. Carted him off from the Drovers last night. Arrested for the murder of Vera Broderick. Well, if she was really Margaret Gittings, like they say, can you blame him?"

"I'm not blaming anyone for anything just yet, Sue. But Bryn? Seriously, do you think he would have been capable of it?"

"Strong man, Bryn, even when he's drunk."

Gethin sighed. Bryn's guilt would let Lisa off the hook, wouldn't it? But Bryn... Oh hell.

"And that's not all," said Sue, almost gabbling as the excitement increased in her voice. "It was on the wireless. Would you believe it? I can hardly credit it myself."

"Believe what?" Gethin had guided her back into the house. His father was already up and dressed, as keen to give the news as Sue had been.

"They've found the bodies, that's what. On the news. Dug up a book with all the burials in it. Not Bryn's girl, not yet, but the others, over in Lincolnshire.

257

How about that, then? I'd call that an almighty coincidence."

"Yes." Gethin sat down. "Isn't it?" He frowned. "Did they say… It wasn't Lisa who found it, was it?"

"Oh, no, some retired policeman, apparently. Walking his dog. Dog walker; I'd call that a bit of a cliché."

"I don't know about the cliché, but coincidence, yes. Bodies found the same time the killer's mother is murdered. It's all… Well, it's just weird, isn't it?"

"I can hardly believe it," said Sue, handing Gethin a bacon buttie, still warm. "Can't get my head round it at all."

Gethin took a bite, chewing slowly. He wasn't sure he wanted to get his head around any of it. Something was going on. Something very complicated, and that convinced him Bryn Davies couldn't be responsible. Bryn was a broken drunk, capable of a wild burst of anger maybe, but not remotely capable of an intricate conspiracy.

* * *

There he was at the police station at Abergelyn again. Gethin had hoped he'd seen the last of it, but once more he was entering of his own volition and asking to speak again to DS Armstrong. He had a ten-minute wait, staring at posters about crime prevention, before Armstrong appeared and ushered him into an interview room.

"Remembered something new, Mr Matthews?"

"No, I told you every single detail that I knew,

yesterday. I've really come about Bryn Davies. You've arrested him."

"He's helping us with our enquiries," corrected Armstrong. "He hasn't been charged, if that's what you're thinking."

"It couldn't have been him. I've been thinking about it, and it really couldn't have been. And you know, he's been through enough in his life, without piling this on him as well."

"We're aware of what he's been through. More than most people could cope with. I'm guessing a jury would consider that a very convincing motive for murder."

"Yes, well, yes, maybe. But what about the other relatives? They've been through the same, haven't they? They'd have a motive, too. Bethany Davies wasn't the only girl murdered."

"She was the only one in these parts. Or at least the only we know about."

"Yes, but, look, I've been asking around. You picked Bryn up from The Drovers in Nantfuan, didn't you? Right. I went there, asked Mandy Jenkins, the landlady, and she said Bryn had been there all the previous evening, in that storm. He practically lives in the place. Didn't leave till…" Gethin hesitated.

"Well after official closing time?"

"Er, something like that."

"It may come as a surprise to you, Mr Matthews, but it did occur to us to make the same enquiries. Yes, Bryn Davies was at the Drovers until eleven thirty, when a Mr Rogers kindly drove him back to his home in Brongarn."

"Okay, that proves it, doesn't it? He couldn't possibly have killed Vera."

"Nothing to stop him leaving his house again, in the night."

"But he couldn't have reached her cottage. The bridge was blocked. I didn't clear it until the morning, just before I found Vera, and it meant the road up the valley was impassable."

"Probably someone on foot could have found a way. Up through the trees. Besides, are you certain when the bridge was blocked?"

"Well, no, but… oh come on, Bryn would have been blind drunk. You're not saying he managed to walk four or five miles, at night, in pouring rain—"

Armstrong held up a hand to stop him. "All right, Mr Matthews. No, we're not saying that. And although we had reason enough to question him, we are not considering him as our prime suspect. When I said he was helping us with our enquiries, I meant just that. Other enquiries. We are now searching for the remains of his daughter, in woods at Brongarn."

"Oh."

Armstrong sat back. "I assume you've heard the news. Timothy Gittings buried a record of his victims and their graves, and the book has been unearthed, in Lincolnshire. We've received copies of the pages relating to Bethany Davies and we are now using them, with the help of her father and other residents in Brongarn, to identify the place where he buried her."

"Oh. Thank God." Gethin whistled his relief. He really hadn't wanted Bryn to suffer any more. Even if it meant…

"Closure at last, we hope, for one very painful old case," said Armstrong.

"Yes, at last."

"However, we still have a rather more pressing case to concentrate on. The killing of Margaret Gittings."

"Yes."

"And assuming we discount Bryn Davies as a suspect, for now, who do you think we should be looking at?"

"I really don't… Do you know when she died, exactly?"

"Initial tests suggest some time in the evening of the third. Undoubtedly before midnight but we should have a more accurate assessment soon. Tell us about your relationship with Lisa Craven, Mr Matthews."

"Lisa? It was hardly a relationship. She came to lunch, once. We took a walk. Went to the pub a couple of times. That's about it. She told me she was writing a book. There's really nothing more I can tell you about her."

"Fair hair. A scar on her cheek."

"Yes, barely visible." Gethin touched his own cheek.

Armstrong considered him for a moment, then opened a file and produced a photograph. "It wouldn't be this woman, would it?"

Gethin stared at the picture of a petite, middle-aged woman with fair hair and a noticeable scar on one cheek, her face strangely expressionless, almost childlike. She was clinging to the arm of a man of similar age, forties or fifties. "No. No, nothing like her. Much younger for a start. Who is she?"

"Since you've confirmed that she is not your Lisa Craven, we can eliminate her from our enquiries. No need to drag her into a story that she knows nothing about, but we had to check. This one is Timothy's sister. She was born Clare Louise Gittings, although she was given another name when she was fostered. She was taken into care after she was mutilated as a baby. The details are on record. Your description of Lisa Craven raised the possibility that she might be Margaret's daughter, seeking revenge on the mother who failed to protect her. I think we can discount that, now. But we still need to find the real Lisa Craven. Or rather, the real woman claiming to be Lisa Craven. A woman who came, out of the blue, to rent a cottage next to Margaret Gittings, and who seems to have vanished without trace on the very night Margaret died violently in such extremely suspicious circumstances."

"Yes." Gethin gave in. Armstrong had a very convoluted way of saying that Margaret Gittings had been murdered, but there it was. Lisa. Stop trying to dance around it. It had to be Lisa. "I know. I know."

"And just a few hours before the buried record of Timothy Gittings" crimes is unearthed in Lincolnshire."

"I know," repeated Gethin. "I know and I don't know. It either makes no sense at all, or too much sense."

"And you really had nothing more to do with Lisa Craven than a casual drink and a stroll on the hills?"

"What more could I have had? I only knew her a few days."

"Are you sure? You hadn't, perhaps, discovered Margaret Gittings" identity and alerted someone who you knew was hunting for her?"

"No! I didn't have a clue about who Vera Broderick really was. Not until my father came out with it yesterday, and he only knew because he'd had tea with Bryn. And Bryn knew nothing about her until I mentioned her at the pub. He must have made the connection."

"Yes, he is quite a mine of information on Margaret and her family. Hardly surprising, of course. She destroyed him. Meanwhile..." Armstrong rose. "The hunt goes on for Lisa Craven. A nationwide alert has been issued and we're going to find her sooner or later. I'm sure you appreciate how very anxious we are to speak to her, so you will inform us if she makes contact, won't you?"

Gethin hesitated before replying. "Yes, of course," he said.

Polite queries

Barbara straightened her jacket, composed her face, then opened the door with a look of mild surprise. "Ah. Sam, isn't it? Or are you here in your official capacity as DI Willis? Do come in."

"Hello, Barbara." Willis carefully wiped his feet on the map. "Is Malcolm here?"

"I believe he may be around somewhere."

Willis grinned. "You never rely on belief, Barbara. I'm sure you always know exactly where he is."

"Oh." She laughed. "If only."

Malcolm had already appeared from the kitchen.

"Detective Inspector Willis. What a lovely surprise." His deadpan expression dispelled any notion that the surprise was genuine. He offered his hand.

Willis shook it. "Stick to Sam, on this occasion. Call it a courtesy visit prior to a formal interview."

"I see." Malcolm showed him into the lounge. Barbara followed them in and seated herself primly, with knitting that looked as if it was brought out only for such occasions.

Willis sat down and looked at them both. "I'm surprised your very, very clever dogs aren't here, too. Eager to be just as helpful as before."

"They're chasing each other round the garden," said Barbara. "I can fetch them in if you like. I'm sure they won't mind being interviewed. Malcolm will be happy to interpret. He's quite fluent in Canine."

"Yes, I expect he had no trouble issuing them with precise commands in Hackling Wood."

"Just the usual," said Malcolm. "Sit, stay, you know."

Willis continued looking from one to the other. Neither blushed. "Come on. You just happened to find Timothy Gittings" book at almost the exact moment Margaret Gittings" body was discovered."

"In one of the Welsh mining valleys, wasn't it?" asked Barbara. "Such a coincidence. I was quite astonished."

Malcolm frowned at her. "All right, yes. What policeman worth his salt ever believes in coincidences?"

Willis's fingers toyed with the air. "Just to get it clear, before we go any further, I am assuming that you deny having any part in Margaret Gittings' murder?"

Malcolm glanced at the books on the shelves. "I'd swear on oath, on the Bible, but there doesn't seem to be one to hand, so I can give you nothing but my word that I had no part in it. Nor did Barbara. It would have been physically impossible. We were both here on the third. Dinner with neighbours after delivering a supply of applewood trimmings for the village Guy Fawkes night extravaganza. We were with Phil and Anne until…" He glanced at Barbara for confirmation. "Tennish? And off down to Welsey the following morning, as you know."

"I accept that physical involvement would have been impossible, yes."

"And there was no involvement of any other sort.

Not in murder. We had no inkling such a thing would happen, and I am not convinced that anyone I've had any dealings with intended it, either."

"Who exactly have you had dealings with?"

"Well, there's Anne and Phil next door," said Barbara, brightly. "We talk to them almost every day. And Gill and Jerry Brown, of course. And do we count the postman, and Mr Giles at the corner shop?"

"Thank you, Barbara." Willis smiled. "I was referring to dealings concerning Margaret Gittings, not groceries or chats over the fence. How about dealings with a woman calling herself Lisa Craven?"

Malcolm drew a deep breath. "I had never heard that name until it was mentioned on the radio."

"But you might know her by another name? Five foot six or seven. Fair hair. Scar on her right cheek?"

"No. No one of that description." Malcolm caught Barbara's look of puzzlement and discreetly shook his head. Not discreetly enough. Willis caught it.

"Someone of what description, then? Come on, Malcolm. Can we stop these games? The Gittings woman was murdered and suddenly you take it into your head to rush down to Hackling Wood and miraculously find the book her son buried there. Aren't you stretching credulity beyond its limits?"

"Yes. I think I probably am. Okay. Yes, I knew someone was urgently trying to track down Margaret Gittings, in the hope of discovering the whereabouts of the missing girls. I told her everything I knew. That's all. I don't believe for one moment that she had any thoughts of killing anyone. She just wanted the book. She found it. They fought over it and she took it. She later found Margaret, dead. That's what she told me and I believe her."

"Oh you do, do you?"

"Yes. She did contact me, that night. She was distressed. She told me a courier would deliver the evidence to me and, well, I knew what to do and I did it. Barbara had no idea about any of this."

"Oh bullshit," said Barbara.

Willis rolled his eyes. "The album was the evidence that allowed us to find the bodies. You could have handed it in to us as soon as you received it. Why couldn't your mysterious huntress have taken it straight to the South Wales police? Or just told them that she knew where it was? Let them carry out a proper search, no need for breaking and entering or violence or—"

"Because there was no time! We had to get straight in and find the body of—"

"Rachel Redbourn." Willis finished it for him. "I understand. I take it you've heard?"

"Yes. Jennifer Redbourn died early this morning. Her brother phoned to tell me. I think it was only the desperation to hear what she needed to hear that kept her hanging on that long. She's asked that Rachel's remains be buried with her."

"I am sure that can be arranged."

"You know, don't you, Sam, that going through proper channels, arguing to reopen an ancient case, applying for warrants – it would have taken too long for Jenny. That was what all the deception was about. Nothing more sinister than that. There was no conspiracy to murder Margaret Gittings. It was just about getting hold of the book and finding Rachel in

267

time – with the added bonus of finding the others too."

"Yes, all right. No conspiracy to murder, you say. But she was murdered, and there is now a nationwide hunt for the elusive Lisa Craven. Would you like to fill me in on that?"

Malcolm hesitated, then shrugged. "Rosanna Quillan. Former police detective. Brunette. No scar."

"Thank you."

"I suppose you'll want me to come to the station for the formal interview. As I told you, Barbara had nothing to do with it."

"Oh, utter nonsense," said Barbara. "As if you could do anything without me knowing about it. I'll fetch my coat."

"Why not?" said Willis, pleasantly. "To save us wasting any more time, have you had any further contact with this Rosanna Quillan?"

"Yes. We spoke on the phone this morning."

"And do you have any idea where we might find her?"

Malcolm pulled on his jacket and checked his watch. "I'd say your best bet, about now, would be Abergelyn police station."

Confession

Gethin emerged from the dreary police station and leaned against the wall, head bowed, contemplating his hands and the evolving mysteries of this case. Bryn didn't seem to be a serious suspect and that was good. But Lisa. If she did contact him, what would he do?

No point trying to dwell on it now. He straightened up... And found himself looking at Lisa Craven.

She paused on the steps, as taken aback as he was. "Gethin!"

He opened his mouth but couldn't think of anything to say.

"I'm sorry," she said.

"Tell me you didn't murder her."

She shut her eyes for a second. "No, I didn't.

Whether anyone will believe me is another matter. It's out of my hands now. All I can do is tell the truth."

"They're looking for you. The police, up and down the country, apparently."

"Yes, I know. I would have handed myself in soon anyway, but when I heard they'd taken Bryn Davies in as a suspect—"

"He's not. Not anymore. They're looking for his daughter."

"Thank God. Still..." She braced herself and came on up the steps. "I'd best get it over with." She paused at the door. "Would you mind coming in with me?"

"Me?"

"I'll understand if you'd rather not."

"No, no, I'll come." More bewildered than ever, he followed her in, hovering behind as she approached the desk.

"I believe you're looking for me," she said.

The desk sergeant had already summed her up.

"You're Lisa Craven?"

"I'd like to give a statement."

"Yes, we'd like you to, as well."

"And I'd like Gethin Matthews to be there. The explanation is for him as much as for you."

* * *

"Your name, for the tape," said DS Armstrong.

"Rosanna Elizabeth Quillan."

"Not Lisa Craven?"

"No. Sorry."

"Why the alias?"

"Because I thought I might find myself involved in criminal activities."

"Such as murder."

"No! Such as theft. Breaking and entering. Nothing violent."

"But you did come prepared to break the law."

She gazed at the ceiling. "Yes."

"Been engaged in much crime before?"

"Not as a criminal, no."

"Oh?"

"I was with the police for a while. I last served as a detective constable with Thames Valley."

"No shit!" said Gethin, under his breath.

"Oh, did you?" Armstrong braced himself against the table. "Well, well. And what induced you to change sides?"

"The need to get some sort of closure for a mother before she died."

Armstrong studied her through narrowed eyes. "Jennifer Redbourn, I suppose you mean."

"Yes. There was..." Rosanna shrugged. "No time for the niceties. She died this morning."

"So I've been informed. All right. Let's hear it then. Your story, please."

Ex-police detective Rosanna Quillan delivered her story precisely and succinctly, sticking to the salient points. There was no need for prompting from Armstrong, and Gethin kept silent, although he was open-mouthed at times.

Rosanna finished. "I opened the shed door and found her hanging. It was obvious she was dead." She waited.

Armstrong sat back, perusing the desk. Finally he looked up. "And you seriously expect me to believe all that?"

"No. I have no expectations. I can only say what happened, and it's up to you what you believe."

"All right, having found her hanging, you did what?"

"I drove on. I knew the evidence in the book could identify Rachel Redbourn's grave, and time was running out, so I found a courier to deliver it to a contact in Lincolnshire immediately." There was no emotion in her voice. Her statement was prepared.

"A courier."

"Yes. Twenty-four-hour emergency service. He collected the package from Cardiff Gate services."

"And your contact in Lincolnshire?"

"Malcolm Cannell. Retired Detective Superintendent Cannell. I phoned him to say it was on its way."

"Ah, the dog walker. Of course."

"He had no idea how I'd come by it. I suggested he pretend to find it, to speed up the discovery of the bodies. That's all he did."

"All right. Who else was helping you in this noble enterprise?"

"No one else. I phoned Superintendent Cannell this morning. He said I should give his name."

"Very considerate of him. Anything else to add to this cock and bull story? You and the murder victim are the sole residents in a valley cut off by floods. You turn your back for five minutes, and she's mysteriously hanged by person or persons unknown. Am I supposed to believe the fairies did it?"

"No. Person or persons unknown."

"And you saw no one else in the vicinity?"

Rosanna drew a deep breath. "I saw a car. A vehicle, anyway. I didn't think about it at the time. When I ran to my car, to get away from Margaret, I caught a glimpse of something parked a long way up the lane, at a farm entrance. After I'd found her hanging, I drove up that way to get away, and it wasn't there then."

"A car or some sort of vehicle."

"It was dark, stormy. I saw a light. Interior, I think. That's all."

"And you didn't hear it drive off?"

"Hard to say in that storm."

"All right. Let's say the murderer was in that car. Do you have any idea who that might have been?"

"No. No idea at all." There was a distinct obstinacy in her voice.

Armstrong rocked back in his chair. "Congratulations. I can't remember ever coming across quite such an improbable story." He glanced at Gethin.

"Can you, Mr Matthews?"

"Er, well I always thought the magic bullet theory in the Kennedy assassination was totally improbable," said Gethin, not daring to look at Rosanna. "That would be my benchmark."

She shrugged apologetically. "Sorry, Gethin. I really didn't like deceiving you. But what I've said is the truth, I swear, whatever the police conclude."

"Yes!" He faced Armstrong. "I believe her. It makes perfect sense."

Armstrong laughed. "I'd say it made no sense at all. I'd say it's all complete bull, if it weren't for evidence that's cast a slightly different light on the death of Margaret Gittings."

"Oh?"

"The autopsy was as thorough as you'd expect, and very illuminating. The victim's hands were bound – you'll both have noticed that. But it seems they were bound post-mortem. What do you make of that?"

Rosanna stared at him. "When she was already dead? To make it look like an execution?"

"Like removing the stepladder she had kicked over in her thrashing when she jumped off it. A splinter from it was found in her leg, which would be improbable if someone had simply pulled it from under her. But it was stacked neatly, well away from her, as if someone wanted us to rule out any idea of suicide."

"Yes, but… How could it have been suicide? Her face, her mouth, there was blood. She'd been beaten."

"Her body exhibited scratches and bruises that would match the scuffle she had with you, if we are to believe your account. But she probably caused the blood herself by swallowing sharp objects, immediately before she died. I don't think it would have been possible for someone to force her to swallow them."

"I don't understand. Why would she swallow…" Rosanna gasped. "Toys! His trophies. There was a tin in that cupboard, as well as the book. She was keeping his toys safe for him, too. Is that it?"

"Yes. It looks like it. A pink plastic hair slide has already been identified by a school friend of Bethany Davies. Bethany was wearing it on the day she vanished. There was also a silver cross matching the description given by Rachel Redbourn's parents, a crushed bangle, a rabbit badge and a diamond ring. Swallowing any of them could have torn a few blood vessels, I imagine. The real damage, which would probably have proved fatal even without the noose, was the kitchen knife she managed to down. Not very efficiently. She was no circus sword swallower. Made an unholy mess of herself with that one."

"Knife?" whispered Rosanna. "The knife he used on Laura Wakefield was never found. Oh, Jesus."

"The supposition is that, regardless of whoever attempted to make the scene appear like an execution, or rather a lynching, Margaret Gittings actually died trying to conceal the remaining evidence of her son's crimes. She'd already lost the book she'd been hiding for him. Perhaps she thought swallowing his treasures would keep them secret. She must have been totally unbalanced, as you've already said. It does mean that, while I'm sure we can come up with a great many offences to charge you with, Miss Quillan, murder will probably not be one of them."

"You think not," said Rosanna, staring at the floor.

There was a tap on the door and a constable peered in.

"Yes, Trevor? What is it?"

"They've found her, sir. Remains. Woods across the river in Brongarn. Couple of locals recognised the spot from the photo."

"Okay. Good. Jones is dealing with the press, isn't he?" Armstrong turned back to Rosanna. "I'll have more questions for you, Miss Quillan. A lot more, but no need, I imagine, to cart you off to the custody suite to clutter up one of our cells. As you came here voluntarily, I assume you're not planning to leave the country in the night."

"No. I'll stay until you decide what to charge me with."

"Where will you be staying? A genuine address, this time, please."

"I'll find—"

"She'll be staying with me," interrupted Gethin. "Hendy, Pontgwartheg."

"No, you can't," Rosanna began.

"Yes, don't be daft. You don't want to be stuck in

275

some hotel, all alone."

"I'll trust you to keep her safe and available then," said Armstrong. "Give her time to think about who else might have been in that car up the lane."

* * *

Rosanna followed Gethin out into the November gloom.

He glanced at her as they reached the bottom of the steps. "Got your car?"

"No. I came by taxi. I wasn't expecting to be leaving."

"The Land Rover then. This way." He gestured along the street. "Car park. A bit of a hike, sorry, but at least it's not raining."

She fell into step beside him. "You shouldn't really be offering to put me up. Not after what I've done."

"But what have you done? If you'd murdered her – I mean, obviously you didn't, that goes without saying…"

"No, it doesn't."

"Well, I know you didn't, but you never expected the police to believe your story and you still handed yourself in, which is pretty brave, I reckon. Now they know you didn't murder her—"

"But I did. That's the trouble. I thought, when I came in, that whatever else I'd done, at least I hadn't been the one to kill her. But it was me all along. Not that obscene window dressing afterwards, but I killed her."

"It was suicide. That's what Armstrong said, didn't

he?"

"But I drove her to it, that's the point. I played on her maternal loyalty, I stole the book she'd been guarding sacredly, all these years, stole her only reason for existing, however insane that reason was. I knew how disturbed she was. I should have guessed what she'd do, once I'd taken that album. I watched her crawl up to that shed and I just drove away."

"You took the evidence she'd been holding back, leaving all those families in torment, when she could have eased their grief years ago. You saw what it's done to Bryn Davies. At least he'll have some sort of closure at last. Closure that Margaret Gittings had been denying him. You can't blame yourself for her actions, Lisa. Rosanna. Sorry, do you mind? I can only think of you as Lisa."

"You can call me anything you like. I can think of some names you'd probably like to use. I am sorry I was lying to you from the word Go. I didn't anticipate…"

"Having a nosy neighbour pestering you from the moment you arrived?"

"If things had been different…"

"You were really a detective?"

"Not for very long. I became disillusioned with the sort of justice the system delivers. I'm not sure now that alternative forms of justice are any better."

"I'm not a philosopher, so I'm not even going there."

He turned onto the High Street. "I'm just going to Hendy, and you're coming with me. Nice and simple, eh?"

"Even after me deceiving you right from the start?"

"Not maliciously, though, was it?"

"No. I hated doing it."

"I understand that. But we ought to be thinking about what now. If the police want to talk to you again, you ought to have a solicitor. My father uses Evans, Price and Garth. We could—"

"It's okay. I won't need a solicitor. I'll simply be telling the truth. No more lies."

Justice

The winter's chill was alleviated a little by a welcome glimpse of the sun. It was outdone by the blaze of a thousand daffodils, bunches of them along with wreaths and sprays. The steep cemetery of Hebron Chapel, rising above the grey village of Brongarn seemed to be in bloom. Everyone wanted to pay their respects as Bethany Davies was laid to rest at last, beside her mother.

Rosanna stood in the corner of the graveyard, with Gethin. She hadn't attended the service in the chapel, but she had to be here to witness this. Most of those who had come to join in the hymns and prayers, filling the chapel for the first time in years, and spilling out into the street, were already wending their way home. Reporters were packing up their cameras and recorders.

Bryn Davies, looking lost in his best suit, was standing at the grave surrounded by a few family members, and by a cluster of people who had become a second family because of events more than a quarter of a century earlier. Crippled families of lost girls. They all hugged each other, shook hands, clapped Bryn on the shoulder.

One looked her way, spoke, and they all turned. Rosanna waited as they approached. Peter Fitzpatrick, Sharon Knowles, Amy Redbourn – the same angels of retribution who had met her at Andrew Rollinson's house. They exchanged glances then faced her.

"You were at Jodie's funeral," said Fitzpatrick. He had lost the intense rage that had burned in him at their last meeting. There was a hint of quietness, if not peace, in the bleakness of his expression. "I saw you there, but you didn't come up to speak."

"She was at all of them," said Sharon. "Weren't you?"

"Yes," said Rosanna.

"You got the book from the evil bitch."

"From Margaret Gittings, yes."

"And the police think you were responsible for what happened to her. Bryn said they'd questioned you when they finished with him."

"Once they'd ruled him out, I was the only obvious suspect left," said Rosanna.

Sharon gave a twisted smile. "Only you? Didn't you suggest any others to them?"

"No."

"Why not?"

Rosanna shrugged. "I didn't want to cause trouble for people who had already suffered enough pain."

"We were questioned," said Fitzpatrick. "We all had alibis."

"Good."

"Fake alibis. We called in favours. You don't look surprised."

"I thought you would."

"We're going to put it right, now. We'd have done it before, but we wanted to see our girls laid to rest first."

"Of course."

Fitzpatrick studied his clasped hands. "We shouldn't have left you to stew. We knew you were looking for her round here, so we came too, spoke to Bryn. He told us he'd just learned where she was living, and that she had a woman living next door. We didn't know it would be you, and that you'd already found the book. If we'd known, we wouldn't have gone near the place."

"Yes, we would," said Amy Redbourn. "I wanted her to pay, regardless."

Sharon put an arm round her. "We were angry. We were going to kick the truth out of her. We didn't want to leave the car outside her house where the neighbour would see it and start getting suspicious, so we parked up the road and walked down."

Amy laughed shortly. "In a bloody thunderstorm, Got fucking drenched."

"We planned to sneak round the back and surprise her, but then you appeared, running for your car. We couldn't have been more than a hundred yards away, but you didn't see us in the dark. You headed off down the road."

"Then we thought, to hell with being quiet," said Sharon, coolly. "Went straight up to her door and hammered on it, rapped on the window, yelled for her. No reply, so we broke the door down and ransacked the place."

They stood in silence for a moment, huddled in their thick coats, remembering.

"You didn't kill her," said Rosanna, quietly.

"No," said Fitzpatrick. "She'd killed herself. They know that, don't they? Would we have done it, if we'd found her alive? I don't know." He frowned, then repeated it. "I don't know. I don't know what we would have done, if we hadn't found the letter."

"Letter!" Army snarled. "A fucking scrawl, blood-spattered, shoved in an envelope, addressed to that evil bastard in Rampton. What did she think we'd do? Stick a stamp on it and post it for her?"

"What did it say? You did read it, didn't you?"

"Of course!" Fitzpatrick shook his head, remembering his disbelief. "We thought it would be a confession, explaining where all the bodies were. An apology for all those years of grief and misery she'd caused us. But no, it was all apologies for betraying him, and telling him she'd make sure his treasures would never be found. You know about his trophies? The bitch had actually swallowed them! We've been asked to identify them. Jodie's badge... The woman didn't seem to grasp that if she killed herself, she'd be opened up in an autopsy. Sick bloody gesture. All she kept saying, in the letter, was that she was sorry, sorry, sorry, for letting him down."

"Sorry!" Amy's fists were clenching. "Sorry for him! Not for us. Not for anything he did, not for everything we'd had to go through. He destroyed us, wrecked our lives! My mother was on her deathbed because of him, and that cow could have told the truth, but no, she was just sorry that she'd let the evil bastard down!" Her voice had risen almost to a scream.

Sharon hugged her tighter. "Hush. It's okay. It's over." She looked at Rosanna over Amy's head. "It was me, all the execution palaver."

"No, it was all of us," insisted Fitzpatrick, but Sharon shushed him.

"Tied her hands, moved the ladder, scrawled the verdict on the wall. Had to, you see. She had no right to kill herself for betraying her son. If she was going to die, it should have been for our girls, for us, for years and bloody years of not knowing and no one caring."

There was silence again. Gethin squeezed Rosanna's hand.

"It seemed bloody pointless after we'd done it," Sharon said at last. "But we couldn't undo it, so we scarpered. Argued the whole way home about how stupid we'd been. And the next thing we knew was the discovery of our girls' remains, all over the news."

"We heard the report of Margaret Gittings being murdered," said Fitzpatrick. "But all we could think about, at that stage, was our girls. We just wanted to claim them, have them home, get them properly buried. But now it's time to confess. It's not as if it matters any more. All we wanted was our girls back, and we've got that. We don't mind paying for the rest."

Rosanna smiled. "I'm guessing the CPS will take their time weighing indisputable evidence against an almost certainly sympathetic jury. I don't imagine the price will be too high."

"No matter," said Fitzpatrick, taking a deep breath. "It's done. It's finished. There's nothing more."

* * *

Gethin walked back to his Land Rover, still holding Rosanna's hand.

"Did you know it was them?"

She nodded. "It had to be."

283

He whistled. "You could have cleared your name at the start."

"I know."

"You are a glutton for punishment, I'll give you that. But at least you'll be cleared now, and like the man said, it's finished, there's nothing more."

"But there is," said Rosanna, climbing into the passenger seat. "Another girl that no one's ever looked for, because we didn't know. She's unclaimed. No one ever reported her missing, but there she is, in the book. It can't be right that—"

"Oh no!" said Gethin, starting the engine. "You're not going to beat yourself up over that one, too."

"No. But I can't help thinking about it. Perhaps it's the saddest case of all."

Part 6: LOOSE END

Diamonds Are Forever

"It might be called wasting police time," said DI Willis.

"Nonsense." Malcolm bent down to fondle his dogs" ears as they strolled around Thresham's village green. "It was quite the reverse. Anything I did merely saved police time."

"You lied," Willis reminded him.

"In a good cause."

"Maybe. Fortunately, we have more important things to deal with, now the inquests are out of the way. You know we've had a possible breakthrough on the sixth victim?"

"The owner of the diamond ring?"

"That's the one. Turns out it's been on the database of stolen goods all this time. Reported stolen by a Mrs Ogilvie, back in 1992. Inscription inside, and the diamond and the hallmarks match."

"Essex. Tell me It's Essex."

"Yep. Down Harlow way. Local police have gone to check up on it."

Malcolm nodded. "I knew it. Margaret Gittings had a cleaning job there for a while. But if this Mrs Ogilvie reported the theft, she can't be victim number six."

"No, she can't, but maybe she'll know who is."

* * *

Mrs Jane Ogilvie was a little deaf, but her memory was as sharp as ever. "Yes, of course, I recall it perfectly. My mother's engagement ring. Naturally it was insured, but it had a sentimental value."

"And the people who you're convinced stole it?" asked the police constable, depositing the fine bone china cup of Earl Grey on the mahogany coffee table to extract his notebook.

"Disgusting people. Gypsies."

"I don't think they were, Mum," said the younger woman, sitting across the room. "Not real Romany."

"Well, layabouts, then. Drop-outs, criminals, they're all the same, aren't they? They were camped on the roadside. Unsavoury. That's the only word for them. They had the ring off my foolish daughter, and the next moment they were gone." Mrs Ogilvie frowned at her companion, who looked slightly shamefaced.

The constable was puzzled.

"Emma Wright," said the younger woman, with a smile. "Née Ogilvie. I was only eight or nine at the time. My mother had told me that I should have Gran's ring, but it was too big for my finger and I put it on my charm bracelet. I'm afraid I didn't appreciate its value, so I gave it to a girl I met on the green, and she gave me a string of beads in return."

"Beads!" snorted her mother. "Mouldy acorns, would you believe. That little hussy saw you coming, and no mistake."

"I was in almighty trouble about it," said Emma.

"You reported it as a theft." The constable was tapping his notebook.

"Because that's what it was: theft," said Mrs Ogilvie. "Trickery. And in return for acorns!"

The constable looked questioningly at Emma.

She shrugged. "My mother says I was naïve, and I'm sure I was, but she didn't seem like a thief to me. Just a lonely girl looking for a friend to play with, and I felt sorry for her. She was rather grubby. A bit smelly, to be honest."

"Could you describe her?"

"Not really. It was thirty years ago. She was very thin, I remember that. Fair hair, like me, but hers was rather tangled. Quite small. I can't think of – oh yes, she said she was eleven but I thought she looked more like my age. That's right, I was nearly nine. It was my birthday a couple of days later and that's when Mum discovered that I'd given the ring away. I'd asked if I could invite Lolly… Yes! Lolly! I remember now. That was her name. Well, it was an odd name, wasn't it? I called her the ice cream girl. Lolly, ice cream, you know?"

"God knows what her name really was," sniffed Mrs Ogilvie. "A born liar. She'll have made up something ridiculous, just to mislead Emma. How did you find the ring, at long last? It was fenced to some crooked dealer, I imagine."

"Er, possibly not." The constable stood up and strolled to the window of the large lounge, squinting across shrubs and lawns and through wide gates to the main road and the wood beyond.

"These travellers camped along the road, you say. That road?

"No, no," scowled Mrs Ogilvie. "On the Harlow Road, other side of the common. It goes without saying they left the place an absolute pigsty."

"The road beyond those woods?"

"That's right."

The constable looked at Emma. "Did this girl, this Lolly, come and visit you here, at all?"

"No. Why?"

"If she had, might she have cut through the wood, to get here?"

"Er, yes, I suppose she would. There is a footpath through it. But she didn't. I'm sure I'd have remembered, if she did."

"No. I see. And she never got as far as this house."

"No. But there was no break in, so why do you ask?"

"Just making general enquiries, madam."

"What are they doing?" demanded Mrs Ogilvie, poking at the curtains with her walking stick.

"I don't know," said Emma, at the window, staring out into the night. "They've got lights in the woods. And police vans, and dogs. Russell went over to ask, but they've got it all taped off, and they wouldn't tell him anything. It doesn't sound good, does it? What on earth does it have to do with Gran's ring? And that girl. Do you think something happened to her?"

"Nothing she wasn't asking for, I'm sure," said Mrs Ogilvie. She scowled at her daughter. "Don't look at me like that. That sort, you know what they are."

"Mum." Emma shook her head. "I know what you

are, that's the trouble."

Mrs Ogilvie hauled herself up. "If you are going be all prim and censorious, I am going to bed. Good night."

Of All The Trees That Are In The Wood

DS Harry Singh, of Essex Police, spread his arms wide as his boss studied the photograph for the umpteenth time.

"We're ninety-nine percent certain that we've got the spot, Guv. The bend in the path, the type of trees, that bank exactly there." He frowned at the cross crayoned onto the picture. "Even a bit of rope embedded in a branch exactly where you can see that swing, there." He pointed to the arc of a suspended tyre at the edge of the photograph. "It has to be that spot. But we've dug and there's nothing. The geophiz hasn't picked up anything in the surrounding area. The dogs haven't had a whiff of anything. It's a blank. Do we carry on searching the entire wood?"

His DI sat back and folded his arms. "Hard to justify the resources if the one definite clue we have is a dead end." He caught Singh's wince. "Bad choice of words?"

He pulled out a second photograph of a grubby and under-nourished fair-haired girl gazing quizzically at the camera. Hard to tell if her expression was puzzlement, surprise or terror. "No post-mortem shot of this one, so was this bank just where he killed her and then he carted her body away in his van? It's bloody frustrating. I'd give my eye teeth to be the one to find Gittings' last missing victim."

"Superintendent Cannell suggested launching a

public appeal, Guv."

"Yes! I'd like to remind him that he's retired, and this never was his force's case, anyway. It's ours."

"Still worth thinking about, though, Guv? Her family must have missed her, surely."

"But we have no girl reported missing in that time slot."

"If they were as criminal as Jane Ogilvie seems to think, would they have reported anything to us? Even a missing child?"

"Probably not. But yes, okay, a national appeal might do something to identify her at least. Give her a name, other than lollypop."

"Lolly, sir."

"Yes, well, Lolly. A name like that would surely mean something to someone. I'll ask the Superintendent – retired Superintendent – to address the nation. He can mention the ring. It's been in the papers already, anyway."

* * *

"Just an orange juice, thanks," said Singh.

"Of course, you're on duty," said Malcolm.

"And I don't drink."

"Well, if I can't get you drunk and worm the truth out of you that way, I'll just have to resort to asking you politely."

Singh grinned. "As long as you're not asking for anything that would have the guv feeding me to the lions. Okay, you want to know how the case is going."

He followed Malcolm to a table by the pub

window. "Your appeal has had results but I'm afraid it seems to have netted the usual haul."

"Timewasters, attention seekers, and old dears desperate to be helpful. Ah well, it was worth a try. She's out there somewhere, and if we can't find her body, it would at least have been something to be able to give her a name."

"You've found the others. That's more than anyone was expecting, after all this time."

"I know. Even so…" Malcolm took a swig of his beer, watching as the pub door opened and a woman looked in, gazing round the bar, obviously seeking someone. He glanced over his shoulder to see if there was a lone male waiting. No one obvious. He turned back to Singh to find the woman looking straight at him, brows raised. Medium height, slim build, short fair hair, fortyish. Neither bashful nor brazen. Malcolm half-rose as she was heading his way.

"Are you looking for me?"

"I don't know." She squinted at him. "Are you Superintendent Cannell?"

"Just mister, these days, but yes, that's me."

"I saw you on the telly."

"Yes?" He pulled another chair to their table.

"I asked at the police station and they said to come back after lunch." She sat down. "I thought I'd look around the pubs and cafés nearby and see if I could find you."

"Well done. You should be a detective."

"No thanks!" She pulled a face. "Sorry. Anyway, I'd rather talk to you here."

"Talk away then. Can I get you a drink first?"

"No, I'm okay, thanks. Thing is, it's about the girl you want to identify."

"You think you know who she might be?"

"Yes. Me.

Malcolm exchanged glances with Singh. For a moment he'd fancied there might be a genuine lead to follow. She hadn't looked over-excited or over-imaginative. "I see. And who are you?"

"Holly Watson. You said she was possibly called Lolly, and I was when I was young. Rhyming slang, I suppose."

"Yes, I see. But I'm afraid the girl we're looking for is dead."

"You mean you think she was killed by Timothy Gittings? In a village, Hayford Green?"

"That is what we believe, yes."

"And there was a diamond ring. You said he'd taken it from her as a trophy."

"Yes."

"That's what made me think. When I heard you mention the ring, I looked up the Timothy Gittings case. There was a picture of him and I'm sure it was him. The man I met in the woods. It makes sense."

"You met a man in the woods in Hayford Green?"

"Well, it was a wood by a village green. I couldn't for the life of me say where exactly, but it was where I mislaid my mum. We lived in a van, and she was mostly stoned. It's quite hard remembering exactly what happened, but it was the last day I saw her. I did try to find her years later, but she'd died. An overdose."

"You looked for her even though she abandoned you in the middle of nowhere?"

Holly smiled. "I'm afraid it was more like me abandoning her. My dad – well, I had two of them, sort of, but they were both a couple of crooks. Don't ask me what they were up to. I was far too young to understand anything except that I was always hungry and we were never in one place for more than a few days."

"I see. When was this?"

"Well, I think '92. It was summer, I remember that. I met a girl on the common. I didn't get the chance to make many friends and it was nice to have someone to talk to. We exchanged presents, and she gave me a ring." Holly laughed. "I gather it was valuable? I had no idea. It was just a sparkly gift from a friend, as far as I was concerned. Anyway, I have an idea I was going to visit her? I knew where she lived, in a rather grand house, and there was a footpath leading through woods. That's where I met this strange man. Boy, really. He wasn't very old. Gangly, you might say. Longish fair hair, like in his photograph. He was odd, but everyone I knew back then was odd, which is why it didn't bother me that much.

"We talked, but I don't remember it making much sense. I was used to that with my mum. What I do remember was that he said I was his sister and he wanted me to come home with him and live with him and his mum."

Both Malcolm and Singh were leaning forward, feeding on her words.

"And I said yes," said Holly.

"You said yes?"

"I know it sounds daft, but I thought having a

brother and a proper family sounded like a really nice idea. I didn't particularly want to go back to the van."

"No, I see. Go on, what happened?"

"You have to understand that this was all thirty years ago and my life changed after that. I've had to rack my brain dragging it up and trying to get it straight. I remember we played on a swing. Or a rope or something. And he took a photograph of me. That must be the one you showed on the telly. I think I would have gone with him. He was really excited when I said yes all right. A bit sad, really. But then things started getting weird. He said if I was his sister I had to be cut. He kept touching my cheek and saying, over and over, "If you're Clare you have to be cut." That's when I got frightened."

"I'm not surprised!"

"My limited experience of life was that if people threatened violence, they wanted to take something from you, so I offered him the ring. I thought he might just go away. He was really pleased with it, like nobody had ever given him a present before. But no, that wasn't enough. He kept on about me needing to be cut. "She won't believe you're Clare if you're not cut." That's what he said. Looking back on it, I do appreciate he was just... what's the nice way of putting it? Mentally disturbed?"

"You must have been petrified."

"I don't know. Frightened enough to want to get away, but I was used to wanting to get away, and avoid being hurt, so I sort of played along. He told me to stay there and he'd go and get a knife from his van. I said okay and I waved as he walked away. Then as soon as he was out of sight, I just ran for it. I fell into a ditch and I crouched there. I peered over the edge, through a bush and I saw him come running back and just stop. Like he couldn't believe I wasn't there anymore. He started sobbing and then howling. I actually felt sorry for him and I nearly climbed out, but then he calmed down. He paced around for a bit and then he went away. That's all. I didn't do anything. I might even have gone to sleep. I remember going back to our van in the dark, but it had gone. No sign of my people, so I wandered on up the road, and I got offered a lift by some guy in a big car. I was cold and hungry so I got in." Holly pulled a face. She took a deep breath. "Maybe I will have a G'n'T, after all."

Singh rose. "I'll get it."

Malcolm nodded. "Want to go on?"

"Yes." Holly shrugged. "You know, until I heard you talking on the telly, the thing that stuck in my mind about that day, or rather night, was that man who picked me up in his car. That was when I was really frightened and hurt. I still panic when I smell a sheepskin coat."

"Can you tell me what happened?"

She gave Malcolm a quaint look. "Seriously? What do you think happened? I'd rather not go into details, if it's all the same with you."

He patted her hand. "Not if you don't want to."

"Later on, he pulled in at a petrol station to fill up. He locked me in while he went to pay, but I managed to get a window open and I wriggled out and ran to hide in the ladies' toilets."

"Smart thinking."

"That's where Ruby found me. Ruby Bakare. She and Dr Bakare took me in. That's the sort of thing they did. Three kids of their own and four they'd scraped up off the streets. We were one big happy family, the first I'd ever had, and I never looked back."

"Dr Bakare?"

"Reverend. Thanks." Holly smiled at Singh as he placed a glass beside her. "Dr Bakare ran a church in Brixton. They looked after me, cleaned me up, taught me to read and write. Ruby taught me to cook – she used to say when I first joined them, I did nothing but eat for a fortnight. I certainly never went hungry again. I got a job in a restaurant, went on to be a qualified chef, got married, three kids, the oldest going to uni next year, I hope. I forgot all about the past. I used to have nightmares about the man in the car, but I never gave another thought to the boy in the wood. Isn't that odd, if he really was a serial killer? It wasn't until I caught you talking on the telly, asking for information about a girl last seen in Hayford Green, that I remembered any of it. I never thought of him as a monster."

"Monsters come in all shapes and sizes," said Malcolm. "You met another, just as bad, the same night. But fortunately there are angels in the world as well as devils, and you met a couple of them, too." He drained his pint, wondering if she noticed how tightly he was gripping the glass, to stop his hand shaking. "All right, Holly. When you've finished your drink, I hope you'll be willing to give a formal statement to DS Singh here, at the station. I'm no longer officially a policeman, you understand. But you'll never know how glad I am that you came forward. Glad? No. Deliriously overjoyed would be nearer the mark."

"His life's mission," grinned Singh. "Last mystery finally wrapped up and, miracle of miracles, the girl's alive, after all."

Malcolm laughed.

Holly laughed with him, then noticed the tears in his eyes. "You kept looking," she said, and leaned across to kiss his cheek. "Of course I'll give a statement."

Moving On

"I'm not sure champagne would be appropriate," said Barbara Cannell. "But I can offer wine, whisky or a chilled G&T with ice and lemon. Or there are some Italian beers that my nephew insists on drinking from the bottle."

Rosanna smiled. "A red wine would be lovely."

"We won't call it a celebration," said Malcolm. "Just a quiet mellow ending to long years of desperation, finally resolved."

"With one light shining out of all that misery." Barbara passed drinks around. "Malcolm is ridiculously chuffed that one girl survived and went on to live a happy life."

"A girl who was never even reported missing." Malcolm shook his head. "Some things are very hard to understand. But it's reassuring, just occasionally, to emerge from nightmares and find there's still sunshine in the world. One story that doesn't end in a sad funeral." He passed Rosanna a bowl of nuts. "You must have had your fill of them. You did attend them all, didn't you? All four?"

"Yes," said Rosanna. "*All* of them."

Malcolm regarded her over the top of his glasses.

"Does that mean you attended Margaret Gittings, too?"

"Cremation. No words. I was the only one there. But

yes, I did."

"Why? I assume it wasn't just to make sure that she was really dead."

"No, it wasn't that." Rosanna shrugged. "I set out to find lost girls and I can't help thinking that Margaret was as lost as any of them. She wasn't killed, but maybe her fate was just as bad."

Malcolm shrugged, content to be charitable now it was all over. "I'll grant you, she was unbalanced, if not downright insane, and yes, maybe she did deserve some pity somewhere along the line. If she did, you're the one to feel it, that's clear."

Rosanna gazed into the depth of her wineglass. "She was adrift in a world where she didn't belong. All she ever had of her own were her children, and they were taken from her. She wanted them. She'd do anything from them." She looked up, biting her lip, then went on.

"You see, I had a mother and my father destroyed her, bit by bit, day by day, sometimes physically but mostly emotionally, until he drove her to drink and then, finally, to suicide. I was fourteen and ever since then, I've wanted some sort of justice for her, even if it's just acknowledgement. Because I loved her. But there's a little bit of me that hates her, too. For escaping from him and leaving me. I know that's ridiculous, but…" She shrugged.

"Life is complicated?" suggested Barbara.

"Something like that." Rosanna laughed, embarrassed. "I've never told anyone that. Even myself."

"It's understandable. And I am really sorry about

300

your mother. Which would be awful at any age, but when you were so young. You must have been traumatised. My poor girl."

"I don't know. It had an impact. It makes me feel sort of equivocal about some things. Margaret's refusal to speak was terrible, it caused such pointlessly prolonged agony, and maybe her desperate drinking in the early days did bad things to her children, but she never gave up on them, even though I fully understand her obsession with them was just an aspect of her insanity. So, yes, I went to her funeral."

"Then I hope she's at peace," said Malcolm. "And all the girls, too. I'd like to think there's peace now for the living, too. For all of us." He sat back, smiling. "How about you? What's this about you giving up your flat in Swindon and moving to Wales."

"The bedsitter was only temporary, while I worked there. I'm staying with... a friend for now."

Malcolm's smile broadened. "Not planning to take up sheep-farming as a career, are you? Know much about them?"

"They go baa?" suggested Rosanna.

"Actually, it's more like meeh, so I'd hold off claiming expertise on the subject for now."

Rosanna laughed. "Yes, but I do need to start looking for another job."

"Return to the police?"

She shook her head. "I don't think they'd have me anymore, with my record."

"You weren't charged."

"I was given a caution. I admitted to breaking and entering, and burglary, and I couldn't really claim I was doing it to prevent a worse crime. Anyway, not back to the police."

"Stick to what you've been doing then, since you're good at it."

"What, as a private investigator? There are enough of them around already."

"But not many with your special talents. Don't waste your gift."

"My dogged pig-headedness?"

Malcolm chuckled. "You certainly have plenty of that. No, your gift is that you care."

Barbara nodded. "Do you have any idea, Rosanna, how many hurting people there are out there, needing answers that no one's giving them, and just longing for someone to care?"

"Well then, go out there and care on their behalf," said Malcolm. "Find them the truth they need."

Rosanna looked from one to the other. They looked at her. It seemed impolite to argue. "Maybe."

"No maybe about it," said Malcolm. "You can always come to me for advice, useful contacts, that sort of thing. Consulting partner, you might say."

"Ha!" said Barbara. "I knew it. So much for a quiet, peaceful retirement, once this case was put to rest."

"The cottage in Cornwall?" asked Malcom, warily.

"Do you want that?"

"Not really."

"No, neither do I. Well, that's sorted. More than enough places to walk the dogs round here."

Two tails began to thump the floor enthusiastically, hearing the word Walk.

Malcolm took another sip of wine. "More than

enough. Well then, Rosanna." He raised his glass to her.

"Here's to closure. Time to move on to the next quest."

"Moving on," said Barbara, as they all clinked glasses.

* * *

Life moves on… but not for everyone.

Not for Peter Fitzpatrick, staring at the photo of his daughter on the noticeboard at his gate and telling himself that he should take it down now. But he knows, if he does, he has nothing else.

Not for Amy Redbourn, placing flowers on the grave where her mother and sister lie buried, whispering "Sorry," but knowing that the guilt will never let go.

Not for Sharon Knowles, packing up her photo of her daughter as she prepares to move, placing it next to the half-empty gin bottle. Questions are answered, but still she is left with nothing but a photograph.

Not for Bryn Davies, brooding over another pint in the Drover's Arms, waiting to be shooed home to an empty house.

But it does go on for Holly Watson, as she waves her son off to university, and that, at least, is something.

* * *

Timothy Gittings draws. It's a picture of his sister Clare. She's out there somewhere, but they won't let him go out to look for her, and he can't take any more photos of her, but he can always draw her. He adds a jagged line to her cheek. Like the line his mother drew on Clare with a knife when she was a baby. "She's not his pretty little princess," she said. "I won't let him have her. She's mine! He won't want her now."

His mother's dead. They told him. He doesn't care. She let him down. She let them take him away. He's glad she's dead.

THE END

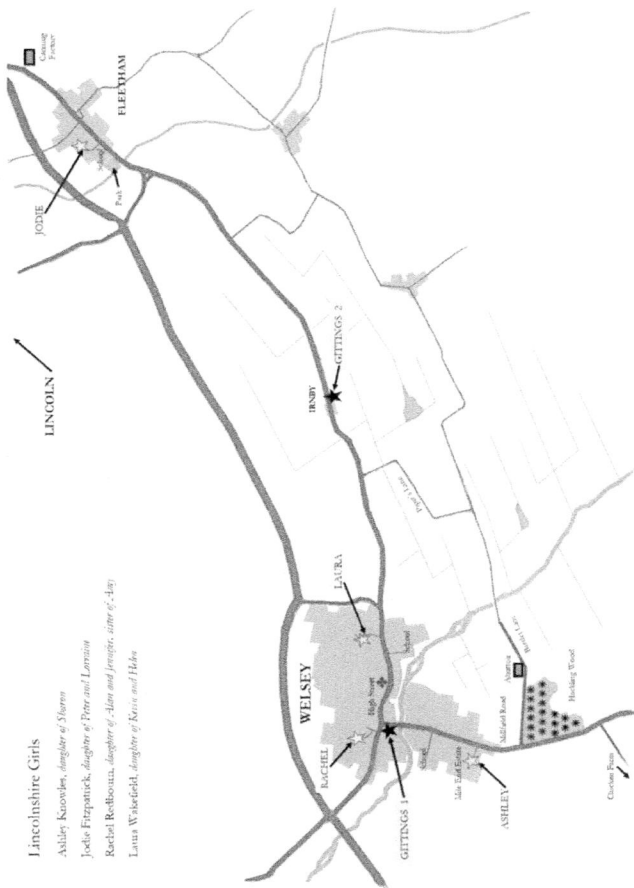

Lincolnshire Girls

Ashley Knowles, *daughter of Sharron*

Jodie Fitzpatrick, *daughter of Peter and Lorraine*

Rachel Redbourn, *daughter of Alan and Jennifer, sister of Amy*

Laura Whitefield, *daughter of Kevin and Helen*

LINCOLN

FLEETHAM

JODIE

Park

Causeway Farmhouse

GITTINGS 2

DENBY

LAURA

WELSEY

RACHEL

GITTINGS 1

High Street

Church

John Tolbert Row

ASHLEY

Midland Road

Bird's Court

Almshouse

Harding Wood

Overton Brook

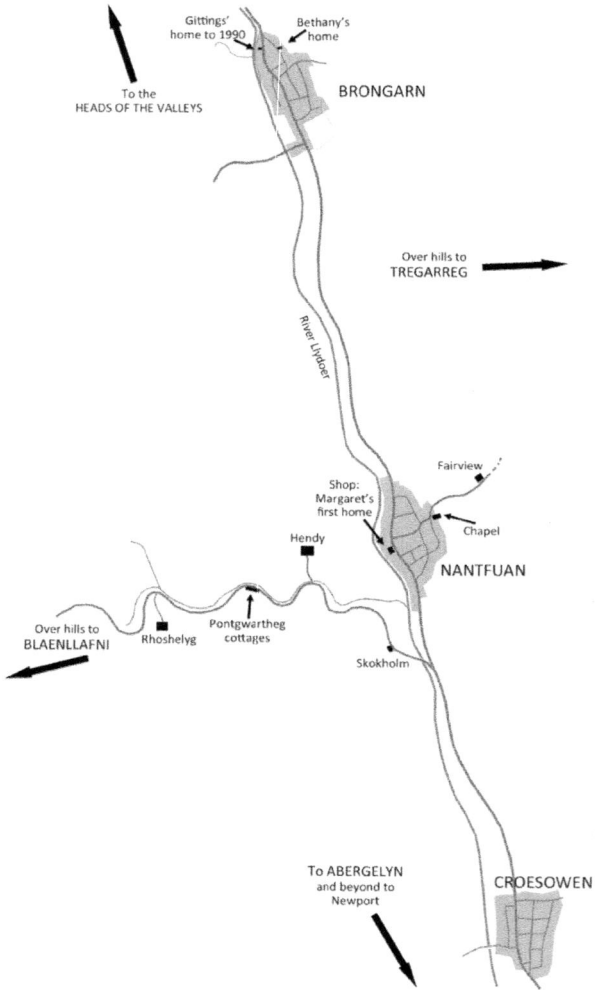

**DIAMOND
CRIME**

Passionate about the crime/mystery/thriller books it publishes

Follow
Facebook:
@diamondcrimepublishing

Instagram
@diamond_crime_publishing

Web
diamondbooks.co.uk

**DIAMOND
BOOKS**

Printed in Great Britain
by Amazon